Ruby Tuesday

A Novel by

Baron R. Birtcher

Copyright © 2001, Precis-Honu Holdings, LLC

All rights reserved. No part of this book may be used or reproduced,
in any manner whatsoever, without the written permission of the Publisher.

Printed in Canada

For information address:
Durban House Publishing Company, Inc.
7502 Greenville Avenue, Suite 500, Dallas, Texas 75231
214.890.4050

Library of Congress Cataloging-in-Publication Data
Baron R. Birtcher, 1959

Ruby Tuesday / by Baron R. Birtcher

Library of Congress Catalog Card Number: 00-2001096201

p. cm.

ISBN 1-930754-11-6

First Edition

10 9 8 7 6 5 4 3 2 1

Visit our Web site at
http://www.durbanhouse.com

http://www.baronbirtcher.com

Book design by:
B[u]y-the-Book Design—Madeline Höfer & Jennifer Steinberg

Christina, who is my inspiration;
Allegra, Raider and Britton, who are my future;
and
Mom & Dad, who are my roots

also by BARON R. BIRTCHER

ROADHOUSE BLUES

ACKNOWLEDGMENTS

The towns of Kona, Honaunau and Hilo, the Four Seasons Hualalai and the King Kamehameha Hotel are real places, though they are used fictitiously in this novel, as are certain other actual businesses and bars frequented by Mike Travis. In all other respects, this is a work of fiction. Names, characters, places and incidents are all a product of the author's imagination or are used fictitiously. Any resemblance to actual persons, living or dead, or to actual events or locales is entirely coincidental.

The author would like to offer a sincere mahalo to Captain Dale Fergerstrom (ret.) of the Kona Police Department for his help, and any mistakes or misstatements with respect to procedures are purely mine. Thanks also to Bob Middlemiss, Editor-in-Chief of Durban House for his wisdom, guidance and insight. A Gentleman and Scholar in the truest senses.

Again, Christina, I could have never finished without your encouragement, and your kind and gentle criticism. You will always be the love of my life.

To Pete Ham, the Stones, and Steve Marriott for the inspiration; and to John Day, Eddie Wenrick, Richard Stekol and Carol Walden for pulling back the curtain.

Mahalo nui special-kine to Lyman & Iaukea, Brad "The King Bee" Freeman, "Wild Bill" Logan, The Polynesian Pirate, and Andrea Hennings.

Thanks (again) to Nancy and Mark Miller for another million and a half copies, a lot of great music, a short lesson in geography, and most of all your friendship.

To Loke Hoohuli for all the word processing help.

To Captain Dave and Rosalie Fink for as many reasons as "Carters has little pills."

To Allegra, Raider and Britton, my constant reminders of who I am, and why I'm here; thank you for sharing the ups, downs and excitement along the way. Aloha pau ole.

Finally, to Mom & Dad, Art & Gaye, Brad & Shelley, Brandy & Dorine, Bob & Wendy, and, of course, Monnie. Me ke aloha pumehana.

She saw the symptoms right away
and spoke to me in poetry
Sometimes the more you wonder why
The worse it seems to get

Duncan Sheik

(from *She Runs Away*)

Ruby Tuesday

PART ONE
STONE BLOSSOMS

NORTH HOLLYWOOD
SUMMER, 1977

1

Nancy Lee tapped her gold Cross pen on the faux-wood veneer of the booth's table top; impatient, waiting on the arrival of her five o'clock interview.

Fuck this, she thought, and pulled another cigarette from the pack.

She slid back the sleeve of her peasant shirt and checked the time. Nearly six o'clock. Almost an hour late. *Five more minutes is all he gets.*

She plucked another match from the book and lit up, blew twin plumes of smoke from her nostrils. She caught her reflection in the mirror behind the bar and smiled to herself. The time that asshole—what was his name?—said she looked like a dragon when she did that. He'd meant it as a racial slur, pissed off about a tough review. *Hell with him. He's long gone, and I'm still standing.*

It wasn't the first time the *Rolling Stone* reporter had been kept waiting by some ego-inflated musician, but her tolerance had diminished with her rising status. Her articles had become renowned for their prophetic qualities. She'd seen the tragedy of Badfinger coming, and written an uncompromising cover piece. She had uncovered rip-offs by unscrupulous business managers that landed a couple in jail. She'd done the last interview with the Supremes' Florence Ballard only days before she died of a heart attack. Hell, she'd even predicted that Frampton would leave Humble Pie.

Nancy took another drag off her cigarette, tapped the lengthening ash away, and flipped open the notebook she carried in her fringed leather purse. She reread the questions she had written there. Her eyes took in her own neat handwriting, but her mind wandered back seven years to the first time she had been introduced to Harley Angell, unofficial leader of the mega-band called Stone Blossoms.

Seemed like yesterday. The chaos inside the Rainbow Bar. His quiet charm had drawn her into a protective cell within which she gave herself over to him completely. Well, almost. They were both so young then. Everything so new.

Stone Blossoms had just finished their first night as opening act for the Allman Brothers Band at the Forum in Los Angeles. The beginning of a fifty-five date summer tour. The performance had blown them all away. Everybody. The screaming of eighteen thousand fans nearly shook the arena apart at the end of the Blossoms' set.

After a ten minute encore jam on Willie Dixon's *Born Under A Bad Sign,* the group was manhandled into a customized Greyhound bus and headed for what became an all-nighter at the Rainbow. The band was still in shock when they pushed through the door.

Stone Blossoms' manager Mark Miller worked the room. He didn't miss a beat introducing the band members to reporters, reviewers, label executives. Knew all of them by name. Kept them moving, making the rounds of all the movers and shakers, trying to keep the band's attention off the groupies long enough to give a few interviews and get a few photos. It had been Miller who navigated Harley Angell through the noisy crowd to the bar stool that Nancy Lee occupied, nursing her beer. Still wet behind the ears in her position with *Rolling Stone.*

It struck her how innocent he seemed at the time; tall and smooth faced, carrying himself in that aw-shucks sort of way he had then. Youthful green eyes complimenting an olive complexion and dark, shoulder-length hair that infused him with rugged Celtic good looks. Shyly uncomfortable and charismatic at the same time.

From Angell's first words, Nancy had been taken by his self-effacing manner, his easy smile, the way he avoided direct eye contact.

Only now did she remember shaking off a premonition that the business would transform him into something unrecognizable, something hollow, hard and cynical.

Nancy exhaled gray smoke and crushed the butt into the ashtray with the others.

A hand touched her shoulder from behind. "Nancy?"

She started, knocking over the remnants of a flat gin and tonic. Melted ice and a wedge of lime slid to the floor.

"God, I'm sorry. I didn't mean to scare you," Angell said. She caught her own reflection in his mirrored sunglasses.

He slipped in along the naugahyde bench across from the reporter. The beginning of their ritual. The exclusive interview he granted her before every new album. Only this one had been a long time in coming.

"No, I was just—" she let it hang.

He reached across the table and offered his hand. It felt warm, dry and strong to her as he enfolded her slender fingers. An unexpected heat on the back of her neck, and she wondered again why she had never tried to sleep with him.

"—I was a million miles away," she finished. "I guess I didn't hear you come in." She gathered her napkin in a ball and wiped up the spill.

He took off his shades and used them to hold back his long brown hair. His eyes were rimmed in red, quarter moons of faded purple beneath. Three days' growth of beard. A tired smile failed.

Angell studied her, appreciating her Asian beauty. "It's good to see you, Nancy," Angell said softly. "You look great. As always."

Always a gentleman. "I wish I could say the same, Harley."

He was silent for a long moment, then shrugged.

There had been growing rumors that the long-awaited new Stone Blossoms album was badly bogged in one of those ugly tangles of "creative differences" among band members. The group had been in the studio for over twenty months, and nothing but negative speculation about the sessions circulated anymore. After a string of enormously successful albums and a sold-out world tour, the burden of living up to its own legend was taking its toll.

"You look like hell," Nancy said.

Red eyes blinked. "Long hours."

His faded denim jacket fell open as he leaned against the backrest and spread his arms. The trademark turquoise choker hung around his neck.

"Getting any sleep?" She tapped the side of her nose.

That tired smile again. "It's under control."

"We don't need any more casualties, Harley." She sounded like a mother. Even to herself.

"It's not me you oughta be worrying about."

Nancy shook another cigarette from the pack, offered it to Angell.

"No, thanks," he said, but reached across the table for the matchbook.

She took one between her lips and allowed him to light it for her. "Kevin Demers getting arrested is nothing new, Harley. Drummers always pull weird stunts like that. Bonzo Bonham, Keith Moon. Same old shit."

"I guess I should be flattered," he smiled. "Our drummer gets DUI'd making rooster tails with his Fatboy on Zuma Beach in the middle of the night—and you worry about *me*."

Smoked offered its twin plumes. "That's different."

"Right." He put up his hands. "Then two days later he's busted at the Riot House with two underage groupies and an eight-ball of Peruvian Flake."

The Continental Hyatt House. Party Central. When the heavy bands were in town, it practically rained TV sets from the windows of the top floor suites.

"Like I said," she answered. "That's different."

Nancy opened her notebook and laid it on the table. She wrote the date and time at the top of the page. "How about we get started by—"

A young waitress interrupted. She stood a moment, then looked at Angell and registered a look of surprise. Sudden recognition.

"Aren't you...?" she stammered.

"Harley Angell," he said, almost a whisper. He extended his hand.
The waitress took it in hers and giggled.

"I can't believe it," she said. She wallowed at the end of his hand, one of the faithful. "I mean, Stone Blossoms is, like…this is just *so cool.*"

"Thanks," he said as he released her. She wouldn't stop staring at him. Awkward moments.

Nancy Lee cleared her throat.

"Oh. Sorry," the waitress said. Still gawking at Angell. "What can I get for you?"

"Bloody Mary, double vodka, heavy on the Tabasco," Angell answered.

"And for you, Ma'am?" The waitress asked without looking at Nancy.

Ma'am? Jesus.

"Gin and tonic."

"Anything else?" Still not looking.

"Not right now," Angell said. The waitress nodded, then slowly retreated to the bar.

After a few beats, Nancy regrouped. She made a gut decision to abandon her set of questions. She'd go for it casually, conversationally. She'd get to that inside edge if things were less structured.

"So what's going on?" She began. "The world is wondering where the next album is, and all there is is rumor and innuendo. None of it good, either."

"On the record or off?"

"Gimme a break, Harley. Why are we here?"

She felt him stiffen.

"Okay, then," he said. "On the record: Recording is going without a hitch, and everyone is getting along splendidly. It ought to be out 'any day now,' and the band is extremely excited to get it into the stores."

The sarcasm was something she'd never seen in him before. He had to be stretched damned thin. But there was something here. She could feel it.

"'Splendidly,' Harley? I hope to God that's not from your lyrics. Come on, for Christ's sake." The vehemence of her own voice surprised Nancy, and she backed off. She had a lot of time invested in this relationship, and this was a big interview. Even for her. No one from the Stone Blossoms' camp had spoken to the press in well over a year. This was sure to be another cover story.

"Listen," she said. "You agreed to talk to me. It's obviously important. The band has been subject to rumors of break-up over this record. Something's got to be said."

Angell closed his eyes and sighed.

Nancy leaned toward him, her tone softer. "There's talk that this could be another abortion like the Beach Boys' *Smile* project."

"Oh, Christ, Nancy. What a crock—"

"—and your drummer's more hell-bent than ever to kill himself. And Lyle Sparks? He's walking around town looking for a solo deal. Then there's you. You look like you don't know what month it is."

Harley Angell met her gaze and nodded, aged five years in that moment. "Can I bum that cigarette now?"

Nancy slid the pack across the table. She waited quietly while he lit up, collected his thoughts.

"The truth is the album's almost done." His words rolled across a blanket of exhaled smoke.

"You're kidding," she said. *That* was big fucking news.

"Not at all. We're at the last stages of mix-down. It's supposed to be this big secret that we're so close, but…" The sentence trailed off into nothing, a shrug, a chord not struck.

She looked at him in disbelief. She hated things that sounded too good to be true. She'd been bitten before.

He read her expression. "I'm not gonna bullshit you, Nancy. It's been torture, but the damn thing's almost done."

"What about all the rumors? All the fights we've been hearing about?"

He took a drag on his smoke as she snuffed hers. "We've had our troubles, sure. But I think it's all just being cooped up in the studio for months on end. That, and not having taken a single break from the recording-touring grind. I mean, how many years has it been?"

She waited him out.

"You know, the Blossoms haven't had any real time off since the first album. That's all the way back in '70. We're all restless as hell. It shouldn't surprise anyone that some of us are getting crazy."

"Go on." The story was already formulating itself. Her brain buzzed. The jazz. She loved when it happened this way. Nancy scratched notes on the pad in front of her without taking her eyes off his face.

"Well, you gotta remember: On top of all that, the albums have gotten more complex, the recording techniques more sophisticated—"

"—Not to mention," she egged him on. "Every new album selling more than the one that came before."

His tired eyes hardened. "You handling me, Nancy?"

"No!"

Angell's fingers drummed a rhythm, something old, Buddy Rich. "'Cause I'm not going to be fucking *handled.*"

"I know."

He glanced away. "Okay—sure, there's a lot of pressure there. Some of it's put on us by our label, but a lot is internal. We create it ourselves, as commercial artists, you know?"

Nancy Lee kept silent, let the interview play itself.

"There's been some tough going this time. Personally, I mean," he continued. "With the records selling so well, there's been more and more internal strain among the band to have songwriting credits. The problem is, you can't just divide up an album and say, 'I'll write three songs, you write three songs and that other guy'll do three more.' It'd be great if you could, but the fact is, not everybody has stuff that fits."

"You mean shitty songs, Harley?"

He laughed for what seemed to him like the first time in weeks. "Okay, yeah, shitty songs. Not everyone writes songs that're strong enough."

"But Harley Angell does," she said.

He looked away. Shades of the old modesty. He didn't answer.

"So the rumors of fighting among the song writers are true?" She persisted.

Angell sat up straight, steeling himself for something. Nancy tensed.

The waitress arrived with their drinks, leaving the glasses at the edge of the table. After a quick sideward glance at Nancy, she placed a plain white cocktail napkin in front of Angell. Some extra sway as she walked away without a word.

There was a change in the electricity between them. Nancy silently cursed the waitress' interruption.

He turned the napkin over without looking at it, his eyes old again as they watched Nancy. Girlish swirls. A name and number. He folded it once and put it in his pocket.

She tried to shape the silence, bring him back on point. *Come on Harley, so the rumors of infighting are true...*

Harley Angell stared his drink, then used a sprig of celery to stir the ice. She saw that he was concocting an answer, privately debating how truthful to be.

"There's a lot of money in song writing," he offered at last.

"And...?"

"And that fed some pretty bitter disagreements over album content. The money, I mean."

The after-work crowd was beginning to fill the place. A group of men in suits, ties pulled down from splayed collars, dragged in the daylight and took familiar seats at the bar.

"But you worked them out?"

"Yeah. We worked 'em out."

He removed the celery stalk, licked it, brought the glass to his lips and looked over the rim at Nancy.

"The celery brings out the green in your eyes," she said.

He laughed in spite of himself. "And you'd *never* write your name on the back of a napkin."

"Hell, no," she smiled. "Well, maybe Jagger."

He laughed again. She had him back.

"What about drugs?" she asked.

"What about 'em?"

"Come *on*, Harley."

"Okay, look. You know as well as I do that drugs are a fact of life in this business. But it's under control. Kevin Demers is insane. And you're right: The things with the hog on the beach and the groupies is just another day in the life for him."

"What about the rest of you? I've heard that there's been some pretty weird shit going on in the studio."

He wiped at his nose reflexively. She was right. There had been way too much booze and coke in the studio over the last few months. Exhaustion suddenly deflated him.

Angell tried for a disarming smile, but looked dismal, drained. "Got any other questions?"

"Sure. Let's talk about songs," Nancy asked, letting him off the hook. "What's the new album going to be like?"

At the mention of the music, a spark lit his features. Harley Angell began an animated monologue about the songs. He seemed genuinely excited. The album was going to be called *Lifeline.*

"Who came up with that?"

He waited a beat.

"I did. It's the title of one of my songs. It's kind of become the central theme of the project."

"How so?"

He stared into his glass. "'Cause it's all I have left."

The stark loneliness of his statement struck Nancy like a fist. "What do you mean?"

"The music. The band. This album." It hung in the air between them until a burst of drinking-buddy laughter rattled across the bar.

Angell straightened himself and absently fingered the turquoise choker around his neck, a finger on the touchstone.

"Please don't print that last thing," he said softly.

"Harley…" she began, but he waved her off. He gathered himself again.

He talked a little more about the 48-track recording methods that allowed the band to explore new musical textures, and expounded upon the "new sound" that permeated the album. When Nancy pressed him further about specific songs and songwriters, he smiled and told her she would have to wait and hear it like everyone else.

After an hour of conversation, Angell was spent. He tipped away the remnants of his third Bloody Mary and looked at his watch.

"I'm sorry, Nancy, but I gotta get back to the studio. I'm gonna hafta split."

"No problem. I appreciate your time." She signaled the waitress for the bill as he slid off the seat. He touched her hand and started for the door.

"Harley?" she said.

"Yeah."

"I'm glad you're happy with the music. I hope it's huge."

"From your lips to God's ears," he smiled. But it was shot through with melancholy.

Nancy Lee felt an indefinable emptiness as the door swung shut behind him.

2

"How'd it go, Mister Angell?" his driver asked.

"Okay, Charles," he said. "It went okay."

The driver smiled. He had really grown to like this Angell guy.

"You want we should go to the studio now?" Six years driving limos in southern California and he still oozed south Chicago.

"In a couple've minutes," Angell said. "I just want to sit here and get my head together first."

Charles caught his eye in the rearview mirror, nodded, and closed the privacy screen between them.

Harley Angell settled against the soft black leather seat and closed his eyes.

He silently reviewed his performance with the reporter, hoped that his enthusiasm for the songs would somehow overshadow the flood of negative speculation out there.

His opinion of the new material was high, but he prayed that the threads holding the band together were not so visible to Nancy Lee. A heavy load of artistic credibility rode on the success of the new album, and he felt the full weight resting on his shoulders. Harley had tried as hard to conceal the animosity that had germinated during the last tour, but it had come to full bloom in the dark confines of the recording studio.

If we can just make it through this album...

He squeezed his eyes tighter and tried to press the creeping dread from his mind. Sounds of passing traffic were dulled beyond the tinted windows. Real life. Normal life. Jesus, how long had it been?

Nancy Lee had been dead right about another thing, too. Drugs had fueled an escalating battle of egos among the band's creative forces, of which Harley himself was preeminent. The group's other songwriting team, lead singer Christopher Morton and guitarist Danny Webb, had been in a constant state of war with Angell over whose songs would go on the album. The arguments were arbitrated by their producer, Tom Foster.

As the record neared completion, though, it looked like the final product would consist of seven songs penned by Harley Angell, two by Morton and Webb, and one by bassist Lyle Sparks.

It was supremely ironic, he thought, that the same creative energy that had propelled Stone Blossoms to five consecutive multi-platinum albums—the two most recent setting world-wide sales records—was turning out to be the catalyst to the band's self-destruction. Harley Angell's talent had brought them here, and petty jealousy was threatening to tear them apart.

Combined, the last two albums alone had sold more than 55 million copies. Songwriting and publishing royalties alone were worth over $1.5 million *per song* at those sales levels. It was no wonder that battles were waged where album content was concerned.

Angell pulled a small brown vial from his jacket, unscrewed the lid and scooped the white powder with a miniature spoon, fed each nostril. He returned the vial to his pocket then leaned forward and knocked on the divider. His signal. A crystalline thrill shot through him as the limo pulled away from the curb.

But the overall quality of the album had to prevail, right? Otherwise sales would disappear and the gravy train would be over for everyone.

Instead of being jealous, the bastards ought to be grateful.

Palm trees cast long shadows across the boulevard and the setting sun burned the Hollywood hills dark orange. He wished the drive was longer as he opened the vial and bumped his nose one last time before he had to face the bad vibes inside HitMan Studios.

As the car slid into the parking lot, he felt the old anxiety rise inside of him. He never knew what to expect of any particular day's sessions. They had ranged from ridiculous to deranged, from grudging collaboration to petty name-calling. Twenty months in those cramped rooms had taught him to expect the worst.

The car rocked to a stop; the driver slid the divider down.

"We're here, Mr. Angell."

Harley steeled himself and reached for the door.

"Thanks, Charles," he said. "I'm gonna be awhile, so you can take off."

"Call me when you're done?"

"Yeah, or I can get a ride from somebody."

The driver arched a brow. He'd seen the bad blood.

"Okay," Angell said. "I'll call you."

He walked the short distance from the limo to the unmarked door of the studio, felt the dying day's heat off the asphalt come through the soles of his leather sandals.

A uniformed security guard waited inside, acknowledged Angell with a casual nod, and let him pass through the first of two heavy doors that separated the lobby from the main control room. Harley snapped off a salute and a smile crossed the guard's eyes.

As the second door opened, Angell was confronted by the loud recorded strains of his own searing lead guitar work set against an intricate backdrop of keyboards and acoustic guitars. The volume was extreme, but necessary in order for the producer to scrutinize the mix for flaws.

Tom Foster punched a button and the wall of sound disappeared into a vacuum of silence.

"My man," the producer said.

"Hey, Tom," Angell answered. They shook hands.

Angell turned his attention to a younger man hunched over, examining something beneath the tape machine.

"What's happening, Dennis?"

Dennis Farr, the engineer, looked up.

"Howzit going, Harley?" He flashed a smile and returned to his work.

Ignoring his arrival, Chris Morton and Danny Webb sat side by side on a red leather couch in front of the mixing console. They stared sightlessly into the dark and empty studio beyond the glass panel that separated the control room and the studio.

What childish bullshit.

Dim light from the mixing console's VU meters bathed the control room in a yellow glow. A thin gray ribbon of sweet smoke rose from a bomber joint that sat in an ashtray next to Webb.

"Hey, Danny," Angell said. "Hey, Chris."

Webb picked up the doob, took a theatrically leisurely hit, then passed it to Morton.

"Hey," Webb exhaled. A cloud drifted to the ceiling.

The silence that followed lasted long seconds.

"So what's the fuckin' deal here," Morton said, agitated. "Let's get on with it."

Foster looked at Angell.

Angell shrugged. They'd been through all this before.

"Where are we, Tom? What's going on?"

"The Suits from the label," Foster began, "are *demanding* to hear a rough mix of the album by tomorrow morning at ten."

"Jesus," Angell said. "Can't we—"

"They're not fucking around anymore, Harley."

"Can we do it? That's hardly any time."

Harley Angell touched his pocket, felt the reassuring little bulge of the vial.

"I've gotten through four tracks already. Six more to go. We can do it, but it ain't gonna be easy."

The engineer nodded, his face drawn. Webb and Morton sat in stony silence.

Angell, Webb, Morton, Foster and Farr worked through the night.

The frequent disagreements over the mix and finally, the song sequence, were mediated as always by Foster. At one point well into the night Morton and Angell nearly came to blows over the vocal mix in one of Morton and Webb's songs. Nerves were frayed, tensions were high. The blow put a metallic edge on everything.

But at five o'clock the next morning, amid a room strewn with fast food garbage, empty beverage cans and overloaded ashtrays, Tom Foster declared the mix complete.

For the first time in over a year, Webb, Morton and Angell shook hands. They had finally finished what had become one of the most anticipated albums of all time. And, by far, the most expensive.

Outside in the parking lot, Angell looked at the moon that still lit the sky over L.A. He breathed deep, deciding to let Charles off the hook at such an early hour.

Thoroughly exhausted, Angell took a cab through the purple predawn to the hotel where he had been living for the last twenty months. He needed a few hours sleep before unveiling *Lifeline* for the label execs. It was always worst for him the first time outsiders heard the music. Harley fucking hated it.

Two years ago, they were kissing his ring like he was the pope. Twenty months and a couple million in studio expenses later, he was practically a leper. Their patience had blown away with the budget, and the only thing that mattered to them now was delivering a new Stone Blossoms album to the stores before Christmas.

So strong was the band's following that the label was planning to raise the retail price of the album by a full dollar over competitive product. If *Lifeline* sold even *half* of what its two predecessors had sold, the price increase alone was worth nearly $10 million to the company's bottom line.

Of course, they were expecting a hell of a lot more than that. The release was expected to make it the label's most profitable year ever.

At 9:30 that same morning, with less than four hours sleep, Harley Angell was back in the HitMan lot. It was empty but for

the marked patrol unit driven by the security guard. He went to the door and found it locked.

Annoyed, Angell killed time walking. The day was already hot and he squinted against the glare that bounced off the glass storefronts he passed.

As he worked off his irritation, a combination of relief and an odd creeping depression took its place. The studio's demand to hear the final product had come so suddenly that he hadn't had time to assimilate his new reality: The *Lifeline* project was finally behind him. Twenty fucking months of blood, sweat and tears. It had cost him his relationship with his live-in girlfriend, and likely any future that Stone Blossoms might have had.

At least there was one thing. After a storm of gossip in the trade press, Angell looked forward to his public vindication. The album really was the best work they had ever done. A genuine goddamned rock masterpiece. Up there with *Pet Sounds,* or *Tommy,* or *Dark Side of the Moon.* Foster had even said as much, and he wasn't a man given to overstatement.

By the time Angell got back to the studio, two more cars occupied the lot. He recognized one of them as Tom Foster's. The other, he assumed, belonged to one of the Suits. There was still no sign of Webb, Morton or the others. Of course, he hadn't seen Lyle Sparks or Kevin Demers in weeks.

Time to get this over with.

He strode to the studio as he fought down a sudden wave of nausea. Months of writing and recording; basic tracks and overdubs; the fighting, pressure, compromise and adaptation. Then came the sudden recognition that no amount of preparation was sufficient to shield you from the moment when the waiting was over. It didn't matter that he had done this same thing on five previous albums. The first exposure was always hell.

He swung the door open and was confronted with the sound of heated conversation.

"—sure as hell better come up with something." An anonymous voice. One of the Suits.

"Listen, I'm sure—" It was Tom Foster.

The conversation broke off and three men came from the studio into the anteroom.

"What the fuck is this, Angell, some kind of goddamn joke?"

The Suit was a man Angell had seen before, but whose name never stuck. A vein pulsed in his temple. The other one stood silently, his hands in his pockets. He didn't look angry. He looked tragic.

"What are you talking about?" Harley said. He could feel his own pulse racing, but didn't know why.

Tom Foster came over, took Angell by the elbow and turned him, their backs to the two executives.

Foster leaned into Angell's ear and whispered, "Where're the tapes, man?"

"I don't know what you're talking about. They were in there," Angell answered, hooking a thumb over his shoulder, pointing to the control room. "Right where we left 'em when we finished mix-down this morning."

"Then we got a problem, my man," Foster said. "A big *fucking* problem."

They both turned back to the record company men.

Angell felt a sudden rush of blood heat his face. His vision began to pinwheel, its field of focus diminishing. He made his way to the control room, followed closely by the executives and Foster.

Harley Angell went directly to the empty tape deck upon which had lain the reels of brown tape that were Stone Blossoms' new album. He pointed, but didn't trust himself to speak. It was unthinkable that almost two years of gut wrenching work was no longer there.

Foster shook his head.

"It's gone, man."

This was Harley Angell's worst nightmare realized.

"What about Webb or Morton? Or Farr?" Angell asked, pleading.

"I was the last guy out of here this morning, Harley…" Foster said.

"What about the guard. Security would know if somebody—"

"I already talked to them. Said they didn't see anybody since we left."

"Mr. Angell," the first man said. "The tapes are insured, so the company can recoup at least part of the goddamned fortune you've blown here. But I hope you understand that you're contractually obligated to deliver a finished album."

"What the hell is that supposed to mean?" Foster said, before Angell could speak.

"What it means is that Stone Blossoms will have to start over. It's not as if they haven't had time to—"

"Oh, *Jesus,*" Angell croaked. "There's no fucking..."

He felt his knees go weak, and the nausea he had experienced earlier as nervous anticipation returned in a rush of terror. He ran to the door, his hand covering his mouth; to the sun, the fresh air outside.

This wasn't happening.

"Harley, listen—" Foster began.

But Harley Angell didn't hear. Time went still.

Angell had a moment of perfect clarity, knew what had to be done. He walked purposefully to his waiting car, the voices of the three men calling after him.

Everything in slow motion.

"Mr. Angell?" The driver said. "You all right?"

Angell was mechanical, unthinking.

"Fine, Charles. Take me home."

The angry label man strode across the parking lot toward the car.

"Now, please, Charles."

The car pulled away as Angell took the vial from his pocket, snorted messy piles from the back of his hand. Blurred images of passing cars, tall palms, billboards, passed in his peripheral vision.

Minutes or hours later, the car pulled to a stop. Angell got out without waiting for Charles.

"Mr. Angell?" The driver called after him.

He was an automaton. He went through the lobby to the elevators, through long narrow halls, past rows of identical doors.

He removed the key ring from his jeans, unlocked his suite and entered.

His head swarmed with music and the din of a million voices. He tasted a tear as it fell on his lips. He tore at his pocket for the vial, found it empty, and threw it against the wall. God damn it.

Harley went to the dresser and threw open a drawer, tossing its contents to the floor. His hand shook as he extracted a small metal box and took one of the tightly rolled joints hidden there. He lit it and took a deep drag.

Harley Angell went to the balcony door and pulled the curtains aside, opened it. He had always loved the view from up here. The sunrise when he returned from the studio. The cool breeze against his skin. The sounds of the street floating up.

He took another hungry hit and watched a pair of seagulls rise on the thermals. They called to each other until their cries were enveloped by the wail of a passing siren. Lonely sounds.

A warm gust tossed his hair as he leaned out over the rail, let the smoke roil away on the wind. He closed his eyes and swallowed hard against the dry lump in his throat.

Harley Angell took a long look across the rooftops of the city he thought he had come to love. A city that had embraced and shattered him.

From behind, he thought he caught a glimpse of someone coming toward him, but he couldn't be sure.

He didn't have time to turn.

It happened fast.

The wind whipped and tore at his clothes, but his mind was void. Empty. He never heard the horrified screams of the woman who witnessed his descent. His outstretched arms orchestrated a diver's floating moments before infinity.

PART TWO

RUBY TUESDAY

PACIFIC OCEAN
200 NAUTICAL MILES ENE
OF HAWAIIAN ISLANDS
SPRING, PRESENT DAY

3

I emerged from the master stateroom of my seventy-two foot, custom-built blue water sailing yacht, the *Kehau*, at exactly 4:00 a.m. I made my way through the galley and salon, came out onto the open afterdeck to relieve one of my two-man crew from his midnight-to-four watch. The sky was blue-black, mottled with stars, and just beginning to show signs of false dawn.

The three of us had been at sea for nine days, making our way south and west from Santa Catalina Island, off the southern California coast, to Kona, Hawaii, a trip of about twenty-five hundred miles. It was no accident that I had chosen the most remote islands on the face of the earth to sail to.

Until a few months ago, I had been a retired LAPD Homicide detective minding my own business, literally, running sporadic but expensive live-aboard sailing and scuba charters that catered to southern California's rich and famous. Mostly rich. The business provided a few extra dollars to augment my pension from twenty years as a cop, and kept me from dipping into the trust fund that my father had set aside for my brother and me prior to his death.

But the previous summer I had let my former partner, Hans Yamaguchi, talk me into coming back to LA to assist on a ridiculously sensationalized serial murder case. The Lizard King Murders. Jesus. The outcome had made me famous, a condition I wanted no part of, and didn't want to talk about anymore. The cost had been too goddamned high.

I was now sailing my yacht, and my life, in search of some anonymity and a fresh start.

"Morning, Yosemite," I said.

The morning's first breath of tropical sea air tugged at my hair. He nodded. "Four ayem already?"

Dave's tanned face was etched with deep lines that mapped his forty seven years, though his blue eyes, paled by years of squinting into the California sun, held the vigor of a man twenty years younger. Unruly graying blond hair and a long drooping mustache brought to mind the cartoon character Yosemite Sam, and had earned him his nickname. He was wearing a navy blue T-shirt. Across the back, in block letters, it read: WE HAVE ENOUGH YOUTH. HOW ABOUT A FOUNTAIN OF SMART? Amen.

An experienced charter boat captain, Yosemite was one of two friends and drinking buddies who had agreed to crew for me. The other was a marine engine mechanic, boat skipper, and ex-navy SEAL named Rex Blackwood. He was still in the rack below after taking the eight-to-midnight.

"I'm gonna check our GPS and start up some tea. Then I'll be back to relieve you," I told him.

I'd braved a month of caffeine withdrawal headaches kicking a two pot a day coffee habit I picked up from the job. Herbal tea was part of the new start I was trying to make. But the nine-millimeter in my nightstand, and the Beretta Bobcat I kept stashed in the galley drawer told the rest of that story.

"Bring me a mug when you come topside."

I put some water on the stove, then headed for the navigation desk at the rear of the salon.

I had personally designed the *Kehau*, and took pride in the workmanship that had realized it. All four staterooms were spacious and accommodating, and the main salon and galley were well-equipped and plush. I justified the expense in her construction by telling myself that it would make her a more popular charter. Of course that was a load of crap, but I didn't spend a lot of time worrying about it.

The communications and navigation area occupied a space at the foot of the stairs that descended from the afterdeck, and contained the most sophisticated communication, navigation and computer systems available. It was my post-retirement intent to sail her around the world, and this trip was her first serious voyage.

I checked our position on the GPS and translated the coordinates to the nav chart. After noting our location with a pencil mark and reviewing our progress, I pressed my face against the black rubber eyepiece of the radar screen and mentally noted the positions and distances of the other vessels in the area. Returning my attention to the chart, I did some quick calculations as to our speed during the night, and the remaining distance to Hawaii. It appeared that we had continued to make good time, with fair weather and following seas for most of the crossing.

I stowed the chart beside the nav table and heard the teapot spit and boil over. I filled a thermos with Mango Ceylon, grabbed a pair of plastic mugs, and returned to the afterdeck.

"Looks like we should make Kona by tomorrow morning." I said.

Yosemite nodded, stood up from the captain's chair, and shifted his gaze back to the horizon line just beginning to appear beneath a deep blue pre-dawn. I took the helm and lapsed into a contemplative silence.

Yosemite made his way to the bow, allowing his mug to sway with the gentle motion of the swells, careful not to spill it over his bare feet. I engaged the auto-pilot after checking the fishing gear we had been trolling since departing Avalon, then sat cross-legged in my chair.

I turned to face the emerging light of morning and practiced emptying my mind. It wasn't something that came easily.

Fleeting images passed, beckoned me to latch on and be pulled along in their wake, like the lines behind *Kehau*. Twenty years on the street careened through my head, slipping on a slick of black blood; the bone and gristle on the walls of a suburban apartment where a young mother and baby girl had been shotgunned by a jealous lover; the wrack and twist of a body taking a round through the chest; a young patrolman bleeding out in my arms after taking a bullet through the femoral artery, staring at my useless tourniquet; my first partner eating his gun when he ran out of things to give a shit about.

And there was more. Plenty more. Dreams, too. Lots of fucking dreams. But I refused to go.

The familiar rush of the sea against the *Kehau*'s hull blended with the creak of ropes and wind in the sails, and called me back. I breathed heavily and opened my eyes.

A dark red line had insinuated itself between the black of the ocean and the glowing sky. Thin clouds, stretched from tufts of cotton, reflected shades of purple, red and silver.

The abrasive whine of two Penn International reels woke Rex and brought him running full speed from his stateroom below. Yosemite reached the first one about the time Rex grabbed the other. I pulled *Kehau* into a tight turn to starboard.

The ex-SEAL was a big man. At six-four and about two-forty, he had me by two inches and thirty pounds. His heavy jaw was stubbled with the new growth of reddish beard, one he had begun at the outset of our trip, and a blond ponytail reached his shoulder blades. A bizarre tattoo of a bearded old man in a hooded robe, a walking staff in one hand and a lantern in another, swelled with the motion of his beefy arms.

"Hoooo-Ya!" Rex hollered. "Hell of a way to wake up!"

"Fuckin' A," Yosemite laughed. I maneuvered the boat while Rex and Yosemite made their way to opposite sides of the transom working to keep their lines as far apart as possible.

Ten minutes later I was washing the blood of two ahi tuna, each no less than sixty pounds, off the deck. Rex and Yosemite grinned like idiots while I went to work cleaning the fish, making filets of the dark red meat.

"That was bitchen," Yosemite said finally.

Bitchen. He was single-handedly working to bring the word back into fashion.

Rex went below to get dressed while Yosemite took the wheel. I took three thick ahi steaks below and threw them on the grill for a breakfast of eggs and fresh fish. It was my turn. As with the watches, we took turns with the meals.

"The fuck are you doing?" Yosemite protested. The three of us were seated in the aft cockpit. Yosemite had brought lunch up from the galley, and we were just getting started.

Rex grabbed the fork out of Dave's hand and tossed it overboard with the peach still attached to its tines. Dave watched it arc away from the boat.

It was coming up on noon and the sun beat down from a cloudless sky.

I heard the fruit hit the water.

"No fucking canned peaches in the field. Last time I had peaches," Rex moved a hank of hair behind his ear and revealed an ugly, jagged scar. "This happened."

"Okay, I'll toss the goddamn peaches. Try to relax, bro," Yosemite said. One by one he slid them off his plate and over the side.

I shrugged and tossed mine overboard too. Rex grunted and went below muttering about peaches and beer.

Rex brought three bottles of Asahi back to the afterdeck, where I was lazily allowing the auto-pilot to do the work. Rex handed one to me and the other to Yosemite. Rex twisted the cap off his and tossed it over the side.

"We'd just got back from a couple days' R&R in Saigon," Rex began abruptly. Dave shot a furtive glance at me, then turned back to Rex. "When this cheesy REMF comes to me and another guy from the Teams—"

"REMF?" Dave interrupted.

"Rear Echelon Motherfucker," Rex said. "Desk jockey. Anyway, dude says our SEAL Team is gonna be taking him and this other cat into the field so he can meet up with this big-time village chief. The story smelled like shit, but we'd been down in the Special Zone—this defoliated piece of fucking swamp—running ops for weeks and we were all ready to *didi* out of that place."

I took a slug of my beer and pictured a younger Rex. A man trained as a member of one of the most feared military units in the world.

"So we get briefed by this REMF who calls himself Mr. Green, and this other spook, Mr. Gold. Both of 'em are wearing mirror shades, man, just like the fucking movies."

Dave pulled at his beer, wiped the foam off his mustache.

"It gets better," Rex said. He reached into his shirt pocket and pulled out a cigar. "Want one?"

I shook my head.

Rex looked to Yosemite and held the smoke out to him. "You? It's a Macanudo."

"Naw," Dave said. "Go on."

I don't know how many hours I'd spent with these two guys over the past couple years living in Avalon. But most of it had been spent in Pete's Roadhouse, my bar of choice. It struck me then how little I really knew about their lives. Nor they mine. But we knew one another's reputations. And that had been enough. But nine days in the middle of nowhere was forging something else.

Rex slipped the cigar from its white tube, bit off the end. He didn't light it, but rolled it between his fingers as he spoke.

"We ran this early morning insertion into the mountains. I remember thinking that everything sounded different up there. Different birds, I guess. Smelled different, too. I'd heard stories of the Montagnards—these indigenous mountain tribes—and how we were trying to use them for intel. Goddamn 'yards knew everything, and neither the VC or ARVN could get control of 'em.

"After about four-five hours of humping the jungle, the spooks want to stop for some chow just outside this 'ville. Team leader tells the spooks they're outta their fuckin' minds. I mean, we don't know what we got in that 'ville. You can smell the cooking fires and hear the goddamn chickens, we're so close."

I took another pull off my Asahi and scanned the horizon. There was a pair of lights off to starboard that I'd need to identify on radar before long. Rex saw them too.

"See the lights?" he asked.

"Yeah, I'll check them out in a minute. Go on," I said. "Finish your story."

He pulled a stainless steel Zippo from his pocket and lit his cigar. The smell of lighter fuel reminded me of the squad room. It whipped away on the breeze.

"Mr. Green opens his rations and starts eating. When Green gets to the peaches, Sully Tyler, our Team leader, tells him to toss them. It'd been a superstition in the unit for a long time about eating fucking peaches in the field. Green tells him to fuck himself, and Tyler's about to go after him. But before he could, Green shoves one of the things in his mouth and starts chewing and smiling. Juice is running down the guy's chin, and Tyler's about to kick the shit out of the guy. 'See,' the spook says, 'nothing to it.' Tyler slapped the can out of the spook's hand and said, 'It's on your head, motherfucker.' Something like that.

"Not fifteen minutes later, we're reconning the 'ville and this dink pops up outta this spider hole and puts a round right through Green's throat. All hell breaks loose and the place turns into a free-fire zone. I mean there's shit coming down from everywhere. I see Tyler disappear into this cloud of smoke coming from a hooch and I follow him in. My eyes are burning from the smoke, and I can't hear nothing but grenades and small arms fire. Just as I enter the hooch, I see Tyler laying there on his back. His leg is gone from the knee down, and he's pointing at me. His mouth is moving, but I can't hear a thing. All I'm thinking about is getting Tyler outta there. And the fucking peaches. I can't stop thinking about the goddamn peaches.

"I grab Tyler by the collar and start dragging him out of the hooch when I feel something behind me. That's what Tyler was pointing at. Two VC are right behind me coming through the smoke. I gave 'em a burst of full rock & roll and turned 'em to pink mist. But I kept pulling Tyler by the collar until I got him outside. The Team medic sees me and helps drag Tyler to the treeline. I ran back toward the ville and took up a new firing position. I'm so pissed. I'm thinking about that cocksucker CIA spook and his goddamn peaches when I get a pair of rifle butt strokes in the back of the head. Crushed my skull and left me for dead. After that, everything is a blank. I wake up in Saigon with my head shaved bald and a headache so fierce I can't hardly open my eyes."

Blue cigar smoke floated across the transom like a spectre, and the water slipping beneath the hull was a strange silence after the firefight in my head. Rex smiled bitterly.

I went below to check the radar and mark the distance and heading of the vessel whose lights I had seen earlier. Different course, no threat. I grabbed two more beers and went aft again. Rex and Dave were silent as snipers, watching a group of sea birds work a school of bait.

I broke the silence. "You come home after that?"

"Naw. I spent three weeks in a hospital in Bangkok and went back to my unit. But it was never the same after that. We lost Tyler and that asshole Green on that op. I was the only wounded. But I started having these weird visions and shit."

"Hallucinations?" Dave asked.

"More like out-of-body experiences."

He sighed and plucked a piece of tobacco off his tongue, then spat over the side.

"They got so bad that they took me out of the field…"

Rex looked up then, glanced from Dave to me. "Fucking spooks were crawling all over 'Nam at that time. They took me out of the field. Somebody heard about my OBE's and this extremely scary dude from Langley had me transferred from the Teams to this special unit stateside."

The big man puffed his cheeks and blew a series of smoke rings that the wind pulled apart.

Dave looked at me, then at Rex. A stray cloud passed in front of the sun and threw us briefly into shadow.

The tip of the Macanudo glowed an angry red as Rex pulled at it one last time. He exhaled a cloud and tossed the butt over the side. A fiery trail of ashes floated down behind it where it died with an audible hiss.

"You were never over there were you?" Rex asked.

"Too young," I said. "Missed the draft by a few years."

"You'd think it'd pass after all this time."

"We've all got ghosts, Rex," I said.

It was coming up on midnight and Dave was about to wake up and take the watch. Rex turned and looked squarely at me. His face glowed orange in the pale light of the compass.

"What about you?" he asked.

Good fucking question. "I'm a rich kid who thought he could make something of himself by changing his name. Go it on my own."

"You were a good cop." The way he said it sounded like a question.

I had done twenty years with the LAPD in an attempt, in some way that still eluded me, to set things right. I'd seen a dozen lifetimes of misery. Seen so much it felt like the darkness was coming in on me. I felt it for the last couple years on the job. Felt my tolerance begin to slip, becoming a violent threat to the assholes I collared up. A dangerous man.

"Yeah," I nodded. "I was a good cop."

"Used your gun some, I heard."

And a spring-loaded sap, a nightstick, a gun-butt, a beer bottle, my fists. "Yeah. I used my gun," I said.

"Then you know." Rex nodded to himself, and looked to the sky.

I went below and grabbed us a couple beers. His watch was over and mine didn't start until four. I cracked one and handed it to Rex.

"Thanks, man."

"When I was a rookie," I said. "I spent my first tour in a squad car with this red-faced vet named Gilley. Real old school. We get this call-out in a nasty section of South Central. Pull to the curb of the building and this pair of badass motherfucker gangbangers is standing at the door. One's got a sweatshirt hood pulled up over his head, you know?"

"Asshole punks," Rex said.

"This one dude makes the hard eyes at Gilley, and Gilley doesn't even break stride. Goes right up to the asshole and looks right into his face, doesn't even blink. They stand there for a good twenty, maybe thirty seconds, and the shithead breaks it off. Gilley laughs as the guy walks off. 'Who was that?' I asked him. Gilley says, 'Who the fuck knows, kid.' And we went upstairs to answer the call."

I heard Dave rattling around down below and looked at my watch. Ten minutes to midnight. This time tomorrow we'd be in the islands. A long damn way from South Central.

"I don't get it." Rex said finally.

"Found out later that the guy Gilley had the stare-down with was this dude he'd busted maybe six months earlier on a rape charge. Story at the time was that Gilley took the guy down in a full-body tackle on the sidewalk in front of the dude's building, pulled down the guy's pants and shaved his pubes for a DNA sample. Does some shit like that and Gilley didn't even recognize the guy just six months later."

The tail of a shooting star sliced a silver gash across the night sky and disappeared without a trace. I blinked away the glow it left in my eyes.

"That's how fucking anonymous it is. How fucking out-of-control."

"That kinda shit'll change you," Rex said.

I started out like ninety-nine percent of my class at the Academy: wanting to Make A Difference. The full magnitude of that vanity was only now becoming apparent to me.

"Without a doubt," I agreed.

The night was warm, and the beer had finally taken the edge off my mood. "I'm gonna get a few hours' sleep," I said.

"I'm still pretty wired. Take it easy, Travis." He leaned against the aft rail and stared out beyond the curling wake as I went below.

I came back a minute later with another Asahi and handed it to him.

"Thanks, man…" he said.

I nodded and turned to go below.

"Not just for the beer," he finished.

"I know."

4

By noon we had rounded Kaiwi Point and were passing into the wide mouth of Kailua Bay. A pod of eight or nine spinner dolphin guided us in, gliding beneath the bow of the *Kehau* as she sliced the turquoise water. From my vantage point at the helm in the upper wheelhouse bridge, I could see their sleek gray silhouettes periodically breaking the surface, and hear the huff of their expelled breath.

The sea shallowed rapidly from sapphire blue to the color of an aquamarine stone as we passed the point. The contours of the sandy bottom were clearly visible, even though the depthfinder had it pegged at nearly sixty feet.

I picked up the microphone of the VHF and switched over to channel sixteen. I notified the harbormaster of our arrival, and requested temporary permission to tie to the pier for an hour or so while Rex, Dave and I offloaded our accumulated garbage and waited for the Agricultural Inspector.

After instructing me to switch over to channel twenty-alpha, the harbormaster asked me a few questions, waived the Ag inspection and gave me a thirty-day permit to anchor in Kailua Bay. By two o'clock we were securely moored and cracking our first Asahi.

"Nice crossing," I said and we banged the bottles together.

Dave was anxious to get ashore, and wasted no time in making it known.

"Let's get into town and drink us some personality," he said.

Rex and Yosemite went below to their showers, but I stayed behind for a few minutes to myself. The tradewinds blew gently through a stand of coconut palms on the shoreline. The pointed steeple of the old Congregational church spiked into the sky behind the trees like a prudish chaperone. The swells breaking against the seawall showered white foam on unsuspecting tourists.

Low-slung buildings traced the shoreline in both directions, and disappeared behind the bulk of the King Kamehameha Hotel which occupied the northernmost end of the bay. Ancient banyan trees spilled shade between groups of palms and plumeria that lined the frontage road.

My mind formed an image, like a sepia print, of this same coastline; pristine and lush, the way it must have been in the time before the arrival of the first Europeans, missionaries and Americans. I saw an uncluttered coastline, striped with fields of green taro stretching up the slopes of Hualalai, thatched huts dotting the strand. I was struck by a familiar sadness that such an aesthetic and serene culture had been devastated by sailors, whalers, missionaries and businessmen. Old Auntie Malia's stories rang in my ears.

I lifted a silent toast to the sea, and the ones who came before, took a long last pull from the bottle in my hands and emptied it.

We slid across the bay toward the pier in the smaller of the *Kehau*'s two skiffs, a seventeen foot Boston Whaler center console, immoderately overpowered with a 90 horsepower Evinrude two-stroke. I call it the *Chingadera*.

I tied off at a ragged wooden dock that was part of the concrete pier. I gave five bucks to a couple of kids to keep an eye on the skiff, and we climbed the creaking ramp for the hotel. The scent of coconut suntan oil drifted across the beach and drew my attention to a knot of young women sunbathing there. College-aged, I guessed. They waved and made girl noises, then pulled a couple more shiny cans from a cooler.

"Were we ever that young?" Yosemite said.

Rex and I just kept on walking.

Kids splashed noisily as numbed adults pulled on cocktails with fruit and flowers around the rims. A pair of red-eyed and shirtless fat men watched us from their seats at the bar as we passed the pool. Fifty weeks pushing company paper for a ten-day package tour to paradise, sucking up mai tais while the wives collected spoons and salt shakers with pictures of Diamond Head. They looked pissed-off and cheated as they watched us pass into the lobby. Swindled by the choices they'd made.

I approached the dark haired girl behind the koa wood reception desk. She wore a pale yellow print dress with a revealing neckline, and fixed me with brown eyes you could fall into. I couldn't help stealing glances at her cleavage while she gave us a recommendation for a bar that met our prerequisites: women, good music and a pool table.

"I like Lola's myself," she smiled, taking in my bluewater tan.

"Close by?" I asked.

"Oh, yeah. Just down that way." Her breasts rolled prominently as she pointed down the road.

"One other thing," I said. "I need to rent a car. How far to the airport?"

"Not far, maybe six or seven miles."

"Thanks. Maybe we'll see you at Lola's," I said. I flashed her a smile that I hoped didn't look too predatory.

"Yeah. I hope so." More of the brown eyes and white smile in return. Two Dodge van taxis were parked in front of the main lobby. I flagged the first one in line, gave him our destination and we headed down the narrow street that fronted the bay.

He pulled to a stop in a small gravel lot across from a two-story plantation-style building. On street level, a wide lanai was crowded with sun-roasted tourists drinking strange colored drinks from hurricane glasses. The three of us looked at each other blankly. Not a fucking chance.

"Lola's?" I asked the cab driver.

"Upstairs," he answered, pointing at an angle we could not visually follow from inside the cab.

Rex and Dave reluctantly opened their doors, but their expressions changed almost instantly. Loud music and familiar noises emanated from the open-air bar that occupied the entire second floor of the old building.

"Fucking *perfect*, bro," Dave said.

"I'll catch up with you in an hour, hour and a half," I said. "I've got a couple of things to take care of first."

"Later," Rex said. "You know where we'll be."

"Hey, Dave," I called. "You groom that 'stache of yours?"

He tugged on the drooping handlebars and grinned. "Special for the ladies, bro. Mustache rides for one and all."

I had the driver drop me at the airport. Before leaving the counter to pick up a cheesy red Mustang convertible from the lot behind the rental desk, I asked for directions to the Kona police substation.

Since I carried the badge of a retired detective, and the concealed weapon I was entitled to, I felt obliged to check in with the locals and let them know I was in their jurisdiction. It was a professional courtesy, and something I wanted to have taken care of before spending much time in town.

A few minutes later, I parked and walked through dual glass doors. A blast of air conditioning struck me like a body blow. A thick glass partition separated the empty waiting area from the rows of desks and workstations beyond.

The officer manning reception, a twenty-something kid with a military cut, gave me an expressionless once-over. The nameplate on the pocket of his dark blue uniform said Kealoha. I leaned toward the glass and asked for five minutes of the watch commander's time. Kealoha picked up the telephone, spoke briefly in a voice I couldn't hear, and turned back to me.

"Your name?" he asked.

"Mike Travis."

"Travis?" He asked like he hadn't heard me right.

"Correct. Mike Travis."

"Hang on," he said and resumed his *sotto voce* conversation with the phone. A moment later he hung up and said, "Captain Cerrillo will be with you in a few minutes. Have a seat over there." He pointed to a row of uncomfortable looking molded plastic chairs that lined the wall across from the main entrance.

Fifteen minutes later, I had read the local paper from cover to cover, and scanned the classifieds for a used car. I jotted the numbers of two likely prospects on a corner of the last page and tore it off.

I was stuffing the scrap in my wallet when Kealoha told me the captain was available see me. He buzzed an electric lock, and pointed the way to a closed door at the far corner of the room. The work area was quiet and orderly. It didn't look anything like the one I came from. A couple of cops in street clothes stood beside a copy machine at the rear of the room and watched me approach the captain's door. I rapped firmly and the two resumed their work.

"In," a voice commanded.

I opened the door and nodded a greeting.

"I'm Mike Travis, Captain. Thank you for seeing me."

"What can I do for you, Mr. Travis?" He was stocky, maybe five or six years older than me. He rose from his seat and extended a hand, but not without giving me the same once-over I had gotten up front. The grip was firm and dry, and his thick, muscular neck looked to be more the product of manual labor than the gym. He wore a dark blue uniform, open at the collar, yellow captains' bars embroidered on shoulder epaulettes, and a no-bullshit expression on his square face.

"I wanted to introduce myself," I said. "I used to be on the job. LAPD. Detective. Retired." I waited through a thick silence, Cerillo's expression unchanging, then continued. "In any event, Captain, I came only as a courtesy, and to let you know that I have a carry permit."

He was still for another long moment. I reached into my pocket, withdrew my wallet and volunteered my identification and permit.

"Narc?" he asked. He searched my face carefully, reconciling the clean-cut photo on my ID with the weathered face in front of him. A man with shoulder-length sunbleached hair, aloha shirt and rubber flip-flops.

"I was a detective for fourteen years, Captain, after six riding a patrol unit. Three years in Narcs, three in Sex Crimes, and eight more in Homicide."

Cerillo nodded and handed my ID back.

"What do you carry?" he asked, still standing behind his desk.

"Depends. Sometimes a nine," I answered. "Beretta Model 92. Sometimes a Bobcat."

"Hmm," he grunted. "How long are you here for?"

"Indefinitely. I sailed over from California and arrived earlier today. I'm anchored in Kailua Bay for the next month or so. Boat's called the *Kehau*."

Cerillo nodded and finally sat down. He motioned me to do the same.

"What kind of work are you doing over here, Travis?"

"I don't know exactly what I'll be doing yet."

Cerillo frowned. I could read his mind. Just what he needed: a gun-toting, unemployed, ex-cop roaming his quiet streets.

"I used to run a charter and scuba business in Catalina," I said. "I don't know if I'll be doing the same thing here or not. I'm just going to wait and see. Just minding my own business."

"Uh huh," he said with an undertone of skepticism. "Where will you be heading after you pull out of Kailua?"

"My family has a house down near the Place of Refuge. I may stay, may move on. I don't know."

At the mention of a home at Pu'uhonua 'O Honaunau, Cerillo's eyes registered faint surprise. That area was both remote and exclusive, not a heavily populated place. Particularly not a place where many *haoles*, whites, would live. To my knowledge, there were still only three houses there: the one belonging to my family; a small coffee shack occupied by a close family friend; and a third, dating back to the early 1900's, once owned by descendants of the *Ali'i*.

"I know that area. You must have that big plantation house, huh? Do you know Tino Orlandella? He lives down that way."

"He lives next door," I said. "He looks after the place for us."

Cerillo looked surprised. "Your mama was a Kamahale. Married the rich *haole*."

"That's right," I said. "Lily Kamahale. She drowned there when I was a boy."

"I remember. My auntie was good friends with your mom." His eyes grew distant for a moment. "I'm sorry."

I was the one who found her. Floating face down in the bay just off the shore. A gray and humid day. Sirens and red lights. Ambulances and cops. I was thirteen when they covered her with a thin white sheet and left me standing on the stoop.

"Thanks."

The cop face came back. "You talk to Tino?"

Tino Orlandella and I had been friends since we were boys. My brother and I had spent every summer with our parents at the house on the beach, and Tino had become a good friend. The last time I had seen him was about four years after my mother died. We were both about seventeen or eighteen. My father was giving it one last try with my brother and me, but it wasn't the same. It was the last time my father ever took us back to that house, though he could never bring himself to sell it. It was too much a part of her.

Tino was getting ready to leave for the army that autumn. Just out of high school, we spent a lot of time surfing, diving, and chasing girls that summer. I had only come back twice since then. My brother had never come back.

"I'm driving down there tomorrow."

Cerrillo nodded. "He's been in some trouble lately. You know about that?"

"No. What kind of trouble?"

"He can tell you if he wants to. When you see him, tell him to keep his shit together, okay?" The captain's message was clearly intended for me as well, and I didn't like the tone.

I stood. "I appreciate your time, Captain."

"You got a number if I need to reach you?"

I took a pen from the holder on his desk and scratched my cellular telephone number on the back of one of Cerillo's business cards, took a clean one for myself. When I finished I tossed it on his desk, turned and opened the door.

"I don't want any trouble," he said. "You pass that on to Tino, too."

"I also monitor VHF channel 19," I said over my shoulder. "You can raise me that way too."

I tossed a ragged salute to Kealoha at the desk on my way out and headed back to Lola's to join Yosemite and Rex. I glanced at my watch and hoped I hadn't fallen too far behind.

5

I groped blindly for the Tag Heuer diver's watch I keep on the nightstand. Not there.

My headache pounded. I pried my reluctant eyes open and finally located it on my wrist. 4:37a.m. Heavy rain beat against the teak deck above, and the *Kehau* moved restlessly against her mooring. It reminded me of that night in Avalon. That kind of rain always would.

I sat upright amidst a clammy tangle of sheets, ran my fingers through damp hair. My pulse drummed behind my eyeballs, my mouth tasted raw.

Red eyes gazed back at me as I splashed cool water on my face. A little too much celebration at Lola's. It was all coming back. I brushed my teeth, and opened the portholes in my stateroom. The Hawaiian air felt cool against my skin.

I crept down the companionway to check on my crew. Loud snores came from both guest staterooms. Good. Rex and Dave were both aboard. I sure as hell didn't remember coming back from the bar.

I climbed the stairs to the galley, passed amid a static hiss from the VHF radio that I always leave on, and went on deck to see if the *Chingadera* was tied alongside. It was, but I didn't remember doing that either. I watched it bob and tug with the rhythm of my pounding head. It was going to be a long day.

I sat cross-legged on the deck and let the rain drench me. The heavy drops soaked me to the skin, but it felt good to have

42

something natural, something normal and grounding, happening to me. I needed to re-orient after the previous night's debauch. Another twenty five hundred miles between my old life and the new one. Between LA Homicide and me.

After a half hour or so, I went below, toweled off, then dressed in a pair of shorts and olive green T-shirt. By the time I returned to the galley, I felt my shirt beginning to stick to my back despite the air conditioning inside. I found a bottle of aspirin, shook out three tablets, and washed them down with a cold Asahi.

The beer found my raw stomach.

I opened a can of tomato juice, poured it in a large tumbler, tossed in a handful of ice and filled the rest with beer. My old standby hangover remedy. Hair of the dog.

By five-thirty the rain had stopped. Patches of purple sky glowed between the parting clouds. Dawn. My talisman. I took a towel to the afterdeck, wiped down a space, and lay down in the cool morning air.

I must have fallen asleep, because the sun was well over Hualalai volcano when I reopened my eyes. I stood up with a commendable sense of balance, then went below to fire up my laptop. After logging on through the on-board satellite system, I checked for e-mail, then got my day under way.

I had planned on making the hour-long drive to check on my family's old beach house, and seeing my friend, Tino. I hadn't seen the place in over twenty years. I tried to pretend it was something else, but it was a pilgrimage.

I turned off the main highway onto a one lane surface road that veered off toward the ragged coastline. I worked through the sharp twists and turns. Dense groves of coffee and macadamia nuts blanketed the mountain behind me. Spindled trunks of papaya and palms spread out ahead amid purple and white orchids growing wild along the road.

About four miles down toward the ocean a yellow sign marked the entrance to a private road where the pavement turned to dirt. A canopy of monkeypod overgrew the road and formed a tunnel. Pinpoints of midmorning sun filtered through and dotted the road. Imprints of tires were visible in red-brown earth. About two hundred yards on, the road ended in a cul-de-sac carved from a coconut grove.

I parked and rolled down the window, letting the engine idle. The fragrance of plumeria filled the air and triggered a rush of memories. Memories I had called upon for years, retreated to, when times were bad.

But it was harder than I thought coming back. I could still see the red strobes of the ambulance on the side of the house. The cops. My mother's shrouded body. But the place held power. An indelible piece of my past, laid down like tire treads.

I looked off into the shady space between our house and that of our neighbor, Tino, and recalled happier times. Games of war we played as kids. Later it was spin-the-bottle with Ruby Duke and Laura de Stefano. The excitement of first touch, innocent.

I could remember the first time I felt I was in love. It was Ruby. The summer I turned seventeen. My mother was dead, and my father, brother and I had returned for the first time since.

Tino and Ruby had long since married and lived in the house given them by Tino's family. A lot of time had passed since I had seen either of them.

Tino was a construction laborer by trade, but looked after my family's house in a casual arrangement where he'd let either my brother or me know if anything needed repair. Tino wanted nothing in exchange. A friend. But I always saw to it that they were taken care of every Christmas.

Our place was simple, two stories, constructed in the late 1950's; basically a large square with a wide lanai surrounding the front and sides. Oversized windows opened onto a tranquil lagoon. Red and yellow hibiscus surrounded the wooden railing that ran the perimeter of the lanai.

I switched off the ignition. A brief silence was overtaken by the clatter of mynah birds. I stepped from the car and walked barefooted across the sandy soil to the door of my family's plantation-style house.

I stopped for a moment at the landing and looked for the initials I had carved into the concrete with a nail a lifetime ago. *MTKV*. Mike Travis Kamahale-Van de Groot. My last two initials had since been swept away by the flood of water under the bridge.

I took out a key and inserted it into the keyhole. As I turned it, the door abruptly pulled inward. A stink of old cigarettes and stale liquor assaulted me and a shirtless man wearing faded cutoffs peered through the screen at me. His hair was tousled and unkempt, eyes yellow and bloodshot.

"Haul ass," he said, shutting the door. The voice was like gravel. "Get the hell outta here."

Cold rage surged. This place was almost sacred to me.

I pulled the screen open and pushed through. He jumped back just in time to keep from being hit by the swinging door.

"Who the fuck you think you are, dude?" he said. Surly, but shaken.

"You're in my house, asshole." I planted my bare feet, ready to put out the guy's lights. I was expecting him to throw a punch, but he surprised me by laughing instead.

"Fuck off," he said, and began to shut the door again.

I took hold of his unshaven neck. I found the nerve ends, dug in, and walked him backward. I bounced him off the couch and he landed hard on the floor.

My stomach heaved. The room was musty and closed, littered with empty bottles. The only fresh air came in through the door behind me.

"How about we start over?" I said.

The man rubbed his throat and eyed me furiously. He pushed his words around the bruises. "Do—Do you know who I *am*?"

"No. I thought you understood that."

"I'm Danny Webb."

I shrugged.

"Fuck you, man. I'm a guest of Valden Van de Groot. It's his house."

I should have guessed. My brother and I don't always communicate well.

"You're the rock star," I said. He looked familiar, but hard living had left its mark. Keith Richards without the class.

"Yeah. That's right." Self-importance lit in his bloodshot eyes. It was a look his face was comfortable with.

"I thought you were dead." I didn't really. But he looked like he was working at it. And using my family's house to do it.

He rubbed his throat angrily. "You fucked up my vocal chords."

"Nothing permanent."

He started to stand up.

I took a long step and pushed hard on the top of his head. He slammed back to the floor. His face turned an angry red.

"I'm Valden's brother, the *other* owner of this house. Now just sit tight there, friend, and we'll get this taken care of."

He took out a pack of cigarettes and lighter, shook one loose, and pulled it from the package with his dry lips.

"No," I said.

Webb glared, then put the cigarette in a dirty ashtray, unlit.

I stepped over a pile of dirty laundry and walked to the phone in the kitchen. I punched out the number for VGC's New York headquarters.

"Van de Groot Capital," a nasal voice answered after two rings.

"Valden Van de Groot, please," I said.

"One moment." An electronic click was followed by muzak-on-hold.

A cockroach shot across a pile of cardboard take-out boxes. A stack of dishes sat in gray water.

"Mister Van de Groot's office." A woman's voice. Officious, precise. An I've-already-got-you- by-the-balls voice.

"I want to speak with Valden," I said.

"I'm sorry, but—"

"Let's not do it this way, okay? I'm Mike Travis, Valden's brother. I'd like to speak with him *now*, please."

"I really don't think—"

"Now. Please."

"Ju—Just a moment." She retreated into the silent power of Van de Groot Capital.

There was another click and a full two minutes of muzak. He came on the line. Harried, edgy.

"You'll never guess where I am," I said.

"Listen, I don't have time for—"

"I'm in the kitchen at the beach house," I finished.

"Oh." His tone suddenly sheepish. "I can explain—"

"I doubt it. I stopped by the place this morning. You know what I found, in addition to the wreckage from a three day bender? Some burned-out jerkoff telling me to…" I took the phone away from my ear and looked over at Danny Webb. "How did you put it? 'Haul ass?' Was that it?"

Webb watched me. He was cooling off, starting to think.

"Look, Mike. I know we have an arrangement. I know you were planning on using the place, okay? But we're in the middle of an important deal with the guy, and I let him use the house for a couple weeks. Sort of a goodwill gesture. That shouldn't be too hard for you to understand."

I couldn't imagine what Danny Webb could possibly have that would interest Valden and VGC.

"No. Not difficult to understand at all, Valden. But I don't really care how important your deal is, I think you friend here is king of the shitheads. The place is trashed, and no telling what felonies have been going on in here. I want him gone."

"He's not standing right there, is he?" My brother sounded as sick as I felt.

"Want to talk to him?"

"Oh, Jesus, Mike. You talked about him like that right in *front* of him? Oh my God. Do you have any idea how important—"

"Fill me in later. I'll put him on, and you can arrange for his departure." I handed the receiver to Danny Webb.

Webb looked at me with loathing.

"Yeah," he said into the mouthpiece. Mr. Charm.

I watched him listen, grunt periodically, nod. He finally looked over at me, tried to give me a hard look that didn't quite come off. "Yeah, okay, Valden, no hard feelings. Friday's cool. Later." He hung up.

The stairs creaked as someone descended the staircase. I turned and saw another haggard looking man in his late thirties, early forties, shirtless, wearing only a pair of faded swim trunks. He absently scratched his balls and yawned, a skinny arm draped over the shoulders of a girl that couldn't have been over seventeen. She looked stoned to the gills.

The guy looked at me, then at Webb.

"What's going on, man?" Thin nasal voice. Rock star hanger-on.

"Nothing," Webb said, annoyed.

I turned and started to leave.

"Clean this place up good, rock star," I said. "You live like a pig."

I could feel his eyes boring into my back. As I got to the door, I turned to face him again. "One more thing."

"What?"

"Get that girl back home or I'll see you do time for statutory rape."

Outside, I saw Tino sitting in a beat up wicker chair on the lanai in front of his house. His had been built, I guessed, in the 1930's. It was constructed of wood with a corrugated metal roof that had long since rusted to a ruddy brown. A classic Hawaiian coffee shack.

Recognition finally crossed his face, like moving from shadow to sunlight.

"Hey, Mik*aaay!* Howzit, brah?" he said as he rose unsteadily from his seat.

"How you, bruddah?" I responded in the easy pidgin prevalent among locals.

"Long time, brah! Let me look at you," he said, stopping about three feet from me and giving me a theatrical once over. "We all grown up now, huh, Mikey?" He embraced me with his thick brown arms.

"All grown up," I said.

Tino was constructed of geometric patterns. His head was a wide oval balanced on a solid square torso between broad shoulders. His neck was lost in there somewhere. He had legs like tree stumps and his whole body rocked from side to side when he walked. A thick tangle of black hair stuck up in unruly tufts, like he had just woken up. He wore only a pair of tattered blue shorts and rubber sandals.

"You look good, Mikey," he smiled and patted his bare brown stomach. "I come fat."

"Too much kaukau," I said.

"And beer," he added with a laugh. "Come sit, man. Let's talk story, yeah?"

I followed him to his house. "So where's Ruby?"

"She's workeen', brah. Cleaneen' houses, yeah?" His voice inflected like a question, but it wasn't. "She be back in a while. Can you wait around? She'll be mad she don' see you."

"I'd like to see her, too." I asked what he was doing home so late.

"Things been slow for me. Not much work, you know? If you don't got one gover'ment job, things real slow," he shook his head sadly as he looked at the scarred wood floorboards between his feet.

"Anything I can do?" I offered.

"No, man. Thanks. We be fine."

The rattling of palm fronds sounded like rain above my head. In the distance, swells broke on the shoreline.

We spent the next hour talking, dusting off old reminiscences, becoming friends again. He told me about becoming a father, and how strange it is to see his child grow up. Ruby and Tino had one daughter, Edita. She had just turned fifteen, and was named after Tino's mother.

But I felt there was something dark beneath the surface. Something brooding, caged. I could tell things were much tougher for him and his family than he was letting on. Maybe some trouble with his daughter. I remembered Captain Cerillo's admonition to tell Tino to stay out of trouble.

"I met Max Cerillo yesterday," I said. I saw Tino stiffen.

"Yeah? What for you wanna see him?"

"Professional courtesy. I wanted the locals to know I'm here."

"Yeah, sure. I forget you're a cop sometimes," he said almost apologetically.

"Was a cop. I'm retired now."

"Yeah sure. Okay."

A displaced tension hung between us.

"You sure everything's okay, Tino?"

"Look—" he started, annoyance bordering on anger colored his tone. He caught himself and re-started. "Look, Mike, everything's cool. Really. Hey, how about—"

Tino was cut off by the barking of a dog that had just rounded the corner of his house at a full run. Misjudging its own speed, his rear end slipped out from under him in a cloud of dust. The dog recovered its footing, then ran directly to Tino, all tongue and wagging tail.

"Hey, boy," Tino crooned, as he scratched behind its droopy ears. "This is 'Poi Dog'."

Poi Dog broke away from Tino to sniff curiously around me. I took the dog's face in my hands and scratched him, removing the dog's long nose from my crotch.

"Nice dog," I said. "What is he?"

"A poi dog, brah. A mutt. A little of everything."

"Stray?"

"Naw. Edita brought him back from town when he was just a puppy. Somebody was giving them away. I was kinda pissed at first, but the goddamn thing is so friendly, I couldn't stay mad. I let her keep 'im."

A dirty Japanese sedan, one hubcap missing, pulled up and parked next to my rented Mustang. A cloud of dust rolled away as the engine dieseled to a stop.

The woman was tall and slender. She leaned in to retrieve a bag of groceries, tucked it under her arm and approached the lanai where Tino and I sat. I felt Tino's discomfort immediately.

Realizing she must be Ruby, I rose from my chair. She wore short cutoff jeans and a sleeveless white cotton blouse, her lissome figure only beginning to show the effects of encroaching middle age. Dancers' legs were still well-toned, and a familiar hibiscus tattoo that she had had since she was fifteen ringed her ankle. Long copper hair in a ponytail. Loose strands across her cheeks. Oversized dark glasses.

When Ruby finally recognized me, her back became rigid and she stopped in her tracks.

I approached her, smiling.

"It's been a long time, Ruby."

"Look, baby, it's Mikey Travis," Tino put in. A false good humor laced his voice.

I hugged her gently, the bag of groceries perched awkwardly between us. Stepping back, my hands moved to her upper arms, and I looked her squarely in the face. Keep smiling, Travis, until you get this figured out.

I felt Ruby shudder as she broke free. She angled her head down and moved quickly to the house without so much as a word.

As she brushed past me, I noticed the lingering green and purple marks beneath her eyes.

"Tino?"

Tino looked away.

"Talk to me." I felt bile in my throat.

Tino watched the dog. "I got drunk, Mike. I don't know what the hell happened, man, but she must have pissed me off—"

"Bullshit." My hands were squeezed into fists.

"I've never been so fuckin' sorry in my life, Mikey. It's just that…" He blinked back his humiliation. "It's just that with no work for me, and Ruby having to clean houses for people…"

"Lots of people live like that. They manage."

"She even cleans up after that asshole in your house three times inna last week! God, it's just too damn much some times…aw, fuck it, you wouldn't understand." He backhanded a tear as it leaked down his face.

"You been drinking alot, Tino?"

"How the fuck do I know? How much is alot, man?"

"You beat on your wife. That's too fucking much."

"Now you gonna judge me, eh, Mike?" he asked angrily. "Why don't you just fuck off then. Mind your own damn business, huh?"

"No hitting."

"I think I heard enough now. I said I was sorry. The fuckeen' cops came, humiliated me in front of my daughter. I said I was sorry then, too. Shit! What you all want anyway? Go on, now. Leave us be."

He turned and stalked off toward the beach. Poi Dog nipped at Tino's retreating heels.

I looked across at their front door, still standing open, wind flapping the screen. I looked at my house, shut tight against the day.

With nothing left to do, I made the drive back to Kona. I drove slow, feeling sick, realizing that things are no longer as they once were.

Hell, maybe they never were.

THE EASTERN sky glowed red the next morning. Sailor take warning, the saying goes. I was drinking a cup of Mango Ceylon and checking the pressure in the scuba tanks I was planning to use later with Rex and Dave.

In the salon below, my cell phone rang.

"Mike Travis," I said.

"Travis? This is Captain Cerillo. We spoke yesterday?"

"Yes. 'Morning, Captain—"

"I'm afraid there's been some trouble. We need to meet." Cop voice.

All my senses jolted. Something ugly washed down my body in a rush of ice.

"What kind of trouble?"

"There's been a murder at your house at Honaunau. Multiple murders, actually."

"Jesus—"

"I'll pick you up at the Kona pier," Cerillo interrupted. "We'll ride down together."

6

Cerillo was leaning against the front fender of his white Ford Explorer as I tied the *Chingadera* to the pier. A Styrofoam cup of coffee was steaming in his hand. Another cup sat on the hood of the truck.

"Coffee?" he offered. He pointed to the cup on the hood as I approached.

I shook my head.

"No. Thanks anyway."

Cerillo shrugged and put it in the cup holder between the seats.

We were silent for a full five minutes as Cerillo made way from Kailua village up Palani Road to the main highway. Once we had passed through the traffic signals near town and headed south, I broke the silence.

"Can you fill me in on what happened, Captain?"

"No," he answered. It sounded like that was all I was going to get. "You were a homicide dick, right?"

"Yeah. D-three."

He arched his eyebrows.

"I want you to see the scene cold," he said. "No preconceptions. I figure I might as well get some of that big city insight." An undertone of sarcasm on that last part.

A solid line of traffic passed us going the other way, out toward the resorts. Where the work was.

"You strapped?" Cerillo asked.

I patted the right pocket of my shorts. "The Bobcat."

"Give it to me," he said. "I'll give it back when we're through."

I took it out, checked the safety, and handed it to him butt first. He didn't look away from the road as he palmed it.

"Did I do something to piss you off?" I asked.

The question dangled in empty air.

"Travis, I'm not sure what to make of you."

I felt my neck get hot as blood rushed to my face. The vehicle's tires hummed against the pavement as I fought for control of my temper.

"You think this has something to do with me," I said finally.

The Captain shrugged. "Maybe not."

The dirt and gravel parking lot between the houses was crowded with vehicles. Big Island cops don't use marked patrol cars. Instead, each officer uses his personally owned vehicle as his radio car, a blue light literally strapped to the roof. I stopped counting at seven, differing makes ranging from a Trans Am to a Ford Bronco. They were parked at odd angles, clogging the turnaround.

A cloud of dust rolled on ahead of us as Cerillo pulled to a stop. Poi Dog scuttled back and forth between the two houses looking agitated and confused. When we approached the door Cerillo gave a curt nod to the uniformed patrolman that controlled the entrance to the crime scene. My house.

I knew the drill. Before I entered, I gave my name to the officer, who made note of it, together with the time, on his log. Captain Cerillo's name was entered immediately beneath mine, and we crossed the threshold.

It was only 8:45 in the morning but already hot. The interior of the house humid and cloying, alive with the buzzing of flies. Cops and crime scene people were everywhere.

I don't know what it is about human entrails that stinks so badly, but I breathed through my mouth despite the flies and tasted death in the back of my throat. The dense, unmistakable smell of spent gunpowder and the copper acridity of blood.

"Good Christ," I said to no one.

The couch was askew from its normal position, a man sprawled across it, his chest blown to hamburger, covered with sticky red tufts of pillow-stuffing. His head dangled at a severe angle over the backrest so I couldn't see his face.

The cocktail table had three glass tumblers sitting in runny pools of melted ice and condensation. An ashtray sat beside an open pack of Dunhill's and a gold lighter. It contained the butts of at least a dozen cigarettes. A small mound of white powder sat amid a larger area of fine white residue, a single-edged razor and tightly wound bill of currency beside it on the far corner of the table.

"You ever see anything like this?" Cerillo asked.

I'd seen some pretty mean shit. "Yeah," I said. But it hadn't been in my own house. The smell assaulted me as I spoke.

A viscous spray of black blood and meat spattered the back wall behind the couch. A man I took to be a detective was looking at the floor beneath it and sketched something on a pad. The couch was in the way, so I couldn't see what he was looking at.

Flashes from a camera held by a uniformed cop stabbed at the dark corners of the kitchen area where a pair of bare feet protruded from behind the counter. A filthy patchwork of black splotches marred the walls and door frames, the smudged trail of fingerprint collection.

A youngish Asian man rose from behind the couch where he had been kneeling. He looked hot and uncomfortable in a lightweight sport jacket and tie. He saw Cerillo and strode over, stepping carefully over pools of coagulated blood and shotgun shell casings.

"Detective Moon, this is Mike Travis. He owns the house," Cerillo said.

"Mr. Travis," Moon said.

"He's a retired L.A. cop," the captain added. "Homicide. Detective third, he tells me."

"Hmm," Moon responded, this time offering his hand. "Hell of a mess."

Moon was small and wiry, bristling with kinetic energy. His thick, black hair cut short, military style. A cliché hatchet face, thin lips and hard black eyes.

"You know these people?" Moon asked.

"Don't know yet. Let me take a look," I answered, stepping closer to the couch.

It was the skinny guy from the day before, Danny Webb's friend. His mouth and milky eyes were open in an expression of bewilderment, tongue and teeth stained with the blood of his last breath through exploded lungs. It had been the force of the blast that had blown the couch out of position.

"I don't know this one's name," I said. "Saw him for the first time yesterday. I think he was staying here with a guest of my brother's."

Moon wrote in his notebook.

I moved around behind, where Moon had been kneeling, and found two more bodies. I could see that one was male, and one female. Clouds of green flies buzzed greedily around ragged wounds.

As I stepped closer, I saw that the face of the female victim had been completely obliterated. The male had been cut nearly in half by close-range blasts of a shotgun. Spent shells cluttered the floor between them.

I looked at him closely. He had been shot twice. What I guessed to have been the first blast punched the hole. His genitals were gone. The second round took him high on the chest, just below the neck. His face was serene as a Renaissance angel. It happens sometimes.

"This one is Danny Webb," I said.

"The rock star?" Moon said, surprised.

"Yeah. The rock star." I said.

"That won't be good," he said, eyeing Cerillo. It would be national news when word got out.

"What about the woman?" Cerillo asked.

From where I stood, I couldn't see much but the head and torso, so I moved around beside her. And when I did, I saw it, and my knees went weak. The flower tattoo. Ruby Orlandella. Ruby Duke, my childhood friend.

"What is it?" Moon asked. "You know who this is?"

I held up a hand. "Gimme a minute." Let memories subside, reality settle in.

"This is Ruby Orlandella," I said finally.

"You sure?"

"Yes, I'm sure. The tattoo," I said. I pointed at Ruby's ankle.

I stood, carefully avoided stepping in the blood, and went to the front door. I pushed past the uniform, out to the lanai and leaned against the rail, gulping outside air.

Moon followed me out.

"You okay?"

I spat the yellow taste of acid from my mouth, then turned to face him.

"No, I'm not okay." I shouldered past him and down the stairs toward the dirt lot. He caught up with me as I walked in aimless circles. "She was a friend of mine."

He shook his head and walked back toward the house, turning once to look at me over his shoulder.

I stood there in the rising heat of morning and stared into the thick jungle where we used to play. To the lanai where we had danced together as teenagers. To the secret spot beside the bay where we had tugged and fumbled until we lost our virginity together.

A ceiling of clouds was gathering over the volcano and moving toward me. I watched them bloat and pull and tear while I took a few clean breaths. Five minutes later, I went back into the house.

"Okay now?" Cerillo said.

"Yeah," I said. "Let's finish this."

"There're two more in here," Moon said.

On the kitchen floor were another pair of bodies. Again, one male and one female, both Caucasian. Each appeared to have been shot in the back, and lay face down on the white tile floor. A wide pattern of blood and tiny buckshot holes perforated the thin white cotton of the man's shirt.

Two more shotgun shell casings lay beside the victims. I read the black lettering on the one nearest me. *Winchester Upland.*

"You know who these two might be?" Moon asked.

I shook my head. "Not from behind like this."

Moon looked at the officer nearest the bodies.

"You through taking pictures? Can you turn 'em over yet?"

"Yeah. We're done," the young cop answered, then called across the living room toward another uniformed officer. "Hey, Makana, give me hand over here!"

A stocky Hawaiian crossed the room, absently pulled at the open end of the surgical gloves he was wearing, then knelt down to help roll the male victim over.

Rigor had set in. Lividity purpled his face.

I shook my head. "Never seen him before."

Cerillo shook his head.

"Okay. Let's take a look at the woman," Moon said, pointing to the second body.

As before, the pair of patrolmen rolled the body over.

The blast had taken her from behind, straight through the lungs, leaving her limp in a deep pool of blood. There were smeared black stains on her hands and on the white kitchen cabinets nearest her.

"Took her awhile to die," I said. I imagined her trying to pick herself up as she slid across the floor on a glaze of her own blood, clawing at the cabinets.

"You know her?" It was Cerillo this time.

"Sorry, Captain. I don't know this one, either."

"Weren't these people guests of yours?" Cerillo asked, eyebrows arched.

"They were guests of my brother's," I said. "Danny Webb and the other male victim, anyway."

Cerillo shrugged.

"And you know who Ruby Orlandella is," I said.

Moon shot Cerillo a glance.

"What was she doing here?" Moon asked.

"I have no idea. Why don't you ask Tino," I said. He was beginning to piss me off.

"We have," Moon said, staring me hard in the eyes.

"And what did he say?" I asked, not breaking eye contact, not about to allow him the satisfaction of a petty game of intimidation. Thoughts of vet cop Gilley, the stare-down with the punk rapist, and how long ago it seemed.

Moon ignored my question. "Were Webb and that other guy lovers? Homosexuals?"

"How the hell should I know?" I answered. I was tired of this. I wanted to see Tino, find out what had happened.

"Don't get testy with me, Mr. Travis, I'm trying to determine if there's a sexual angle to this."

"Okay, give it a rest guys," Cerillo said, breaking the growing tension between Moon and me. Cerillo looked at me then. "So, tell me, how do you read this?"

"The whole scenario?"

"Yes," Cerillo answered. "Tell me what you think."

I walked back toward the front door, took in the room again. I tried to envision how the room looked, felt, sounded before someone had come in and blasted five lives away. The two detectives remained silent. The hum of crime scene processing continued around me as I pulled the scene together in my mind.

"It looks like we had the five victims standing or sitting around the living room area. Some kind of party, judging by the cocktails and the coke on the table there. It is cocaine, right?" I asked.

"Yeah, it's coke," Moon answered.

"Okay. So everybody's talking, partying when somebody comes busting in the door here," I hooked a thumb over my shoulder toward the front door.

"Takes them by surprise," Cerillo said.

"Yes," I nodded. "And blows away the first person he sees."

I looked at Moon and Cerillo.

"The guy on the couch," I finished.

Both of them were nodding, too.

"Go on," Cerillo said.

"Maybe the others don't see or hear the guy until he fires the shotgun—" "That's consistent," Moon interrupted. "The first officer on the scene said the stereo was going pretty loud when he arrived."

"Anyway," I continued. "I'm thinking that the shooter headed directly to Webb and Ruby. They were probably standing there talking. The shooter says something. He wants something."

The incongruous sound of laughter drifted in from outside. I glanced around and saw a pair of cops taking a cigarette break.

"He tells the two over there," I went on, pointing toward the kitchen. "To put down their drinks and stay put—probably right there in front of the partition between the kitchen and the living room."

"The two glasses sitting on the counter," Moon said.

"Right," I said. "While they stand there with their hands in the air, he talks to either Ruby or Webb. My guess is Webb."

"Why's that?" Cerillo asked.

"Because Webb is the only one who appears to have been hit twice, where he would have survived the first shot. The way I see it, the gunman asked him something, didn't like the answer, then shot Webb in the balls. Webb's in shock at that point, but still alive."

"Christ," Moon said.

I walked over to where Webb and Ruby lay, and went on. "Ruby starts screaming, and he turns the gun on her, shoots her in the face to stop the noise, again in the stomach as she goes down."

More laughter from outside. Cerillo leaned through the door and told them to shut the hell up. The tension, the stifling heat, was getting to us all.

"Go on," Cerillo prompted, agitated.

"Webb's on the floor," I said. "And the shooter gives him another chance. Shooter doesn't hear what he wants, then finishes the job, shoots him in the chest."

"The other two?"

I walked toward the kitchen, Moon and Cerillo right behind. I noticed Moon had stopped taking notes.

"These two here," I said. "They see how it's going to end, and try to make a break. They start to run. The wide pattern on the male victim's back suggests he was shot from farther away." I pulled my arms up and made like I was holding a shotgun. "The gunman probably just swung the shotgun around and shot them both while they tried to get away."

"Interesting," Cerillo said. "What do you think, Detective Moon?"

"Could have been like that," he said. His tone said he thought it was bullshit.

I turned to face him. "Then how do you read it?"

"Pretty much the same as you, except that the shooter was after the woman—Ruby Orlandella."

Moon led us back to the front door and walked us through his version.

"The killer comes in," he went on. "He's pissed—in a rage— he blows away the skinny one on the couch, then beelines over to Ruby and Webb. He's jealous. He thinks Ruby and Webb have been getting it on."

I looked out the window toward the water, turned my attention back to Moon.

"Killer blows the guys balls off, then puts one in his chest," he said. "The woman is screaming. The other two guests are screaming. The shooter lets the two in the kitchen have it, then starts in on Ruby. He's still in a rage and mutilates the woman—blows her face clean off."

"You think it was Tino." I said. It wasn't a question.

Neither of them responded.

"Who called it in?" I asked.

They glanced at each other, then Cerillo decided to answer.

"A nine-one-one from the girl next door. The daughter."

"Oh, shit," I sighed. I'd forgotten about Edita. "Where is she now?"

"We don't know. She's gone," Moon answered.

"What the fuck do you mean 'gone'?"

"Gone. Not here," Moon answered. "She wasn't here when the first officers arrived." Giving me the impatient treatment again.

"Don't get testy with me, Moon." I stabbed a finger at his chest. "I'm trying to help you determine the whereabouts of a fifteen year old girl who just got to see her mother without a fucking face. So back off, okay?"

"Big city attitude, huh? Big city *po*-lice detective gonna tell me what's going on," Moon said.

I shook my head.

"This isn't Mayberry," he spat.

A weight came over me like a blanket. Like a straightjacket. I had discovered my own mother's body floating in the bay not a hundred yards from where I stood. I had an idea of what the girl was going through.

"We'd like to talk to her, too, so relax Mr. Travis," Moon said. "We'll find her…In time."

"Call me Mike, okay. No more of this 'Mr. Travis' shit. It's condescending."

"Fine, Mike," Cerillo said. The peacemaker. "We'll also need to speak with your brother. Do you happen to have his number?"

I turned toward Cerillo.

"Why don't you let me call and tell him what happened. Otherwise, he'll dodge your call for days."

Cerillo and Moon did that looking at each other thing again.

"Yeah. Okay," Cerillo said. "If the detectives are through lifting prints off the phone, we can call from right here."

Moon moved off toward the kitchen, spoke briefly with an officer, then motioned us over with a wave of his hand.

"But when we're through with the call," I said, walking back to the kitchen. "I'm going to go find Edita."

I was not asking permission.

The plush offices of Van de Groot Capital occupied floors thirty-five through thirty-seven of an elegant high rise building on Water Street in lower Manhattan. Highly polished agate flooring reflected the indirect light from sconce lights attached to burlwood walls. Potted ficus and ornamental palms dotted the long corridors where photographs and magazine covers from financial publications hung in matching designer frames.

I envisioned the offices as I dialed Valden's direct line.

The tapping of computer keyboards and muted electronic bleating of telephones mixed classical music to create what Valden Van de Groot thought of as the Symphony of Omnipotence.

Van de Groot Capital had been founded by my grandfather, Clifford B.T.Van de Groot in the late 1950's as a firm specializing in locating investment capital for start-up companies considered either too small, or too risky, to be funded by the larger New York venture firms. Starting with a small investment stake loaned to Clifford by his uncle, he proceeded to build an empire that now claimed sizable ownership interests in some of the world's largest and best known corporations.

By the time my grandfather died, VGC operated offices in both New York and London, and was recognized as one of the finest venture capital firms in the world. With a net worth well into the tens of billions, it was also one of the largest privately held companies in America. The name Clifford Van de Groot was held in great regard by most everyone in the world of finance.

The fact that my brother Valden was not the founder of the company did little to moderate the size of his ego. Nothing pleased him more than to be doted on by sycophants. He loved the fact that even though he stood at something less than six feet tall, had less than a full head of hair, and carried an extra twenty-five pounds around, he could have, or rent, the attentions of some of the most attractive women in New York. The fact that he was married and the father of two teenagers mattered little to him in that regard. Just a sour note in the Omnipotent Symphony.

I glanced down at the rusty stains of blood on the kitchen floor and punched the last digit. I waited through the crack and hiss of an old line as the connection completed.

Valden considered himself above the rules promulgated to keep the rank and file in line. He thought of himself as a Master of the Universe, a term he had run across in Tom Wolfe's *Bonfires of the Vanities*, a book he had listened to on tape since he despised actual reading.

Despite the repeated warnings of VGC's in-house attorneys, Valden could not resist the carnal temptations of the corporate offices. These same attorneys had orchestrated a number of quiet cash settlements with Valden's women over the years, some of them VGC employees, and were likely to continue to do so.

As a fifty percent shareholder, I knew all of it.

After two rings, his secretary picked up, bypassing the main switchboard. I asked for Valden.

"I'm sorry, but Mr. Van de Groot is in conference just now." Another officious female voice to match the hallway frames.

"We went through this yesterday. This is Valden's brother, Mike, and it's an emergency. I need to speak with him immediately."

"I really *am* sorry, but he was very clear in his instructions to me that he should not be disturbed. I can leave a message asking him to—"

"That's enough," I interrupted. "I said this was a goddamn emergency."

"Well—"

"Listen, lady. Do you want to take the chance that he might be more pissed off at you if you *don't* interrupt him? Put him on." After a second, I appended, "Please."

"I'll see what I can do." The please gave her an out.

A few moments of muzak-on-hold. Peggy Lee this time, wondering aloud if this was all there is. Good question.

Valden came on strong.

"You've got some balls, Mike. Fifty percent of everything, and all you have to do is stay the hell out of the way—"

"We've got a problem, Valden," I overrode him. "There's five dead at the beach house. One of them is Ruby Orlandella."

"Ruby…?"

Her name spun down the wire at me. Five dead was too much for him to get hold of, but Ruby he knew. The Master of the Universe was collapsing into microcosm.

"And four others," I said.

"Will it hurt VGC? If this gets out, a connection made—"

"Jesus, Valden, you're unbelievable—"

"I've got the company to think about—"

"Another one down is Danny Webb."

"Webb?" Plaintive.

"The other three are unidentified. Know who they could be? Who hung out with Webb?"

"Gimme a minute here. We need a plan, Mike, we have to—"

"Names, Valden. I need names. What've you got?"

A long moment of hollow silence, then the old Valden, the Machiavellian.

"One is probably Webb's gofer. I don't remember his name. Shit this couldn't be worse timing…"

"Stay with me, Valden. Webb's gofer. Get his name."

"Right. Yes. I'll send one of my people over there right away."

His *people*.

"Somebody close to the deal we were working with Webb," he continued. "Maybe we can still hold it together."

"Valden—" I began, but he went on as though I wasn't there

"I have just the person. I'll have them get in touch with you once they arrive. I've got to go, Mike. There are a million things to do now."

"I don't think so, Valden," I said. "There're a couple of police officers here that have a few more things to talk with you about." Without waiting for a response, I handed the phone to Cerillo.

As I strode toward the front door, Moon called out to me.

"Where are *you* going?"

"To find the girl," I answered without looking back.

Heavy clouds had crept across the sky and cast shadows across the dirt turnaround. The day was darkening in a way that matched my spirit. As I made my way across the crowded parking area toward the Orlandella's home, I saw Tino sitting, unmoving, on his lanai.

When I reached the bottom of the stairs, I saw the glint of dull metal around his right wrist. The other end was fixed to a drainpipe that stabbed through the metal roof and down through the worn wood floor. Tino looked at me with a mix of hostility and shame, then turned his eyes away. Poi Dog was curled at his feet. I heard a low growl as I approached.

"Tino?"

He said nothing, shot me a sideways glance then turned back to the wall.

"Tino? Did you do this?"

"The cops t'ink so," he answered. There was undisguised rage in his voice. "*You* t'ink so, *too*?"

"I don't know what I think. I'm just real fucking sorry right now, and that's about all."

"Well, fuck you den, brah. I don't have nothin' to do wit' 'dis…" his voice trailed off, exhausted, rained.

A uniformed cop came from around the back of the house, zipping his pants. Taking a leak in the jungle.

"All right, Tino. Just tell them straight," I said quietly. "Don't try to bullshit anybody. You try to mindfuck these guys, and they'll see you in lockup. Don't do it."

He gave me a baleful glare. I ignored it. We didn't have time.

"Your daughter needs her dad now."

The cop was coming closer.

"Just get the questioning over with, and get back to Edita. You got a lawyer?"

He chuffed a mirthless laugh.

"What for I'm gonna have one fuckeen' attorney?"

"I was only asking. Just try to be cool, Tino. If you didn't do anything, then you're going to be fine. The main thing is to get back here to Edita."

He looked at me with cold anger, but said nothing.

"Okay, Tino?" I prompted. "I'm trying to help you here. Don't fuck yourself up."

The cop's black shoes crunched across the gravel as I turned to enter the house.

Before I crossed the threshold Tino called out to me.

"Mike?"

"Yeah?"

"I didn't do nothing."

"Okay, brah," I said, and pushed through his front door.

The house was small by modern standards. A kitchen, living room, bathroom and two bedrooms all on a single floor. The furniture was old and faded, but neat. An assortment undoubtedly collected from family leftovers and garage sales.

A thin breeze blew in through open windows, and pushed at the gauzy white curtains like tethered ghosts. A stack of dishes still sat in a drying rack beside the stained kitchen sink.

I thought back to the way it had been when I found my mother in the bay. I recalled how that had felt and tried to put myself in Edita's place.

I remembered that everything had felt completely disjointed to me then, unconnected to the events that began to unravel the instant after my legs gave way beneath me. I remember hearing myself yell for help. I recalled images, a montage, an odd soundtrack of voices, the wail of sirens and cops' questions superimposed over it all. I remembered wanting to run the whole thing in reverse and make it go away, make it disappear. Mostly, I remembered the overwhelming sense of abandonment.

I knew where I'd find Edita.

I walked down the narrow hallway toward the back of the house where I knew the bedrooms were. Both doors were closed. I entered the one on the left, It was Tino and Ruby's room.

The curtained windows were slightly ajar, allowing only a breath of outside air into the small space. An antique dresser placed beneath them, a wedding picture of Ruby and Tino centered upon it. A tarnished silver and tortoise shell comb and brush set on top of an age-yellowed lace cloth. Family heirlooms.

An unmade bed sat opposite the window and dresser, above which was a framed watercolor of a white sand beach lined with tall coconut palms. An empty hammock was strung between two trees in the distance. The bottom corner of the piece showed the artist's signature and date. Ruby Duke, 1977.

Two sets of sliding doors stood on opposite sides of the room, one for him and one for her. I went to the far side of the room and slid the right side open. Ruby's side. Faint but unmistakable female smells filled my nostrils. The clothes were hung neatly in two rows: blouses and shirts on top, pants and shorts below. A long shelf ran the length of the opening just above eye level and held an array of boxes, shoes, hats and other odds and ends. I bent down to see into the small space beneath the lower rung of clothing and shuffled things around. Nothing.

I closed that side and opened the other. The clothes on the bottom rung had already been pushed aside. I looked hard into the gloom. At first I saw nothing. But I knew what I knew, and waited for my eyes to adjust, pushing harder at the clothes. In the far corner of the closet, beneath the bottom rung, protruded two bare and dusty feet. Then the room's dim light revealed the tear smeared face of a teenage girl.

"You're going to be all right, Edita," I said softly.

Her long arms were wrapped around her knees, pulling them up close to her chest. She was rocking back and forth and staring into the middle distance, eyes swollen. I took two steps backward and sat down on the bed, never taking my eyes off of her.

I held out my hand, and for reasons I didn't understand, my mind wandered back to the watercolor painting over the bed. I never knew that Ruby had been an artist. I wondered what else I didn't know, and never would.

My own voice sounded strange to me as I whispered to Edita. I'm not sure what I said, but it drew her from her hiding place.

She came out and sat beside me on Ruby's bed, and I put both arms around her. Her shoulders began heaving and sobs wracked her body. I said nothing, only held her there and shared our loss.

When her sobs began to subside, I talked to her, telling her to stay in the room until I returned. She shook her head violently at first, not wanting to let go of me. I promised her I'd come right back.

I spotted Cerillo outside the house talking to another cop.

"Captain Cerillo?"

Cerillo nodded brusquely, then finished whatever he was discussing with the other cop. When the Captain was through, he started toward me. I moved to meet him half way, out of Tino's earshot.

"What are you going to do with Tino?" I asked.

He took off his mirrored shades and squinted at me.

"Take him in for questioning," he said.

"Then he's a suspect?"

Cerillo didn't answer.

"What about the girl?" I asked.

"Did you find her?" he countered.

I debated not telling him, but the thought didn't last long. She was a material witness.

"Yes."

"Where is she?"

"Listen, Captain, she's damn shaken—"

"Understandably," he interrupted.

"Yeah. Well, how about taking a short statement now, and save the rest for tomorrow or the next day? When she's up to it. I mean, hell, she's only fifteen."

Cerillo looked hard at me.

"You gonna tell me where she is or not?"

"After you tell me what is going to happen to her tonight. Her mother's dead, and by the sound of things, her dad's probably going to be spending the night in a cage. What happens to her?"

He was pensive for a long moment, watching Poi Dog cock his leg, then he answered, "Child Protective Services."

"No."

"What the hell do you mean 'no'?" he said.

"I mean that's a bullshit deal."

He shrugged.

"What are you suggesting?"

"I'll look after her until Tino's released," I said.

His answer was quick.

"No."

"What the hell do *you* mean, 'no'?"

"I mean that's not how it's done, Mr. Travis."

"Neither is finding your mom dead with her face shot off right before you leave for school. Give the kid a break, Captain."

Wheels were turning behind his eyes.

"Ask Tino," I persisted. "If he gives his consent, it would be okay, right?"

I looked over his shoulder and saw the first of a pair of unmarked station wagons, rear windows blacked out, pull into the drive. He followed my gaze.

"Coroner's wagons," he said unnecessarily as they nudged their way into the crowded turnaround.

I didn't blink.

"Okay, Travis," he said. "If her father okays it, I'll remand her to your custody. But you'll have full responsibility to get her to where she needs to be, when she needs to be there. Fair?"

I nodded.

"That's fair, Captain. Let's go get his permission, and get her out of here. She's been through enough."

"Not before Moon talks to her," he countered.

"Tell the sonofabitch to take it easy on her."

"Thirty minutes, tops," he said. "Then you bring her back in to the sub tomorrow. Deal?"

"She's in her mom's bedroom," I said. "I found her hiding in the closet."

Cerillo sighed.

"Let's get Moon started. I want to get her the hell out of here."

8

It was after two p.m. when Cerillo dropped Edita and me at the Kona pier. A group of kids splashed off the end of the wharf, and their noise put a point on our long and silent drive back. Each of us was lost in thought, nerves frayed and stinging.

I talked with Tino before they cuffed and loaded him into the back of a patrol unit, Edita's face buried against my chest where she couldn't see him. He had finally agreed to allow Edita to remain in my custody while they held him for questioning. He said that even I was better than the Child Protective Services system. Besides, he told me, there were no other family members that could have looked after her anyway.

I had no idea in hell how to take care of a teenage girl, but I owed it to Ruby if no one else. A lifetime ago she had been my first love. It had sliced right through me after that summer to learn how quickly she had let me go. How it seemed she had forgotten all about me after I left for the mainland. Now I wondered how long it would take to get the taste of her blood off my tongue.

Edita had fought hard for her composure before being interviewed by Detective Moon in the living room of the Orlandella's house. She had insisted that they let me stay in the room while she recounted the events that led up to her phoning 911, but I remained mostly silent in deference to procedure. Moon had his job to do. Fortunately, he had the wisdom not to push her too hard or too long, collecting only essential facts, taking careful notes in his notebook.

"Edita, I need you to tell me, as well as you can remember, everything leading up to your calling 911, okay?" Moon used a voice that conveyed both efficiency and empathy.

"Okay." Her voice was thin and taut.

Moon waited for her to continue on her own.

"I was out with some friends last night, and got home kinda late." She shifted her gaze to the worn carpet between her bare feet.

"What time was that?"

"Maybe eleven, I guess."

"You sure? The correct time is pretty important," Moon prompted. She didn't look up as her feet prodded the floor.

"Maybe it was more like midnight," Edita admitted.

"And who were you with?"

"Some friends." Her answer was clipped, defensive.

"I'm going to need their names, Edita."

Edita glanced over at me and I gave her a small nod. She closed her eyes.

"Peter Kalima. My boyfriend," she said finally.

"Who else?"

Several seconds passed in silence, then she said, "Nobody."

"How can I get in touch with Peter?" Moon asked.

I watched her wrap her arms around herself as threat closed in. It wasn't about being out when she shouldn't have been. It was the chain of events that led away from it, the terror, the images seared into her brain. She looked at me with anxious eyes, but all I could do was allow the truth to drain out at its own pace.

Moon waited, a hatchet face revealing nothing but smooth patience.

My sympathy went out to her. Adolescent concerns roiled against the nightmare of murder; guilt rode her hard as her worry for Peter Kalima weighed her down, even as her mother lay unburied, unsanctified. The ugliness of it all tore at her spirit. She struggled, arms still wrapped tightly around herself, awaiting a warmth that would not come.

"Edita?"

The phone number slipped loose on a rasp of breath. Then the address.

"So what happened when you got home?"

"Peter dropped me off about fifty yards up the road. I didn't want to get caught coming in late, so he turned off his headlights and coasted down. He dropped me up there."

She pointed vaguely toward the back of the house, where the road led down from the main highway.

"What happened then?" Moon was going smooth and slow.

"I came down the road to the house," she said, her fingers digging into her arms.

"Did you notice anything unusual?"

"Like what?"

"Were there any lights on? Anything like that?"

She hesitated, quiet, fingers digging into flesh.

"Edita?"

"Yeah," she said. "The lights were on at the other house, and I could hear music playing inside. Well, maybe not really music exactly, but I could sort of hear that thumping sound like when somebody's got a stereo on real loud."

"That's good," Moon encouraged her. "Were the lights on all over the house, or just in one area?"

"Just downstairs, I think."

"How about at your house, Edita. What was going on in here?"

She stiffened, and I felt the negative charge in the air that I had when I last saw Ruby. It was sudden, visceral.

"The lights were out," she answered after a moment's hesitation. "Except for that one lamp over there by the couch." She pointed to a blue-green ceramic lamp that sat atop a beaten end table beside the couch. "The TV was still on, and my dad was laying on the couch."

"Did he say anything to you when you came in?"

Edita hacked out a laugh.

"No. He was drunk." Her arms dropped to her lap. "Like usual."

Moon allowed a few beats of silence.

"Did you see your mom anywhere?"

"I didn't look," she said through a break in her voice. "I guess I thought she was in her r–room…"

Edita kept her unsteady focus to the floor, her hands restless, twisting, trying to reshape the past. I knew she would torture herself over not having looked for her mother. Guilt for a long time to come.

Maybe I could help her, I thought. I knew what it was like. But it passed as quickly as it came. Hell, I could barely help myself.

"What did you do next?" Moon asked.

"I went to my room and went to bed."

A loud scrabble of mynahs pierced the air, then died down just as suddenly. Disembodied voices that I knew to be uniformed cops drifted across the driveway. "And this morning?"

"When I woke up this morning," she began. "I came out to the kitchen. My mom would usually wake me up, but today she didn't—"

Her throat closed around welling tears.

A warm breeze pulled at the curtains that hung over the open window, carrying the fragrances of plumeria and gardenia into the house. The mynahs started fighting again. The jungle was continuing its own cycle of death, reclamation and regeneration, oblivious to the tragicomedy being played out. I felt a disconnected vestige of something like hope in that. That life tries like hell to go on.

I went into the bathroom and took some tissues from a box on the sink. I sat beside Edita and offered them. She dabbed at her eyes and nose.

"Take your time," I said.

She drew a ragged breath.

"But she didn't," Edita continued finally. "She didn't come in to wake me up. That's when I knew something must be wrong. Mom's always hassling me to get up and get to school on time."

Moon and I glanced at each other, both noticing the use of the present tense.

"Uh huh," Moon injected into the silence.

"That's when I noticed that the dishes were still on the counter from last night's dinner. Mom never does that. So I went back to her room, and only dad was there in bed. By himself—"

A car door slammed. Edita startled.

"—H–he still had his clothes on…" Her voice faded into nothing.

"You're doing fine," Moon said.

"Sh–she wasn't anywhere in the house, and I started to get sort of scared, you know? I went next door. I was thinking maybe, like, she maybe went next door to clean house or something…"

Her eyes never rested, searching for purchase, for stability.

"That's when I found them," she finished at last, the words emptying out of her.

"The bodies," Moon said.

"Yes."

"The door was open?"

"Not open. But not locked, either. I knocked, but no one answered; I thought maybe they couldn't hear me 'cause of the stereo. It was still on, so I let myself in."

A car started in the driveway, and the three of us sat silently as it crunched over the gravel and sand toward the highway. Edita wiped her eyes.

"Want something to drink?" I asked. "A glass of water, maybe?"

She nodded and I rose to go get it.

"Did you touch anything? Move anything?" Moon asked as I went to the kitchen.

"Just the door, I think. I don't remember. I just remember I saw the guy on the couch, and I screamed. I could see…Oh, God…"

Her shoulders heaved as great rushes of fear seized her, then primal grief, a sound so painful that I saw Moon look away.

"It's okay, Edita, we're done for now," he said. "You did just fine."

Small brown hands covered her face, a tissue twisted between her fingers.

"You've been a big help," he said, and reached out to touch her shoulder. "I appreciate your talking to me."

She nodded from some imploded place, without raising her head or meeting his eyes.

Moon looked at me and gestured toward the door with a nod. I followed him out the door and across the dirt lot. An ambulance and a pair of vans had arrived to take the bodies away.

"She'll be staying with you, I understand."

"That's right," I said.

"I'm going to want to talk with her again tomorrow."

I looked back toward Tino's house. "I'll let her know."

"I'm going to be talking with the boyfriend in the meantime. I've also got some more questions to ask about her dad, but now was obviously not the time."

"Obviously."

He squinted at me, sizing me up. "We know how to get a hold of you when we need you?"

"Cerillo has my number," I answered. "She's had enough for now."

"For now," he replied. "Bring her over to the sub tomorrow morning around ten so we can finish taking her statement."

I nodded.

Moon walked back toward my family's house and I stood a moment longer in the hot midday sun. I looked over to see a stretcher being pulled through the front door and shook off a mean deja vu.

I followed Edita up the ladder from the skiff and aboard the *Kehau*. I had her canvas duffel and backpack slung over my shoulder. We still hadn't found any words, and without breaking the brittle silence, I tossed her bags on the sofa and poured two fingers of Makers Mark in a glass and knocked it back. My hands had begun to shake and I had to set the glass on the counter in order to pour the second one. I looked up and saw Edita watching me.

"Did you know my mom very well?" Her voice was loud after the silence.

"Since she was younger than you," I managed.

She looked back at me with an expression that seared me. I'd been with crime victims more often than I could count, but this time I was raw and unprepared. I knew she wasn't looking for words, only a connection, something to latch onto in a world that had slid out from under her.

She nodded and looked out toward the shoreline. As I watched her I thought how, in an alternate universe, she could have been my daughter. It struck me like a rogue wave and left me hollow.

"Edita, I'm not very good—"

"Me neither," she interrupted.

I put the whiskey bottle back and went to the refrigerator. I pulled out two Asahis and jacked the tops, handed her one.

"Go ahead," I said. "I'm sure you could use it."

She showed me a small smile that gave some hope for her future, and sipped.

"Let me show you to your room," I said and picked up her things. My words sounded pompous and inappropriate, but she nodded and followed me.

Ten minutes later, she'd seen all there was to see of the *Kehau*, including how to use the stereo and video units concealed behind the wood panels that lined the salon's starboard bulkhead. I opened the first of three deep drawers beside the stereo and showed her a sizeable collection of CDs and DVDs. Anything to keep her mind occupied, reconnect with the ordinary. I knew from experience that she was still in shock. Hell, so was I. When reality came, it would hit her like a train.

"Thanks," she whispered, and knelt before the open drawer.

"Old fart stuff," I said through a smile that felt unfamiliar on my face. "Sorry." Miles Davis, Clapton, the Dead, Little Feat.

She plucked one from the drawer.

"You've got Santana," she said.

The memory flooded back unexpectedly. *Samba Pa Ti* playing on the boombox on the lanai, my arms around Ruby Duke's waist. The smell of her hair, the sound of the waves.

"Want me to put it on?" I asked Edita, praying she'd say no. She waited a moment, then shook her head.

"It reminds me of my mom," she said. "She used to play it all the time." Edita slid the case back into the drawer, and thumbed through the rest.

I took my beer to the afterdeck and the light of a dying afternoon, and watched it fade away.

Love or money, I thought to myself. Murder was almost always about love or money. Sometimes it was a random act of madness, like Manson, but that was mercifully rare.

Hans, my old partner, always said follow the money. Follow the money and you find the motive. Me? I always found passion to be the thing. It was an emotion that cut both ways. Sex could turn to violence. And violence could turn to sex. I'd seen it a thousand times. And I never underestimate the power of passion to obscure reason.

Love or money. This could be either one.

Valden himself had told me that VGC was working with Danny Webb on something. I had no doubt that there were millions at stake on whatever it was. There you go, Hans. There's the money.

But what I had seen of Tino and Ruby cut me to the core. I had seen husbands kill wives, girlfriends kill boyfriends, and every other permutation of assault for much less than what had been going on between Tino and Ruby. And here was Webb living next door, rubbing Tino's face in his own failure to provide for his family, while his wife cleaned up the mess. The Tino that existed in my memory was incapable of that kind of violence, but the local cops thought otherwise.

Love or money.

A shrill whistle from the pier shattered my concentration and I dropped my beer on the deck. It rolled away, the bottle unbroken, a stream of foam bleeding from its neck. I plucked it from the gunwale just before it went over the side and squinted across the sapphire bay. Rex and Yosemite were waving from the wharf. I stood and acknowledged them, only then realizing that I had taken the *Chingadera* earlier that morning leaving the two of them stranded aboard. It hadn't dawned on me that they weren't there when Edita and I returned.

The larger launch, a twenty-one foot Mako, was still padlocked into its davits on the deck above the wheelhouse. I had the only keys. We'd need to get both boats in the water before tomorrow.

I ducked my head into the salon where Edita had a small pile of CD's on the floor beside her.

"I've got to run over to the wharf for a minute to pick up a couple of friends. I'll be right back, okay?"

She looked up, startled, her brown eyes wide.

"I'll just be a couple of minutes," I said. "I'm coming right back."

Anxiety gripped her.

"I want to come with you, Mr. Travis," she said. "I don't want to be alone."

I felt like an asshole.

"Sure," I said. "Let's take a ride."

She sprang up the stairs to the afterdeck and emerged into the fading afternoon. It pulled at my heart how fast she moved. Like she didn't want me to change my mind and leave her.

"Oh, and one other thing," I said.

"Uh huh?"

"Call me Mike from now on, okay?"

She nodded, tested the word.

"Okay...Mike."

She came to me then, buried her face against my chest. She felt small and frail against me, and I shuddered involuntarily, feeling her loss as though she had doused me with it.

She looked up at me.

"Okay?" I said.

She looked at me again, a nod.

"Okay."

9

"She alright?" Dave asked.

"Yeah," I said. "She finally fell asleep." I had sat on the bunk beside her while 20 mg's of Ambien dissolved into her bloodstream. For the first time, as she drifted off, I saw her at peace.

Yosemite passed the Makers Mark to me and I took a hit. We'd dispensed with the niceties and drank our whisky from the bottle on the stern of the *Kehau*. A cooler full of iced Asahi sat on the deck between us. The sky was a cloudless blanket of stars, only a breath of wind to pull at the windsock on the mainmast. It ruffled indifferently in the lazy breeze.

"What happens now?" Rex asked, reaching for the bottle.

"I take her in for the rest of her interview tomorrow morning," I said.

"What about the dad?" Rex asked.

I shrugged.

"I don't know," I said. "I'll find out tomorrow."

"They gonna let him out?" It was Yosemite this time.

"Can't say. But they're gonna want to button this up damned fast."

I scanned the shoreline. Tables were full at the restaurants along the water. Couples held hands and shopped. Groups of young men and women cruised the avenue. Street vendors on the hustle. People out enjoying a tropical evening.

Rex watched my face.

"Tourist towns…" Rex said.

"You know what it's like," I said. "This place runs on their money. Can't let ugly shit like what I saw today go unpunished for long. The tourists'll take their dough and fly someplace else to spend it."

Rex pulled at his beer.

"You gonna be able to do anything?" Yosemite asked me.

The question stung. I'd been thinking about that all afternoon. When you're a cop, you live for the job. It's every minute of every day. It separates you from people who aren't cops. It's *us* against *them*. Now that I was retired, I'm sure I was considered more like one of *them*. Being an outsider made it even worse.

"I can't *not* do anything," I answered. "It's why I wanted to be a cop in the first place."

A heavy bass beat and snatches of music drifted across the bay from Lola's. Business was healthy, lights shone bright. I wished we were there.

"One night when I was a street cop in L.A.," I began. "There was this young dealer. He ran the area near USC. Sold crack and Mexican brown."

Rex stood and leaned on the rail, his back to us. He pulled a cigar from his shirt pocket, bit off the end, and lit it with his worn Zippo. Smoke drifted across the deck.

"They called him Hogg, I don't know why," I said. "Anyway, this guy is a mean motherfucker. Word on the street said he was good for ten, twelve murders, maybe more. But we couldn't get anybody to testify, couldn't even turn a CI. Hogg had everybody scared."

"Make a good politician," Yosemite said.

I tore at the label on the beer bottle and crushed it between my fingers.

"The guy had total disrespect for cops. Taunted us openly, whenever there was a crowd around, knowing he owned the bystanders. For grins, he'd toss bricks from rooftops at passing black-and-whites. Hit a cop on foot patrol once and paralyzed him from the neck down."

I shook my head and tossed the crumpled piece of label into the cooler. A cloud of blue smoke passed between Yosemite and me.

"Every night for a week I staked the guy out when I came off my tour. Got to know his habits, when he was likely to be alone. Then one night I came back to Hogg's neighborhood and waited. Alone. Froze my ass off in a dark doorway for almost three hours."

I pulled at my beer until it was empty. I tossed the bottle in the ice and grabbed another one, cracked it.

"Hogg was alone, too, when he finally came by. It was almost light, I remember. I dragged him into an alley and beat him to a paste. Damn near killed the sonofabitch. Broke his nose, four ribs, collarbone, and both arms. Crushed a cheek so bad he lost an eye. But I let him get a good look at me. He knew who I was. He knew who had his life in his hands."

Rex leaned toward me, the tip of cigar glowing red between his fingers. Ribbons of smoke peeled off in the wind.

"What'd you beat him with, Mike?"

"My fists," I answered. "Fists and feet."

Rex nodded, clenched the cigar between his teeth.

"What happened after?"

"Nothing. And no more bricks from rooftops."

The three of us sat in silence, music and splashes of laughter periodically blew across the bay. Rex worked his cigar, and Yosemite leaned back and gazed at the Southern Cross sinking toward the far horizon. I rolled my beer between my hands and watched condensation make a pool between my knees. I don't know how long we sat like that.

"Pretty bad?" Yosemite asked, breaking the long silence. I knew what he meant. He passed the Makers Mark back to me.

I grabbed the bottle and took another long pull. I watched the bubbles work up the neck, felt the sting all the way down.

"A fucking bloodbath."

"Not what you had in mind for a homecoming."

Not by a long fucking way. The house would never be the same.

"What can we do to help you, bro?" Yosemite asked.

I shook my head.

"I don't know," I said. "Maybe nothing."

"Hey, man—" he started.

I interrupted him.

"Look, you did me a solid and crewed for me. The rest of this shit is on my watch. I'll do what needs to be done."

"We're here, man," Rex said simply.

"I know," I said.

I tossed off the last of my beer, threw the empty in the cooler, and got to my feet. Rex finished his cigar and Yosemite walked unsteadily up the gunwale to the bow, the whisky clutched firmly by its neck. Without another word, I went below.

I opened the door to Edita's stateroom, careful not to wake her. A thin band of yellow light traced the floor and crossed her sleeping face. I could see Ruby there, her breathing counting a slow cadence. The room returned to darkness as I closed the door.

I thought about Tino spending the night on a steel cot in a holding cell. I thought about Valden, and wondered how well he slept that night. I thought about the blood-soaked beach house. I thought about Ruby. And I thought about the past.

As I opened the door to my own stateroom, exhaustion took me. I thought again whether there was one solitary thing I could do to make any part of this goddamn situation any better. Edita, at least, was sleeping the sleep of the angels.

I spent the night with demons.

10

I was up before the sun.

The morning was quiet and the sky over Hualalai was whispering of purple predawn. I put my tea in the holder beside the captain's chair and opened the worn guitar case at my feet. A Martin D-35 I'd been given as a kid that smelled of wood oil and dust. I finger-picked a handful of chords, pulled the high E back into tune, and riffed into an old Neil Young tune. The music drifted across the dull shimmer of the bay.

The sun stole over the volcano as I finished the last of what must have been a dozen songs, and I put the Martin back in its case. I hauled it below, refilled my tea, and went to work pulling air tanks and weight belts from the aft storage locker. I fitted six of the metal cylinders into custom holders and slipped Rex and Yosemite's BCs over two of them. After I tightened the regulators in place, I opened the valves and checked the pressure. Satisfied, I closed the valves and placed the gear in the *Chingadera* along with masks, fins, and wetsuits. I had thrown the last of it aboard when a voice came at me from behind.

"You look busy," Edita said.

Bare feet stuck out beneath the blanket she had wrapped around her. Her hair was tousled, eyes still rimmed with sleep, and something else as she faced a new day.

"You're up early," I said.

She showed me a wan smile and nodded.

"A bad dream woke me."

I climbed the stairs from the skiff.

"How about some breakfast?" I asked her. "Toast? Orange juice?"

She nodded and sat heavily on the captain's seat, swiveled to face the morning sun. I saw her shiver as she pulled the blanket tight around her, but it wasn't from the cold.

A few minutes later, I brought up some juice and two plates of toast, fresh papaya, banana and mango. I sat on the banquette adjacent to where she sat, while Edita balanced the plate on her lap. She picked at it mostly, pushing the food into patterns, taking the occasional bite. The fork went onto her plate with a careful clack, and I watched her drift away.

"I'm scared," she whispered to no one.

The morning was still. Even the waves that lapped the hull had gone silent.

I held out my hand to her and patted an empty place beside me.

"Give me the plate," I said. "Sit over here."

She hugged the blanket around her like a shroud.

"What am I gonna *do?*" she asked as the tears began their slide.

I wrapped my arms around her until she had cried herself out.

I paced the station's spartan reception area while we waited for someone to take us back to one of the interview rooms. Edita sat in one of the plastic chairs and stared blankly at the floor, nervously biting a nail. She looked frightened and small, younger than her fifteen years.

After a twenty minute wait, the desk officer finally buzzed us through the inner door, startled us both with the sound. We followed him through a narrow corridor in single file toward an empty room at the back of the building. I brought up the rear.

A door to our right opened suddenly, and a wiry young man with straight dark hair, baggy pants and oversized white T-shirt came out, followed by detective Moon. The officer guiding Edita and me didn't slow, but the young guy looked up and caught Edita's eye. She froze momentarily in her tracks and stared back. Her face registered a level of surprise that bordered on alarm, but she said nothing.

Her boyfriend. Peter Kalima.

He looked at her with naked contempt.

"Bitch."

She recoiled as if she had been struck.

He turned to look at me and I studied the mean golden eyes. Moon was in my peripheral vision. I could tell by his face that he'd heard it, too.

Edita remained still, in shock. I gestured for her to follow the officer in front of us with a gentle push between her shoulder blades. She locked eyes with her boyfriend as she followed the cop through an open door and into a vacant interview room.

"I'll be there in a minute," I said as she went in.

She nodded blankly, still looking at Kalima.

As the door closed behind her, I put a stiff forefinger square into Peter Kalima's chest, and pushed him back into the room he and Moon had just left. Moon followed us in and shut the door.

"You got something to say, cocksucker?" I said.

Moon weighed the need to step between me and Kalima, but stayed where he was. Kalima tried to stare me down. The whole damned world loves to stare.

"This young man has something he wants to say, I think," I said to Moon.

"I didn't say *nothin'* to this asshole, man," Kalima said. He gestured toward me with a toss of his head.

"Give me a minute, here, Detective Moon?" I said.

Moon nodded, stepped away a few paces, turned his back toward Kalima and me, made a show of looking at something on the table in the corner.

Kalima smirked and started for the door.

I grabbed his shoulder and swung him around. I locked his face in my hand and backed him hard against the wall. I peeled back an eyelid until you could almost see into his brain. Kalima stood frozen, the golden eye looking more like a bruised yellow apple.

"You know that girl's mother was killed."

"Uuunnnhhh…"

"So you'll help out, answer a few questions."

"Uuunnnhhh…"

"Now listen carefully," I said. I squeezed a little harder. "You listening?"

He was turning on his eyeball now.

"I'll say this once: If you touch her, you'll be blinded for life. Got it?"

I shoved some eyelid into the socket. A little bleeding. When I let him go, he grabbed his eye and staggered around.

"Door's over there," I said. He didn't move, just leaned against the wall.

We left Kalima standing in the interview room. As we walked to where Edita waited, Moon turned to me.

"You're lucky that kid's eighteen. I wouldn't have let you do that otherwise."

I glanced sideways at Moon.

"I guess that makes you lucky, too."

The interview with Edita and Moon lasted about an hour.

As before, I remained silent as she retold her story from the beginning. It was the part I'd already heard. Toward the end, though, Moon shifted into a new line of questioning.

"So, you told me before that you got home about…" Moon consulted his notes briefly. I knew this was just part of the show. "…Midnight. Is that right?"

"Yeah," she answered. "About midnight."

"And where was your dad when you got home?"

"On the couch, like I told you before."

He made another show of reading his notes, not looking up. "Ahh, right. Did he say anything to you when you came in?"

"No. Like I told you, he was sleeping on the couch," she was becoming agitated.

Moon pretended not to notice.

"But he didn't even wake up, huh?"

Her face darkened. "No, he didn't wake up. He was *passed out,* okay? He was drunk and passed out! Happy?"

Moon ignored the outburst, but looked up from his notebook momentarily. His forehead wrinkled as he began writing again, the pen scratching at the silence.

When he was finished, he asked, "Does he do that alot, your dad?"

"What? Get drunk or pass out?"

Moon didn't respond, only shrugged.

"Yeah, he does," she said.

Moon looked at her, raised his eyebrows.

"Does what?" he asked.

Edita glanced at me before she answered.

"Both," she said finally. "He gets drunk and passes out."

The pen scratched against paper again.

"He ever hit you?"

"No," she spat.

"But he hit your mom." A statement.

Edita didn't answer. The humiliation she felt was almost tangible. Long seconds ticked by.

"Let's move on to the next morning," Moon said. "You got up, and then what?"

She inhaled deeply and sank a little lower in her chair.

"I went to the kitchen. Mom usually woke me up in the mornings, but she didn't that morning. I thought maybe she forgot, and was busy in the kitchen. Maybe she got up late or something...I don't know..."

"But she wasn't there," Moon prompted.

She shook her head.

"No. She wasn't there."

"Where was your dad?"

A spasm of fear overtook her.

She looked over at me, then answered him.

"I *told* you. He was in their bedroom."

"I thought you told me he was sleeping on the couch."

"He was. He must have gotten up in the night and..." uncertainty rode over the fear.

I looked up at the clock on the wall above the door. I watched a long thirty seconds struggle by.

"Edita?" Moon asked into the silence.

She looked up at him.

"Does your dad own a shotgun?"

She looked at me again, then back to Moon. And slowly nodded her head.

11

Cerillo's office felt close and hot, the blinds across the window behind him losing their battle with the sun. Moon and I sat in matching chairs across the desk from the captain.

"You think Tino good for this?" I asked them. "You think he's even capable of this kind of shit?"

Like most of the cops on the Big Island, Cerillo had grown up here. So had Tino. Their families had known each other. It was a common problem in small town law enforcement—everybody knew everybody else. It was especially true here, where only a few generations earlier the islands had still been more or less communal. People worked together in those times, farmed and fished together, raised one another's children.

Moon, Cerillo and I sat behind a closed door. Edita waited outside in the lobby. After she had finished her interview, I asked to see the captain and Moon alone.

"I don't know," Cerillo said. "He's shown a violent side before. Bad enough to where his wife had to call us out."

"Domestic disputes aren't the same as multiple homicide," I said.

"True enough," he nodded. "But they can turn that way pretty damn fast."

I'd been on my share of domestic call-outs. I'd almost been stabbed when I answered one. By the woman who'd made the call in the first place. She came undone when I started to cuff the husband who'd been beating on her.

"Have you charged him?"

Moon had been silent until then, but I felt his growing hostility.

"Not yet," Moon said. "But we can keep him another twenty-four hours before we have to kick him loose."

"You have to keep him in lockdown?"

Moon shook his head in frustration.

"It's a capital crime, Travis."

I looked at Cerillo. He shrugged his shoulders in a gesture that said, *what did you expect?*

"What did Tino say when you questioned him?"

"For God's sake, Captain—" Moon protested.

Cerillo held up a hand and looked at me.

"The only reason we're having this conversation at all is that you used to be a cop," he said.

"And it happened at my house."

"That, too."

"So what did Tino say?" I asked again.

"Not much," Moon answered. "Says he was passed out. Blacked-out, he says. Doesn't remember shit."

That was a bad fact.

I played it through as a prosecutor would: a recently unemployed man, drinking heavily by all accounts—one who had recently displayed violent tendencies against his wife—*sleeps* through a multiple shotgun homicide thirty yards from his house. His wife is found, faceless, next to the body of a male victim who had been shot in the groin.

Genital mutilation is a classic sign of sexual rage. It wouldn't take much to get a jury to imagine a drunk and jealous husband staggering across a hundred feet of parking lot to blast the object of his jealousy with a shotgun.

What troubled me, though, was the presence of other victims. It didn't fit.

The fact that nothing had been stolen was equally troubling, for reasons that argued against my belief in Tino's innocence. Not even a bill of US currency sitting in plain sight on the coffee table. That pointed to something less planned, a spur-of-the-moment crime of passion.

"Tell him about the shotgun," Cerillo said.

I looked over at Moon.

"We found a twelve-gauge in the garage behind Orlandella's house. Ballistics confirmed it had been fired recently."

"That doesn't mean—" I began.

Moon held up his hand.

"Let me finish," he said. "We also found an open box of shells of the same type we found at the scene."

"Winchester Upland."

Moon nodded.

"And we tested Tino for blowback and powder, too."

"And?" I said.

"Negative."

They hadn't found any powder residue or blood on Tino's hands or body. That, at least, was something.

"Have you identified the other victims?" I asked.

"The male and female found in the kitchen," Moon began, "Were Tom Foster and his wife, Courtney. Lived in L.A. Had a place in Maui."

"How'd you find that out?"

"There was a purse locked in one of the cars in the lot—a rental—and it had wallets and drivers' licenses for both of them."

"Who are they? Why were they there?"

"He was in the music business. Concert promoter. The wife apparently didn't work. As for why they were there…" His sentence was punctuated with a shrug.

"How about the other one? The one on the couch."

Moon flipped through a couple pages of notes.

"Leonard Rand," he answered. "An assistant of Danny Webb's."

"What about prints? Anything usable?"

Cerillo shook his head.

"Only partials. Got 'em off the brass base of the shotgun shells."

"Did you run them?" I asked.

"There's nothing to run. They're shitty looking partials."

"All the shells have them?" I pressed.

"Yeah," Moon answered slowly, suspicious. "All but one."

"No murder weapon?"

Moon made a face.

"The shotgun from Orlandella's house."

"But you can't match ballistics from a shotgun wound," I argued. "It might not be the murder weapon."

"Get real, Travis," Moon sighed.

I ignored him.

"How about the white powder on the table? What'd you do with that?" I asked.

"Cocaine. Bagged it and tagged it," Moon said. "What are you getting at?"

I ignored his question and asked another.

"There was a pack of cigarettes on the table and a lighter, right?"

"Right."

"Where are they now?"

"Evidence room," Cerillo answered this time.

"Did you print those?" I asked.

"Of course. The only prints were Webb's."

"Can I see the cocaine?" I changed the subject again.

Moon hesitated, looked at Cerillo.

"Hell, why not?" Cerillo answered. "We've gone this far. Bring it in."

Moon came back a few minutes later holding two oversized baggies. I looked briefly at the white powder in one bag, then handed it back to Moon. I looked at the contents of the second bag more carefully. In it was a twenty dollar bill, wound tightly into a short tube.

"Did you print this?" I asked.

Cerillo looked at Moon. Moon looked at me.

"We can't. I mean, I don't think we can lift prints off etched paper like that. Not here."

I knew that fingerprints can be lifted from almost any surface. The oils, salts and acids in human skin are extremely resilient. Lifting them from something other than smooth surfaces was a sophisticated process, but mostly a matter of having the right equipment.

"Crime lab guys in L.A. could probably do it. If I can get this printed for you on the mainland, will you?" I pointed at the currency in the evidence bag I still held in my hand.

Moon shook his head, but Cerillo was thinking it over.

"What do you expect to find?"

"I'm not sure. But I can't imagine that the asshole capable of this kind of bloodbath isn't going to take a little toot of free happy dust if it's just sitting there waiting for him."

"And you think they left prints on the currency?" Moon asked, half-skeptical, caught between his not wanting my help, and the assistance it might provide.

"You never know. We've got the victims' prints for elimination. How about letting me make a call?"

They were quiet for a moment, then Cerillo turned his black desk telephone around and pushed it toward me. I punched in the number for the Homicide Bureau in L.A.

After three rings, a voice came on the line.

"Homicide."

"Hans Yamaguchi," I said.

"Hold one," the voice said.

Hans had been my partner for most of my stint in Homicide. He was also a good friend. As I waited for him, I punched the button that activated the speakerphone, so Moon and Cerillo could listen in.

"Yamaguchi." The voice was deep, blunt.

"Hans, it's Mike Travis. I'm calling from Hawaii. I've got you on the speaker with a couple of detectives from Kona."

I made the introductions.

"Well, I'll be damned," Hans said. "We were just talking about you."

"We *who?*" I asked suspiciously.

"Me and a couple Hollywood types. They want to do a movie about that serial case we had." This wasn't the first time either of us had been approached by entertainment people seeking to sensationalize a case.

"Jesus Christ," I said.

We'd seen enough of the spotlight already.

"Got a free lunch out of it," he laughed. "So what's going on? You must need something."

"Yeah, I do," I said. "We need a favor."

Moon filled him in on the murders at my house in Honaunau. He listened to the entire scenario without interrupting. Hans was a good listener. It was part of what made him a good cop.

"So you want some latent prints done up by our lab? Is that it?"

"That's it," I said.

"I don't see a problem with that. Want me to run them through the system over here, oo?"

The DMV, NCIC—the National Crime Information Center— or the DEA's system, NADDIS.

"Do it," I said.

Moon threw a look at Cerillo.

"No sweat," Hans said. "When'll I get 'em?"

The detective was staring at me.

"Tomorrow," Cerillo said through the tension. "FedEx."

I had another thought.

"Hans," I said. "I'm gonna put you on hold for a second."

I punched the phone's red button without waiting. The light blinked as I looked at Moon.

"Have them print the shotgun shells, too,"I said.

"We already did 'em," he answered. Moon was getting pissed. I didn't trust his work.

"I have a thought here that might help," I pressed. "Go with me on this."

Moon held my gaze for a few moments, finally acquiesced with a sour look at his Captain.

I punched the blinking hold button.

"Hans, I'm gonna send you some shotgun shells. Have the lab do those too."

"You got it," he said. "Anything else?"

"I owe you one," I answered.

"One doesn't even begin to cover what you owe me," he said, and hung up.

By the time we arrived at Kealakekua, Edita was worn and empty. But she wasn't going to let me visit her dad without her.

The cells where he was being held were a part of the county court complex, and designed to hold only a few prisoners while awaiting trial. If they ended up bringing charges, he'd be moved about a hundred miles farther away, in Hilo. Knowing we'd be searched before being allowed in, we left all our belongings, including my Beretta, locked in the car. We checked in with a pair of uniformed guards and cooled our heels in a dingy waiting area for almost half an hour before being escorted through several sets of steel wire doors and into a small room.

The only furniture was a worn metal table and four chairs. All the furniture was bolted to the concrete floor. Two windows, opaque with grime, sat high on the wall and were criss-crossed with thick wire. Edita paced while we waited for the guard to bring Tino.

Edita let out a muted cry at the sound of a sharp rap on the door short minutes later. It opened with a metallic squeal and Tino was brought in. He was wearing his own clothes, but had cuffs on his wrists. The officer with him made no move to remove them. Tino must not have been told who his visitors were, because his eyes went wide and tried in vain to hide the cuffs.

"Not wit' her, brah," he said to me. He wouldn't look at his daughter.

"Daddy." The word came out bruised. She went to him.

The guard came between them before she could get there.

"No touching, miss."

She looked at the guard, confused, then to me.

"Sorry," I said. "I should have told you."

"Whatta you bring her here for?" Tino accused.

"She needed to see you, Tino," I said.

"Not like this, brah." He backed toward the guard still standing behind him. "Not like this."

Tino turned his back to both of us.

Edita was lost, the color drained from her face.

"I'll go," she said.

"Tino, for God sake—"

"I said no!" He yelled. His voice boomed in the small room.

Another guard came to the door and escorted Edita back to the waiting area. I stayed behind with Tino. Once she was gone, he moved to the table and sat in one of the chairs. The guard looked at me.

"You gonna be okay?"

"Fine," I said.

"I'll be right outside, you need me."

I nodded as he backed out of the room. I heard the grating of metal locking against metal. I took the chair opposite my old friend.

"You're an asshole," I said.

"I'm not gonna let my girl see me like dis here," he said. He placed his cuffed hands on the table where I could see them.

"You're all she's got, Tino. She needs to know you're okay."

He looked hard at me. The whites of his eyes were yellow and webbed with veins.

"I'm not okay."

"Tell me about the shotgun."

"For hunting, brah."

"They tested it," I said. "It's been fired recently."

Tino nodded.

"I was hunting. I tole you."

"When?"

He shrugged his heavy shoulders.

"I dunno. Few days ago, maybe?"

"Are you fucking with me?"

He shook his head.

"No, brah."

"I want to help you, Tino."

"I know."

The room went quiet. There was nothing more to say. I stood and moved toward the door, rapped three times. I heard the guard's footfalls echo on the concrete floor as he approached from outside. I turned to look at Tino.

"You've got to help me, man," I said. "You've got to help me help you."

He looked resigned.

"If can, can. If no can, no can," he said.

The heavy locks worked inside the door, and it swung open. The guard stood just outside, looking at us both.

"You're an asshole, Tino. But I want you to know something."

"What, brah?"

"Your daughter still loves you."

He looked at the floor. When he looked back, his yellowed eyes were wet.

I stepped out into the corridor and turned back to face him one last time.

"But you've got to give her a reason," I said. "Help her remember why she should."

12

Her face was impassive as we headed back to Kona. The day had turned bright and cloudless while we had been inside, and in some way made it all the worse.

She reached for the dash and turned the radio on. She didn't look at me as she pressed the preset buttons and searched for a song she liked. She'd punched through all of them twice when I reached down and switched it off.

"I'm sorry, Edita."

She shrugged.

"Not your fault," she said. She was looking at me now.

"You want to go back to school?" I asked. I thought it wouldn't hurt to let her get her routine back, a sense of order.

She stared out the window again, and was silent for so long I thought she'd forgotten I asked a question.

"I'd rather go back tomorrow," she said. "I don't think I wanna face all those people yet."

I wondered how much of that had to do with Peter Kalima.

"I understand," I said.

She pulled at a lock of hair and twisted it around her finger as she watched the macadamia and coffee plantations roll by our window. I watched a mongoose slink across the road in the rearview mirror.

"Mike?"

"Yeah?"

"Could we stop off at my house and pick up a couple more things? I wasn't really thinking too clear before…"

The house was several miles the other direction. I pulled to the shoulder and waited for a lull in traffic.

"Only if you let me buy you lunch," I said.

She nodded.

"You'll still take me won't you?" She said. "To school?"

"Sure."

Her hand reached out, fingers too cold for such a bright day.

We pulled into a mom and pop lunch stand that used to be a national chain fast food joint. Now it was local plate lunches; laulau, teriyaki, long rice, loco moco, and huli huli chicken. There was a line at the counter, so Edita went to get us a table while I ordered.

I leaned against the wall and watched her while I waited for our order to come up. Her chin rested on her hand and she stared vacantly out the window. A few minutes later I brought our lunch over to a small Formica table that looked out on the parking lot. Ephemeral waves of heat rose off the asphalt like ghosts. I thought I knew what she'd been looking at. And what she'd been thinking.

We ate in silence for awhile, Edita pushing the food around on her plate again.

"So, do *you* think my dad did it?"

I had wondered how long it would be before she asked me that. I knew that some small part of her felt guilty. On more levels than even Edita herself might know. Guilt that she had not been there to somehow save her mother that night. Guilt that she had been fighting with Ruby so much. Guilt that she was still alive, and her mom wasn't. Guilt as the thought crept into her mind that she wished it were her dad laying dead instead. Guilt that she thinks her dad might have done it.

"I've known your dad a long time," I said. "And it doesn't seem like something the man I know would do." It was a shabby little truth.

She stared blankly through the window, chewed her food mechanically, as if it had no flavor at all.

"That detective thinks he did, though, doesn't he?"

"What Detective Moon thinks right now isn't important. It's up to him to collect evidence and draw conclusions from that. Try not to let him get under your skin."

Her attention went back to the heat phantoms.

"Why won't my dad see me?"

The toughest question. Her father's shame only made him look more guilty.

"He's not ready yet," I answered. "Give him a little time." And it sounded as lame to me as it did to her.

We were back aboard the *Kehau* by three o'clock. It had only taken Edita a few minutes to gather more clothes and school books and put them in a duffel bag. But while I waited in the front room of the old coffee shack, I came across a set of photo albums stacked beneath an end table. I flipped through the pages of one book after another, until I came to the one on the bottom of the pile. The oldest one. The pictures hit me hard, and I closed it quickly. Edita saw my expression and asked if I was all right. I told her I was, but she let me borrow the book. Told me I could keep it as long as I wanted.

I took it below to my stateroom where it would remain in a drawer until I found the courage to open it again.

When I came back onto the aft deck, Rex and Dave were rinsing their scuba gear and laying it out to dry. Edita was in the galley below when Rex asked me if we wanted to join them on an afternoon dive. I glanced at Edita and saw her brighten just a little, a small pulling away from the suffering.

"You guys didn't get enough this morning?" I said.

"Never enough, bro," Dave said. "You can't believe the visibility. Fish all over the place."

"Besides," Rex added, an accusing toss of his head in Dave's direction. "We got a late start."

"Something wrong, Yosemite?" I asked.

An expectant smile formed at the corners of Rex's eyes. He knew what was coming.

"I got myself a job, amigo," Dave said. "I'm staying here in the islands. I'm not going back to California."

The wake of the parasail boat jarred the *Chingadera* and banged her against the hull. I looked over the transom to see that it was okay.

"Tell him the rest," Rex said. He wore a look like he was waiting for the punchline of a joke he'd already heard.

"Got me an apartment, too," Dave finished. "A regular goddamn life-transplant."

I shook my head in amazement. He had lived in southern California all his life, spent the past eighteen years building a solid reputation from which his charter fishing business had sprung. He'd survived economic ebbs and flows, but the comfort I'd always perceived in his life must have been, in actuality, a plodding sameness that he had now chosen to escape. I knew some of that terrain. Another person's life is seldom what it appears to be.

His face reddened slightly as he acknowledged Edita standing beside me.

"Sorry," he said to her. "Didn't mean to cuss."

I brought three beers and a Coke for Edita up from the galley. We drank to Dave's new life as he detailed how, while mooring at their morning dive site, they'd come across some people from Jake's Dive Locker, a local scuba outfit. One of their captains had quit to go back to the mainland and Dave had managed to finagle a job. As both a licensed boat captain and certified scuba instructor, he had been in the right place at the right time.

"I'm tellin' ya," Dave said. "The karma is cracklin' for me, bro. The dude that's leaving for California—the guy that just quit—he was renting an extra room in a house up *mauka* of the airport. I'm taking that, too."

Rex bobbed his head in confirmation.

"Roommate's a babe, too."

I glanced over at Edita. Her face betrayed melancholy, and I thought I could read her mind. Some people get to choose the way their lives go.

"When do you start?" I asked.

"Tomorrow, man. Can you believe it? Four days a week, starting right away."

"Yosemite—" I said.

"Of course," he continued. "I'll have to find a second job somewhere. Part time."

"I think that's—"

"'Bitchen' is the word, bro," Dave said.

I heard laughter for the first time that day.

"You're sure?" I asked again.

"Does a Barbie doll have plastic tits?" Dave said.

He flashed a look at Edita.

"Damn," he said quickly. "Sorry, man."

It was good to hear her giggle.

"So whaddaya say?" Rex asked. "We gonna go diving or what?"

I told them I had some work to do, but Edita moved forward. I knew it would clear her head.

She went below to change, and I helped Rex put together some equipment for her to use. While she was out of earshot, I filled Rex and Dave in on our morning with Detective Moon and the abortive visit with Tino. They continued organizing the equipment while I talked, grunting acknowledgment from time to time, stopping only when I described my introduction to Edita's asshole boyfriend.

"Won't take his eyesight for granted anymore," Rex said, and spat over the side.

I leaned against the bow railing as I watched the *Chingadera* skim across the glassy sea, around the point and north toward Turtle Pinnacles. The sun beat down on my shirtless back and baked the teak deck beneath my feet.

I was restive and tense from too much sitting, and too little exercise, so I dove off the bow and let the ocean cool me down. I swam laps around the *Kehau* until I was out of breath, then climbed the ladder and toweled off. I felt my heart beat against my chest and sat cross-legged on the hot deck while the sun dried me. Then I closed my eyes and thought about what to do next. Moon and his people were putting together their case against Tino, and Hans was pushing the shotgun shells and roll of currency through L.A. forensics. So I decided to get on the computer and do some research on Danny Webb and his band, Stone Blossoms.

I ran my fingers through damp hair as I booted up the laptop and watched the screen flicker to life. A small satellite dish that sat on the crossbars of the mainmast provided me all the satellite communication links I would ever need.

I established a connection with my ISP, typed the words STONE BLOSSOMS into the prompt box and pressed the *Enter* key. After a few seconds the screen showed me a list of websites.

There were seventeen sites dedicated to the band, and I scrolled down to view the name, web address and a brief description of each one. What I was looking for was not the kind of arcana that most of the sites appeared to contain, but a couple of them looked promising.

The first link I went to was one sponsored by the band's original record label, Maverick Records. After a minute of downloading, I was greeted by a screen that featured colorful full-motion graphics and a variety of sublinks to chat rooms, discographies, song lyrics, photo archives, history, album art downloads, and the like. If this was just one of the websites having to do with Stone Blossoms my mind was spinning at how popular the band must be. It amazed me when I stopped to think about what an enormous business enterprise they still were, even after having disbanded decades earlier. I clicked the icon labeled HISTORY, and took notes on a yellow pad on the desk beside me.

It took almost a full hour to digest the information on the first site alone, and I'd already pulled together three pages of hastily scrawled details. I had everything from the names of people associated with the band, to dates of recording sessions, and even the studios they'd used.

I returned to the SEARCH RESULTS screen on the browser, and linked to the next of the Stone Blossoms websites that had caught my attention earlier.

The second one was sponsored, according to the site's main page, by an avid fan. It contained photos, concert set lists, rumors about the band members and their current projects. Other items were much more obscure than the general fan-club type of press information contained on the Maverick Records web site. The subject heading icon that interested me most was labeled STONE BLOSSOMS MYTHOLOGY. It was there that I first learned about the legendary missing tapes from the group's final recording session. And that one of the victims from my house, Tom Foster, had been the group's producer. I wrote both of these items on my legal pad, and circled them several times.

I was nearly finished reading when my cell phone rang. Instinctively, I looked at the clock above the stove in the galley and was surprised to see that over two hours had passed since Rex, Yosemite and Edita had left. I padded across the salon and picked up the phone from the dining table.

"Travis, this is Detective Moon. I'd like to talk with you."

There was something strange in the tone of his voice.

"I'm in the middle of—"

"It's important," he interrupted. "I won't take much of your time. And I have something I need to give you."

"Fine," I said. "But you'll have to come out to the *Kehau*. You know where it is. I'm in the middle of something here."

"No problem. Give me twenty minutes."

I looked at the phone in my hand, glanced back at the clock in the galley, and figured the current time in Los Angeles. Even though it was well after five o'clock in L.A., I decided to place a call of my own while I waited for Moon.

As I expected, Hans was still at his desk. I looked through the notes I had taken from the Stone Blossoms' websites, extracting the names of the people associated with the band that I wanted him to get current addresses for. I wasn't yet sure what I'd ask them once Hans ran them down, but I hung on the hope that something would rattle loose. It had worked for me before. I was sure there was a more plausible explanation for the murders than a drunken jealous rampage. I had a feeling that I might end up being the only hope Tino had in proving his innocence. If, in fact, he was.

Hans huffed a little, but ultimately agreed to help me locate the rock group's old manager, Mark Miller; the recording engineer from the band's last session, Dennis Farr; and the last three surviving band members. But partners are partners, retired or not, and he knew that I'd treat the information with care.

"I'll ring you back tomorrow," Hans said. "The fingerprint work oughta be done by then, too. Should only take 'em a few hours once they get the FedEx."

"Listen, Hans, I don't know how long the locals are gonna let me stay in the loop on this thing—"

"Don't worry about it," he said, interrupting me. "I'll call you first."

"I appreciate it."

"You'll pay me back somehow."

I had just broken the connection with Hans when I heard the approach of an outboard motor. Before I could get topside, I felt the dull thud of a skiff butting the Kehau.

"Hello the boat!"

Moon.

I quickly gathered the notes I had taken, stashed them in a drawer beneath the nav desk, and snapped the laptop shut.

I climbed the stairs to the stern in time to see Detective Moon tying off a small Alii Kai skiff to a chrome cleat attached to the gunwale.

"Come aboard," I said. I gestured toward the short ladder that hung down and nearly touched the surface of the bay.

Moon was dressed in crisply ironed khaki slacks, a blue-and-white aloha shirt open at the neck, and dark brown deck shoes. He held a manila envelope in his teeth as he used both hands to steady himself as he climbed aboard.

"Something cold to drink?" I offered.

"Yeah. Sure. Got a Coke?"

I led the way below.

He took a seat at the edge of the tan leather banquette seat that formed an L-shape around the koa wood dining table. Large tinted windows ran the length of the room and bathed it in afternoon light. A breeze stirred through two sliding sections left open for circulation.

The detective slapped the envelope he'd been holding onto the table directly in front of him. I handed him his Coke, and he opened it with a snick of the poptop.

He looked up from the aluminum can and into my face.

"I'm gonna get right to it, Big City," he said.

"Big City?" I said.

"Yeah," he said. His voice dripped with sarcasm. "That's you. Big L.A. copper in little Kona town."

"Listen, detective—"

"No. You listen, Travis. I'm gonna do what my captain tells me to do on this, but I'm not gonna pretend I like it. Or even agree with it, okay?"

"What the hell are you talking about?"

"I got a couple of things here for you," he said. He gestured with his free hand to the envelope on the table. "But I want to make sure you understand where I'm coming from first."

"Let's hear it," I said.

He took a noisy pull from the soda can and put it down on the table a little too hard. A stream of foam bubbled over onto my table.

"I don't much care for some big city hotshot cop getting involved in my case. You don't understand the islands. You're an outsider. And as far as I'm concerned, we don't need some fucking *haole* come-lately sticking his nose in and screwing things up, cop or no cop."

I let his condescending use of the word *haole*—a not-entirely-benign slang term for caucasians—pass. Ironic, too, given my bloodline.

"I'm trying to help you," I said.

"Yeah, well, if it were up to me I wouldn't be taking any of your help. But the captain did some checking up on you. You got some rep, I'll give you that. And he thinks maybe you can help. He was pretty happy with that fingerprint thing you pulled."

"But you don't need any help, do you Moon."

"That's right, Big City, I don't."

"Well I'm happy you got that off your chest," I said. I let a few beats of charged silence pass before I continued. "Now I'll tell you where I'm coming from, Moon."

A hint of a smile.

"I don't much give a fuck what you want," I said. "All I know is that five bodies were blown all over the walls of my house, one of whom was a friend of mine."

Moon waited.

"What evidence you have is crap, your only suspect doesn't remember a goddamn thing, and there's not a witness in sight. From where I sit, you can use all the help you can get, whether it comes from a 'big city *haole*' or not."

Moon took a long slow swallow of Coke.

"As far as I'm concerned," he said. "I have the shooter in custody. You want to go chasing smudged fingerprints from here to L.A., be my guest."

"You have what?" I asked.

"You heard me. We're booking Tino Orlandella on suspicion of murder," he said. "He'll be on his way to Hilo by this afternoon."

Moon opened the flap of the envelope that he had brought aboard. He withdrew two neatly typed sheets and handed them to me.

The first was a letter granting me temporary guardianship of Edita for the duration of Tino's arraignment and trial, signed by Tino, and countersigned by a family court judge. The second was printed on HPD letterhead addressed to the harbormaster of Kona, signed by Captain Cerillo, stating that, due to police business, I was to be given unrestricted authorization to remain at my present mooring until further notice.

Moon enjoyed the look on my face.

"Like I said before," he said. "The captain seems to think that you can help us on the case. He was real impressed."

"And I'm supposed to look after a teenage kid while I'm at it?"

"That's the way Tino wanted it," Moon watched my discomfort. "And until he's found guilty, he's still her custodian. It's his choice."

"Jesus Christ."

Moon rose to leave. My cell phone rang. I let it go.

"Tino should be kicked loose for lack of evidence. He and Edita should be getting on with their lives."

"I'll see myself out," Moon said, "Oh, by the way, your house is no longer a crime scene. You're free to go back and clean up."

"Got a long memory, Moon."

"Yeah, yeah," he said over his shoulder.

I watched his silhouette in the doorway against the fading afternoon sun.

"Oh, and one other thing," the detective added. "Ruby Orlandella's funeral is day after tomorrow. Yoshoda Cemetery in Kealakekua. Tino wanted me to tell you to tell Edita."

The cell phone kept ringing as Moon disappeared down the ladder.

13

The goddamned phone didn't stop.

I flipped it open.

"Travis."

Silence on the other end.

"Mr. Mike Travis?" The voice was female, businesslike.

"Who is this?" I asked.

"Mike, my name is Marti Batteau," she said. "From Van de Groot Capital."

Just what I needed. A fucked up day getting worse.

"What can I do for you, Marti?"

"Your brother Valden gave me your number, and said that I should contact you with regard to the matter that took place at your family home."

Matter. Not *tragedy* or even *unpleasantness.*

"The *murders,* you mean?"

"It's an open line, Mike."

I waited.

"In any event," she went on after the awkward pause. "I would like to meet with you to discuss it."

"What did you have in mind?"

"Well," she said, "I've only just arrived, so I'll need some time to make phone calls. Perhaps we can meet for dinner tonight. Say six? My hotel?"

"Say six-thirty," I answered. "And what hotel?"

There was a sound of rustling paper.

"The Four Seasons Hualalai. Do you know it?"

"I know where it is, Marti. I'll meet you at the beach bar."

"Fine. Six-thirty."

I snapped the cell phone shut. I had no idea what she looked like, but I figured it wouldn't be too difficult to spot an uptight New York businesswoman with a superiority complex on the beach at Hualalai.

BY FIVE-THIRTY I had showered, shaved and begun to feel like myself again. I threw on a pair of khaki slacks, an aloha shirt with green banana leaves on a beige background, kangaroo skin deck shoes without socks, and a pair of Neptune sunglasses. I opened the drawer beside my bed and looked at the little Beretta Bobcat. I slipped it into my pocket.

Rex, Dave and Edita were still out diving, so I wrote a quick note and left it on the table in the salon before I left.

It was a twenty minute drive to the hotel. I pulled up to the Four Seasons valet stand, left the keys with the attendant and crossed through the elegant lobby to the stairs leading down to the beach.

The sky was hung with the hint of the coming sunset, tinting the clouds in shades of orange and salmon. The mist from breaking waves mingled with earthy scents of pikake and ginger. A breeze ruffled palm fronds overhead and made a sound like falling rain.

I followed a meandering pathway past the main pool, and turned left toward the sound of a trio playing Hawaiian music. Chairs and tables rested on smooth white sand. There were only ten or twelve people seated there, so meeting Marti Batteau was not likely to be too difficult. None of the tables was occupied by a lone woman.

I caught the bartender's attention and ordered a double Absolut on the rocks, no garnish, and took over an unoccupied table on the beach.

The musicians were singing the Sunday Manoa's *Kawika*. I was tapping my hand on the faded wood tabletop when Marti made her appearance about ten minutes later. My drink was half- empty.

"Mike Travis?" she said. "I'm Marti Batteau."

I was taken by surprise by two things: The intrusion on my wandering mind that had been absorbed by the sounds of the shoreline, the music, and the top half of a double vodka; and the woman's appearance. Not even a remote resemblance to the woman of my imagination.

I stood and shook her hand. It was firm, but feminine. I pulled a chair away from the table for her.

"A gentleman," she smiled. "Not too many left."

The real Marti was tall, five-foot-nine or -ten, slender and lissome. Thick mahogany hair fell to her shoulders and was cast with auburn highlights in the unfolding sunset. She wore a linen pantsuit the color of straw, with a deep burgundy blouse that set off a smooth olive complexion. My eyes followed a simple gold chain and pendant necklace down to the swell of her breasts.

Most striking of all to me were her eyes. Some men are leg men, some are ass men, others are breast men. I have always been an eye man. Hers were a deep nutshell brown, large and doe-like. The kind of eyes that could suck you in and convince you of anything. And had you pat your Beretta, just to be sure it was there.

"Thanks for coming," she said. Her voice was honeyed gravel, like a torch singer. Or maybe Lauren Bacall, Kathleen Turner.

"Sure." I signaled for the bartender.

"Your brother Valden told me to look for a tall, handsome guy with a nice tan, sun-bleached hair that needed a trim, and a devil-may-care attitude."

"Statements like that usually comes in crocks," I said through a smile. "My brother wouldn't say any of that."

"How about, 'Look for a big guy with too much time on his hands and a Jimmy Buffett fixation.'"

I raised my glass.

"He's a Master of the Universe, you know."

"What?"

"Never mind."

When the bartender came I ordered another double, and Marti had the same.

"I gather he doesn't impress you," Marti said.

"To each his own."

"And yours?"

"A good boat, tradewinds, and good company."

"I like that better," she said.

I smiled and looked into those brown eyes. "And I like you better."

She watched me.

"The phone call?"

"It wasn't the real you."

"And you're pleased."

"Oh, yeah."

The brown eyes warmed, like she was suddenly free, enjoying her senses. Tactile, soft, interesting.

"So," she began. "Tell me what happened at your family's house."

I was reluctant to get into any details without getting some background of my own. And like a good cop, I answered a question with a question.

"What's your interest in all of this?" If it had been of personal importance to him, Valden would have come himself. Instead, he chose Marti Batteau. I wanted to know why.

She hesitated before leaning back in her chair, swirling the ice in her cocktail. There was a faint air of artifice about her now, a feline awareness of her situation. No longer tactile and soft, more a checking on her surroundings, how she could use them if she had to. Through it all, she exuded that silky-strong sensuality of the predator.

"I'm in charge of an IPO that is very important to Van de Groot Capital. A deal that also involved Danny Webb."

I nodded, but said nothing. I already knew that part. It was a weak start and I wanted more.

"I'm the only female Executive Vice President at VGC. I've been there for almost ten years and I'm the first woman to have ever been put in charge of an IPO. Let alone a deal of this magnitude."

I drank my Absolut and waited.

"You obviously know your brother very well, Mike. You can't think it was easy to get where I am."

"Then why did you stay with them so long?" I asked.

She chuffed out a New York venture capital laugh I'd heard before.

"For the money, of course."

I caught a sense that she had lost control of herself momentarily and let me into a space she kept for herself alone. Something in her reeled itself back in as she looked unblinkingly into my eyes.

"I was not fortunate enough to have been brought up with wealth, like you and Valden," she said. "Quite the contrary, in fact, and I'm not about to go back *there*."

Our drinks were nearly empty, so I signaled the bartender for another round.

"So this deal with Danny Webb was going to be big?" I asked.

"*Is* big," she said. "Present tense. The deal we're working is much too big—and much too far along—to allow Danny Webb's death to derail it."

"I'm not sure I follow," I said. "Then what are you doing here if the deal is not dependent on Webb?"

She appraised me silently. I'd seen that look before. Usually under harsh lights, wire-glass, and two-way mirrors. I waited while she worked it through, deciding how much to reveal.

"You see," she said, "We're preparing to go public in just under two weeks. An IPO. Oh, you probably don't—"

"Initial Public Offering," I interrupted. "I know what an IPO is."

"Ouch," she said. "I'm patronizing. Sorry."

"You're doing fine."

"You're not exactly the margarita-swilling boat bum that Valden would have people believe, are you?"

I lifted my near-empty vodka glass.

"I hate margaritas," I said.

She smiled, but it was careful.

"I take it you know the Stone Blossoms?"

I nodded.

"Danny Webb and Christopher Morton—Danny's songwriting partner from back in the old days—were to be the creative heads of a new entertainment company that VGC is taking public next week. It's going to be into everything from pre-recorded music—"

"CDs and cassettes."

"Right," she said. "From pre-recorded music to film and television production and distribution. They had already amassed a sizable portfolio of music publishing rights, and were going to fold that into the new company as well.

"Down the road, the plan is to have at least one, perhaps two cable TV channels dedicated to baby-boomer music trends—"

"Like VH-1 or MTV."

"Similar, but more sophisticated. Our programming will consist mainly of documentaries and biographies of music acts and artists as well as live broadcasts of concerts."

The bartender arrived with two fresh cocktails. I slipped a hundred dollar bill into his hand and thanked him. He nodded politely and returned to his station behind the bar.

"Not cheap like your brother," she said.

"Better looking, too."

"It makes your head spin to hear the plans for this company," she went on. "When it's matured, it will rival some of the biggest entertainment conglomerates in the world."

"You still haven't answered my question," I said. "Now that Webb is dead, how do you keep your deal together."

"Because the glitz of the deal wasn't in Danny Webb and Christopher Morton, 'the rock stars'." She used her fingers to trace invisible quotation marks in the air. "The sizzle that was going to attract all that new public capital had to do with what Danny *had*."

"Which was what?"

She spun the ice in her glass with a swizzle stick and gazed out toward the horizon. The dying sun had left purple stains on the clouds.

"The key to a successful start-up company," she said, "Is to make a huge splash with your first product. Especially in the entertainment business. If you go big—I mean really big—with your first release, be it a movie, CD, whatever—"

"Then your reputation as an industry 'player' is secure," I finished. "And you can attract the next round of big acts to your company."

"Exactly." She nestled back into her chair.

"You didn't answer my question again," I said. "What did Webb have that was so important?"

Marti looked furtively from side to side and leaned toward me. It reminded me of bad melodrama. She was a strange combination of savvy and innocence. Learned it all by trial and error, up from the wrong side of the tracks.

She lowered her voice to a near whisper.

"He had the lost Stone Blossoms tapes."

"Now I'm impressed," I said. "You sure he had them?"

"We're pretty sure he did, anyway."

The night was suddenly quiet, like those odd random moments when everyone at a party stops talking at once. Even the gentle breaking of waves fell back, muted. The band was on a break, and I hadn't even noticed they'd stopped playing.

The sky had faded to full dark. Fire-tipped tiki torches lit snaking traceries along the pathways around the resort. An outburst of laughter from an adjacent table broke the curious silence, and restarted time.

I let the "pretty sure" part slide for the moment. Marti Batteau was on a roll, getting excited describing the intimate inside details of a major deal, the way big-business types can.

"My God," she said. "It's almost like having the master tapes to a lost Beatles album."

"How much money were you intending to raise with your IPO?" I asked. I was still having trouble letting go of the past tense.

"Two billion dollars," she said through a smile equal parts pride, greed and fear of failure.

"And VGC would get, what, a couple points for setting it up?"

"Seven points," she said, then stopped to let that sink in. "A hundred and forty million dollars in cash and stock. Biggest single deal we've ever done."

"And a chunk of that becomes a nice bonus for you."

The nutshell eyes, the innocence and cruelty. Give me the *Kehau* and a decent wind. Money like that could be poison.

Canned Hawaiian music floated across the sand from the bandstand, and broke the mood.

"Enough business," she said. "I want to know more about you."

Oh, Christ, I thought she had me figured better than that. But I went along.

"Like what?"

"Like what do you do?"

"I used to be a cop," I said.

"And now?"

I was silent a moment. I felt the weight of the little Beretta in my pocket.

"Now," I said. "I'm between things."

"Between what things?" She persisted.

"Between being a cop and not being one."

"And how's it going?"

"Slow."

I took an ice cube in my mouth and began to chew it. She kept staring at me.

"Are you married?"

"Never."

"Never have, or never will?"

I'd seen some of the ugliest shit in the world delivered up in the name of love. And I'll never forget the look of inconsolable heartbreak on my friend's face when he lost his young children in a nasty custody battle. They were constant reminders, lurking in my heart and in my brain.

"Never have," I said finally.

"Hmmm."

She tossed off the remainder of her vodka in one swallow.

"So, Mike," she said. "Care to walk me back to my room? I feel like skipping dinner. It's late where I come from."

I stood and helped her with her chair. She looked up at me briefly before she stood.

"You're very polite," she said.

Polite, but not very nice.

14

I woke with a start, not remembering where I was. The ceiling fan hummed and ruffled the diaphanous curtains, still closed against the morning sun. In the background were the mingling sounds of the ocean and the suite's shower being turned off. A moment later Marti emerged, naked but for a pair of turquoise French cut panties. She was toweling her wet hair.

"Good morning," she purred. The torch-singer voice was still infused with last night's passion.

I lifted myself from the pillow and leaned back on my elbows.

"That's a hell of a sight to wake up to," I smiled.

"Breakfast should be arriving any minute. I ordered room service."

"You have a problem with priorities, don't you?"

She tossed her wet towel at me.

"You and I have some work to do today," she said.

I headed for the shower. She watched me, giving me the once-over, then she was blow-drying her hair.

It was supposed to be afterglow, but she used the torch-singer voice. Take me back to the house in Honaunau, let's look for the tapes...

I wondered who had used whom.

I was spooning at the sliced pineapple and berries when it hit.

"What is it," she asked.

I thought about Edita waiting for me to take her to school. She would be raw-nerved, feeling abandoned again. Christ. I shoved back my chair.

"Something I have to do."

"Go," she said.

"No questions?"

"Go. Talk later."

I went.

The problem was I had the only cellular telephone from the *Kehau*. I'd need to raise her on the VHF somehow. It was long past eight-thirty. At the concierge desk, I explained the problem. The woman there told me that the resort operates both a cruiser and a dive boat of its own. The hotel had a VHF radio in their activities. They got me to it fast.

Fifteen minutes later, Marti and I were in my rented Mustang and heading south toward Kona. Just being outside, the glimmer of the ocean and the clean tropical air, it all helped, but Edita was there like a wound.

"Can you talk now?" Marti asked.

"I can talk."

"So, what's going on?"

I filled her in as we drove. I told her about the murders, Tino Orlandella's arrest, and my having been made Edita's legal guardian.

I slewed the Mustang to a stop at the foot of the pier.

I was helping Marti over the stern rail of the *Kehau* when I heard someone approach me from behind.

"Bad deal, man." Rex said. "Edita was pretty bummed." He gave Marti a quick look, but his attention was on me.

"Where is she?" I asked him.

"At school," he said. "Don't worry, I took her ashore and got a cab to take her. She's gonna have a friend drop her at the pier after school. Four-thirty, she told me."

"Did you go with her?"

Rex looked at me with a *what-a-stupid-goddamn-question* expression.

"Of course I did. She was nervous as hell, and I think it hurt her feelings that you never came back last night. She relies on you, man. You're the rudder, Mike."

"God damnit," I said.

Rex shifted his attention to Marti.

"So are you going to introduce me?"

I did, then we all went below. Rex showed her around while I went to my stateroom to change into a pair of shorts, sun faded tropical shirt, and pair of flip-flops. Marti and Rex were standing on the bow talking when I came back out.

"We'll get going in a few minutes, Marti. I have a call I need to make first."

"No problem," she said. "I'm enjoying the breeze."

I punched Hans Yamaguchi's number, and waited while it rang. Moments later, Hans was on the line.

"Hey, Mike," he said. He sounded animated again.

"You sound happy. What's going on?"

"You remember Reverend Green?"

Hans and I had worked a case a few years back that involved a mail-order minister. The guy ran a "church" in the basement of a run down apartment building on Vermont.

The good Reverend Green and his son, in their zeal to save the souls of their lost heathen flock, proceeded to "convert" about seventeen prostitutes into "nuns." The nuns would "counsel and comfort" male members of the faithful in the apartments upstairs in exchange for monetary contributions. All tax-free. We couldn't touch the Rev.

One day, we got a missing persons/probable homicide call. It was called in by the younger sister of one of the nuns who claimed she had evidence we could use on Green. It involved an alleged homicide. Three days after we interviewed the sister, she, too, went missing.

We leaked the story to the papers, and the next thing we knew, we had a former male member of the congregation come forward and admit to participating in the destruction of two dead bodies, though not to the murders themselves. He was an inmate up in Chino. Seemed he found some salvation of his own through a sentence reduction deal with the DA.

Hans and I interviewed the former parishioner, and he described having taken the corpses into one of the apartments above the church, placed them, each in turn, into the bathtub, then methodically dismembered them.

The bags of body parts were transported to Green's opulent home in Marina del Rey where he had a fifty-three foot sportfishing boat docked out front. There at the house, the bodies were hacked into smaller pieces, doused with kerosene, and burned. The charred bone fragments were dumped off the end of the reverend's private dock where it was assumed that the outgoing tide would scatter and permanently hide the evidence. Why they didn't take the boat out and scatter the ashes, we'd never know. Nobody said criminals are smart.

After being denied a search warrant on two separate occasions, Hans and I decided that maybe I should spend a weekend scuba diving "recreationally" in Marina del Rey. Three hours later I had found enough bone fragments to fill a small sandwich bag.

With the help of the county coroner's office, we painstakingly identified and labeled the burned bone remnants, among which were seven different atlas bones—the small bone at the top of the spinal column upon which rests the skull. A human body only has one atlas per customer.

With these in hand, we found ourselves holding evidence connecting the reverend to at least seven homicides. And a witness to the dismemberments.

Reverend Green and his son were both convicted. The son received a reduced sentence as the result of a deal he cut with the DAs office in exchange for testifying against his own father. The reverend went down for life.

More recently, strong politico-social sentiment had turned Green's first parole hearing into a three-ring-circus. It looked like it could actually sway the tide enough that he might well get released pending appeal.

It seemed like another world.

"Sure, Hans," I said. "What about him?" "He died in prison this afternoon. It's all over the TV news."

I could hear familiar noise in the squad room behind Hans' voice.

"You've got to be kidding."

"No shit, brother," Hans said. "Heart attack while he was sitting on the can. Can you beat that?"

"Too bad. He went too easy. I was hoping he got shanked."

"Yeah, well, any way you slice it, the fucker's gone. Died on the crapper."

"I'll spare you the obvious irony."

"Elvis, I know. And thanks."

"So, you got anything for me on the stuff we talked about yesterday?" I asked.

"Got a couple things. First off, you're not gonna like this, but the fingerprints are shit. Unusable partials."

"Smudgy unusable, or clear partials, you know, with sections missing?"

"Fairly clear, but not enough to run through the system."

He was right. I didn't like that.

"Okay," I said. "What else?"

"I was able to locate the people you were looking for. Well, everybody but one."

"Which one?"

"Mark Miller, the manager. But I'm still waiting. Anyway—you got a pencil?"

"Shoot."

"The first one, one of the musicians, guy named Kevin Demers?"

"Yeah?"

"Dead."

"Fuck," I said. "How?"

"DOA at USC Medical Center about a year ago. Solo motorcycle accident. Apparently, he had a whole chemical lab in his system at the time."

"At least he didn't take anybody with him."

"Next one's Dennis Farr, the recording engineer. Guess what? He's your neighbor. No shit. Seems he was doing some recording work with one of your stiffs, too."

"Danny Webb?" I asked.

"No. The producer guy..." I heard shuffling paper. "Tom Foster. He's in Hawaii."

I remembered being told Foster had a place in Maui.

"Where? Maui?" I asked.

"The hell should I know. Address I got says Hilo. Where's that?"

"Big Island. That's where I am. It's a two or three hour drive from here."

Hans sighed.

"What the fuck am I doing wrong? Everybody's in Hawaii but me," he said.

"Just stay where you are, Hans" I said. "If you came here, you'd lower the average IQ of both states."

"Funny guy. Want the address?"

"No," I said. "Just give 'em all to me at the end. I want to hear the rest first."

"Okay," Hans continued. "Next up is Lyle Sparks. This one lives in Malibu. He's got his own production studio there. Does movie and TV soundtracks."

"Go on."

"And finally," Hans said. "We've got Christopher Morton. This asshole has it made. He's got a place in L.A., one in New York, and one in Caracas."

"Venezuela. Interesting," I said. "Must like fishing."

"Guess so," he said. "Ready for the addresses and phone numbers?"

When I had finished copying the information on my yellow legal pad, I asked for one more favor.

"Hey, Hans, how about sending those prints over to Vonda Franklin at Forensics."

Vonda was a forensic tech in the lab that specialized in photographic and video work.

"I'll call her and tell her to expect them from you," I said.

"What do you have in mind?"

"A last ditch effort. One of the local dicks over here is busting my balls, and I'd like to prove him wrong."

"I'll take them over on my way to lunch," he said.

"Thanks, partner."

The line sounded unusually dead when he hung up.

I looked out the window and saw that Rex and Marti were still content above decks, so I placed a call to Vonda Franklin to tell her to expect the prints from Hans.

I described to her what it was I had in mind for her to do. There was a predictable amount of hemming and hawing, but she finally agreed after I promised her another free weekend on the *Kehau.*

She promised to get back to me the next day.

15

Dinner aboard the *Kehau* was quiet. The yacht rocked gently in the wake of passing boats, rigging clanged in the light breeze that honed the deck. Neither Marti or I could speak openly about the day we had spent at the house in Honaunau looking for the tapes. And Edita was shut down around her fears and sense of betrayal. Nothing cuts quite the same as betrayal in a kid's eyes. But she had that other look reserved for Marti Batteau.

Only Dave seemed unaffected by the taut mood, that or he was trying hard to diffuse it. I was grateful for the distraction as he rambled on about the tourists, his voice muffled whenever he dabbed at his mustache. His first day at his new job. This would be his last night aboard before moving into his apartment.

Marti derailed it.

"So how was it today, Edita?" she asked.

"School, you mean?"

"Yes. Was it rough?"

"Sucked." Edita's eyes were old. I wondered if she'd ever be young again. She stared at her plate.

"Might help to talk about it," Marti said.

"I'm finished," Edita said. She rose and took her untouched plate to the sink. "I've got homework."

"Too soon to push like that," I said when she had gone below.

"You can't mollycoddle her," she said.

"Nobody's mollycoddling her," I said. "She just needs some time to get a foothold. Go easy."

Marti's brown eyes glared. If Edita's were filled with lost innocence, Marti's gave back a lifetime removed from soft sheets and musk and languid touch. There was challenge and hardship there that reminded me how little I knew of this woman.

"Life doesn't provide footholds, Mike. You think those kids at school were easy with her today?"

"Look—" I began

"If she's going to get through this, she's going to have to be tough. That's the way of the world. Especially for a woman."

"I don't see it that way," I said. Not everything had to be competition, life-and-death struggle. A wise bartender I once knew used to say, *"To struggle is a choice."* It comes a little clearer every day.

She tossed her napkin on the table.

"Then we disagree."

There was another awkward silence.

"Let's talk about something else," she said to no one in particular.

"Whattaya think of Rex's tattoo?" Dave said.

Marti stared for a moment, then managed a smile.

Later, when the dishes were cleared and the galley straightened, Rex and Dave took off for another tour of the bars. Marti and I stayed aboard and opened a bottle of Pinot Grigio, took it topside in a bucket of ice.

The moon was nearly new and the stars stuttered between lacy clouds. I uncorked the bottle, poured two glasses, and she followed me to the bow. It was quiet there, and more private. The conversation I wanted to have with Marti was not for Edita's ears.

The deck still held the warmth of the day, so we sat and sipped cool wine, looked across the bay toward town. Water lapped against the hull. Tourist noise and restaurant smells drifted over the black bay.

I'd spent the better part of the afternoon dwelling on the murders and had drawn a few conclusions. I went over them in my head as we sat there in the dark.

First, if the Stone Blossoms tapes did still exist, they were believed to have been in the possession of Danny Webb at the time of his murder. Or soon to come into his possession. If that were true, there was a good chance the killings were not a crime of passion, but a robbery. A good thing for Tino.

The lingering question was why the others had also been gunned down. For that matter, why had *anyone* been killed at all? Wrong place and wrong time? I didn't like it. I rarely liked the simple answers. Too often they involved coincidence, and I didn't like those either.

Second, if the tapes were with Webb when he died, then where were they now? It would be extremely difficult, if not impossible, to convince Moon or Cerillo that there was an alternative motive behind the killings; robbery, not jealousy. Most definitely not without some evidence of the tapes having been stolen. The big problem with that was that no one really knew for certain if the damn things really existed at all. According to the research I had done on the Internet, it was more widely believed that the tapes had been erased, not stolen. If that were the case, then there would have been nothing to steal in the first place. Bad for Tino.

No matter how I turned it over, it boiled down to this: If I couldn't prove the existence of the tapes, then obviously I couldn't prove they'd been stolen. If I couldn't prove they'd been stolen from the house at Honaunau, then I couldn't prove an alternate motive for the multiple homicides that had led to the arrest of Tino Orlandella.

The worst part was that the most plausible legal explanation for the killings rested in circumstantial evidence that placed a drunk and raging Tino at the crime scene, exploding into a jealous fury, and taking the lives of five people. Worse yet was that it would play so well to a jury. It would appeal to their darkest fantasies, illusions that played themselves out almost daily on daytime TV.

It was clear to me that in the absence of a forensic miracle from Vonda Franklin identifying the shooter or shooters, the trail I had to follow was the missing tapes.

"You okay?" Marti said. "You're awfully quiet."

"Just thinking."

"About today?"

"Yeah." I pulled the bottle from the ice bucket and studied the label.

"Are you sure there is nowhere else in that house that something could be hidden? A floor safe? A fireproof file cabinet?"

"We've already been over this," I said. "My father never used the place as an office, much less for storage. You saw yourself what it's like. It's just a goddamned beach house." I buried the bottle back in the bucket.

She frowned. Moonlight caught its shadows.

"It's just hard to believe that a sophisticated businessman like your father wouldn't have had some small place for keeping sensitive items."

"Maybe he didn't have many secrets."

We'd already had that conversation at least twice earlier that afternoon on the drive back from the house. It went nowhere.

Marti had gone over the place inch by inch while I cooked dry coffee grounds on the stove. An old cop trick to neutralize the stench of blood and death that lingered in the confines of a closed-up space. The only thing that was different since the last time I had been there was that the corpses had been removed. Everything else was left where I'd seen it last, where the cops had left them. The glutinous stains on the floor where the bodies had lain, the dark clouds of fingerprint dust on the walls, even the victims' cocktail glasses. I doubted that I could ever sit in that room again without seeing Ruby lying there shattered and lifeless.

By the time I finished scraping remnants of tissue and blood from the walls and floor, Marti had finished rummaging. She silently watched me rinse the stiff brush and bucket in the kitchen sink. In the end, there was nothing, short of recarpeting and new paint, that would remove the black smudges of print powder from the walls, floor, furniture, windows, and carpet. The memory would never be washed away.

We were both silent now, and the sounds of a skiff floated to where we sat on the *Kehau*'s gently rolling deck. I upended my wine glass, drained it, then pulled the bottle from the ice bucket and refilled both our glasses.

"Are you sure Webb even had the tapes?" I asked.

It was the first time I had openly raised my doubts to her. Somehow, back at the house, it hadn't seemed as important. But the longer I thought about it, the more critical the question became.

She tilted her head to the moon laced clouds.

"No. I'm not," she said. "Fact is, we think that's the main reason why Danny was here in the islands."

"What do you mean?"

"We think he was meeting someone. Getting them from him."

"Who?"

"I don't know," she said. "Danny never said. Of course, he never would have told me anyway."

I mulled that over.

"Foster, maybe?" I asked.

The breeze pulled a lock of mahogany hair, draped it across her face.

"Maybe, but he's dead now, too, isn't he?"

She brushed at the strands with long fingers and leaned back again.

"So, you were going to Wall Street with a two billion-dollar IPO, and you didn't even have one of the main assets of the company in your possession?"

She stiffened.

"It's not as if the Blossoms' tapes are the only valuable asset, Mike. They were just our insurance of a profitable first year. It's a highly competitive industry."

Sounded like well-rehearsed bullshit for a shareholders meeting. My look said so.

She breathed a sigh.

"It's like this," she said. "Let's say this long lost Stone Blossoms album were to be released. I think it would also be safe to assume there would be a ton of media hoopla. How many copies would you think it would sell?"

"I have no idea. A million? Two?"

"Two million—double platinum. Not bad for an upstart new record label," she smiled knowingly. "But that wasn't a fair question."

"Go on," I said.

"Let's start with a couple facts: First, the Stone Blossoms never sold fewer than two million records. Second, each of the five consecutive albums that followed their debut eclipsed the prior album's sales."

"Impressive." It was.

"There's more," she said. She held up three fingers. "With the release of each new record, the back catalog—the albums that had preceded the current release—each re-charted and sold in the mid-six figures."

"Okay—"

"Wait, I'm still not finished," she continued, four fingers in the air. "Their last two albums sold twenty-five and thirty million copies—each—worldwide. That's where the band *left off*."

She took a sip of wine and rested her case. She'd told the story before.

"Sure," I said. "But does anybody care anymore?"

"You said it yourself the other night, Mike. With the death and drama surrounding it—hell, even as a curiosity piece—it's the next best thing to a lost Beatles record."

I had said that. And the statistics were impressive, too.

"So," I said. "I'll up my guess to five million."

"That's about what we figure it to be—if it *flops*. Our internal estimates put it more like seven to ten million. Conservatively. So, let's do the math. Let's call it ten million copies—that makes it easier. Let's also put the retail price of a CD at eighteen dollars. You with me?"

"Rock-o-nomics 101?" I said.

"Just listen. Our IPO company—Planet Entertainment is the name, by the way—will be directly involved in the distribution, publishing and the ownership of the album. Each of those areas have their own profit structure, but let's break it down:

"A record company that does nothing but sign the bands, front the money to produce, record and promote an album will make about twelve and a half percent of the retail price in profit. That's after expenses."

I did the math.

"So," I said. "With a CD worth eighteen bucks a shot, retail, the record company's cut alone is worth a bit over two bucks apiece. Sell ten million, you make, say, twenty million."

Her eyes were bright. She loved this.

"Right," she said. "But that's only the beginning. There's probably another dollar profit in distribution—getting the CD's to the record stores."

"There's another ten million."

"Exactly. That's an entirely separate profit center."

I raised my eyebrows.

"Thirty million for your new company," I said. "Not a bad start."

She moistened her lips with her tongue as a night bird soundlessly swept the sky above us.

"Not bad at all," she smiled. "But the best part is the publishing. That's the deal the publisher makes with the songwriter."

I reached across and replenished her wine.

"The publisher administers the song, keeps track of airplay, exploits the printed sheet music, rents the song to movie soundtracks or commercials, you know, things like that."

"I'm with you," I said.

"Well, Planet Entertainment has bought the publishing rights from the original publisher of all the old material, which carries with it the explicit understanding that it will also own the rights to any 'new' material."

She made the quote marks with her fingers, a gesture that usually annoys the hell out of me.

"Of course, the old publisher had no idea that there was any hope of uncovering any *new* material," I interjected. "Especially with two band members dead."

"Go to the head of the class," she responded with a grin. "So here's the deal: The royalties on a song usually amount to about fifteen cents per song, per record sold."

"Who gets that?"

"Ordinarily, it's split between the songwriter and the publisher on a fifty-fifty basis. The Stone Blossoms deal was made way back when they were nobody, so that's pretty much the deal each of the band members had."

She paused. We both drank slowly. She reached across and brushed my hand with hers. Her skin was soft and hot.

"I'm not boring you, am I?"

"Go on," I said. It's interesting." Especially as a motive.

"So now let's figure the profit on publishing. Say there's ten songs on the CD. Each song is worth seven-and-a-half cents to the publisher—"

"And the writer, as well," I interrupted.

"Right. The writer gets his, too. But let's just concentrate on Planet's profit as publisher okay?"

She put her glass on the deck and ran her fingers through her hair. She held it there, back behind her head for a moment, then let it go. It lay softly on her shoulders before the wind pulled at it again. She tossed her head and moved close to me.

"Seven-and-a-half cents per song, times ten songs, equals another seventy-five cents per CD. Sell ten million, that's another seven-point-five million."

"Not bad," I said.

"And that's just the 'mechanical royalties.' There are other royalties paid each time a song plays on the radio, jukebox, or on a commercial. It goes on and on."

"And you can sell all those rights to someone else if you chose to, right?"

"Right. They're an asset worth roughly ten times the revenue stream it produces, maybe more."

"So if you were expecting to be paid seven-and-a-half million dollars in publishing royalties from record sales, you could sell the asset for *seventy-five* million dollars?"

"If the income stream were sustainable over time, quite possibly," she said.

That was a hell of a lot of cash. I counted it off.

"So that's ten million for distribution profit," I said. "Twenty million for record company profit, another seven-point-five for publishing. My God, that's almost forty million dollars for one lousy album."

"Plus the asset value of the publishing, plus the sales of back-catalog CD's. And that's the *conservative* estimate. It will likely be closer to *double* that."

"So you and VGC stand to get rich."

"VGC is already rich," she said.

"I know Valden," I said. "VGC is never rich enough."

"Almost eighty million operating profit off of our first CD, plus another seventy-five mil for publishing. That should do wonders for stock prices," she mused.

"I see why you'd want those tapes," I said dryly.

Her eyes turned predatory.

"You bet your ass," she said. "So where the hell are they, Mike?"

I shook my head.

"Anybody's guess. All I can tell you is that without some proof that the things were ever in the house, the cops can't investigate a theft. Only the murders."

"So…" she prompted.

So, that meant that I needed to investigate the theft. The hell with VGC, it was Tino's only chance.

"I'm looking into it," I said.

"You'll keep me up to speed, right?" She asked seriously. "You can see how important it is. To Valden, VGC, and me."

"It's important to a lot of people," I said. "Enjoy your wine while I check on Edita."

I went quietly below to the staterooms, and saw no light in the space beneath her door.

"Edita," I whispered. There was only silence. I was glad she was asleep. She'd had a hell of a day, and my contributions had only made it worse.

As I moved to turn in the narrow passage, I felt warm breath on the back of my neck. The musk of Marti's perfume lingered while her lips traced a moist, lazy path from the base of my neck to my earlobe.

"I never got to see where you sleep," she whispered.

16

Edita was not excited about sharing the breakfast table with Marti, though I watched a small smile creep across her lips when I loaded Marti into a taxi back to the Four Seasons before I got into the Mustang and drove Edita to school. I was surprised that she had chosen to return to school again, particularly on the day of her mother's funeral. It struck me later that she needed the support of friends and familiar surroundings on that of all days.

The morning was still and heavy, the sky a layer of ashen clouds. It mirrored how I felt. The funeral wasn't scheduled until four-thirty that afternoon, but the gloom was tangible.

At nine-thirty that morning, back aboard the *Kehau*, I placed a call to Vonda Franklin. She told me to hold my damn horses while she gathered up the information she needed to pass along to me.

"I was just getting ready to call you, Travis," she said. "But first of all, you gotta answer me a question."

I knew what was coming.

"Fire away."

"Who's the goddess of forensic technology?" She asked.

"You are, Vonda. You are the reigning queen. The seer of things unseen, the—"

"Damn straight, I am," she interrupted. "But that's enough. You better save some for next time you need something."

"How'd you make out?"

She huffed.

"You never give me the easy stuff, do ya?"

"If it was easy, I'd do it myself," I said.

"I'd love to see that."

I drummed my fingers on the table. She was doing me a favor, so I reined in my impatience.

"Did it work?" I asked.

She hesitated a moment.

"Yeah," she said. "In a way."

I exhaled audibly.

"I'm no lawyer," she said. "But I don't think they'll hold up in court. You know what I mean?"

"They don't need to. I only want them to make an ID. I can take it from there."

"Just so you know, I'll tell you how I got it done, okay?"

I knew that was coming, too. Like most techies I knew, it wasn't enough to tell you what time it was, they needed to tell you how the clock was built.

"There must have been about thirty or so partial prints," she began. "And I had to start by scanning each of 'em into the computer. Then I took the best one of 'em, you know, the cleanest, most complete one of the bunch, and boosted the size and resolution to the max, so I could see it real good. I call that the 'base partial.'"

"I follow," I said.

"Then, using the MERGE program—"

"What's MERGE?" I interrupted.

"It's a piece of software that allows you to overlay graphic images on top of one another. Mostly, it's used by artists and graphic layout people. For artsy-fartsy stuff.

"So anyway, I used MERGE to overlay each of the other partial prints—one at a time, mind you—with the base partial. Once I found an overlay that had lines and swirls that matched a piece of the base image, I knew I had another partial of the same fingerprint."

"Uh huh."

"Just like assembling a jigsaw puzzle, I repeated the process until I had assembled enough pieces of a particular print from a particular finger, to create an intact, complete print."

"Hell of a jigsaw," I said. "How many were you able to get?"

"A lot of what you sent over was total crap—completely unusable. But I was able to assemble two complete prints from what I was given."

"Which fingers are they?"

"One looks like a thumb. The other is probably an index or middle."

"You are as good as they get, Vonda," I said. I meant it.

"You got that right," she said. "And you owe me *again*."

"I never forget my obligations."

"Now what do you want me to do with all this stuff?"

I gave her instructions to fax the two composite prints over to Detective Moon, and send the original evidence back via overnight mail. I thanked her again and snapped the phone shut.

I knew she was right about the prints being unusable in court, but all I needed to do was have the prints run through Hawaii's Justice Department computer and see if we could, at least, identify a suspect to interview.

I phoned Moon next.

He answered after two rings.

"Moon, this is Mike Travis—"

"Well, well, Big City," he interrupted. "To what do I owe the pleasure?"

"Listen," I went on. "I wanted to give you a heads-up on a couple of things."

"Go ahead, impress me."

I exhaled, looked out the window and studied the heavy sky. The air smelled of ozone and wet jungle.

"First, I had the LA forensic tech people look over the partial prints, and they were able to piece together a pair of complete images."

"Uh huh," he said. He sounded unimpressed.

"They should be coming over your fax any time now. They'll most likely be worthless for use in court, but if you run them through your database we might get an ID off of them."

"Go on," Moon prompted, sounding bored. But I knew he would run the prints.

"And there's another angle to the murders that we ought to be looking at, too."

I gave him a sketch of Marti's and my conversation regarding the missing Stone Blossoms tapes. I explained their monetary value, and concluded by suggesting that Moon and I find Dennis Farr and see what we could learn about them. I didn't tell him it was Hans who'd located the band's former engineer in Hilo.

Moon chuckled.

"You never give up, do 'ya Big City? You'll try anything to get your buddy out of the shit. Let me tell you something: Tino Orlandella's staying right where he is."

I said nothing, holding it in.

"If you want to go chase reconstructed fingerprints and recording engineers all over Hell and gone, then be my guest. But I think the whole stolen tape thing is a crock of shit."

Moon paused for a moment, as if reflecting on something.

I waited.

"You know, Travis," he continued. He sounded almost wistful. "I thought you were supposed to be a good cop. A pro. But now you're just wasting my time. It's a little disappointing."

He hung up.

Moon believed he already had his case solved, and was convinced that my friendship with Tino had blinded me to the conclusions he'd come to. I supposed I couldn't blame him. But it wasn't going to stop me.

I made my last call to the recording engineer from the last Stone Blossoms project. The number Hans had given me was Farr's apartment, but the man's wife gave me the number for the recording studio where he was working on a project for Tom Foster. That answered that. I had wondered how Farr had ended up in Hawaii at the same time as Webb and Foster.

I made an appointment to meet him at the studio at eleven o'clock the next morning. Beyond taking my name, he never thought to ask who I was, or what we were to discuss. An element of surprise worked all the better for me, so I didn't offer anything if he wasn't going to bother asking.

Noon was approaching, and I used that as an excuse to meet Marti for lunch at the resort.

After we settled into our table at the Four Seasons Grill, she asked about my progress.

The truth was, I was feeling pretty pleased with myself that the matter with the fingerprints had gone as I had hoped. I shared the outcome with Marti.

I let her know, too, that I had found the Stone Blossoms' old engineer in Hilo, and that I planned to meet him the next day.

Cinnamon eyes watched me.

"You look pleased with yourself."

"I am," I said.

"Know where I've seen that look before?"

"Where?"

"When I seduced you last night."

I delayed my departure as long as I could, anything to avoid thinking about Ruby's funeral that afternoon. It was a burning stone in my stomach.

We spent the remainder of our lunch overlooking the golf course, discussing Marti's work on Planet Entertainment, and the arrangements she'd made to fly Danny Webb's remains back to L.A. for burial. It had fallen to Marti to organize an elaborate service for the dead rock star. It depressed me even more to recognize the irony of the way an asshole like Danny Webb would be memorialized compared with Ruby Orlandella.

"The press has been hounding me for details, Mike."

"And Valden?"

She nodded.

"Yes. He's very concerned about spin control."

I held my tongue.

"There's just not much to tell yet, Marti."

"I know," she sighed. "And I've got another phone interview with the *Post* in an hour."

I looked around and saw that the place was empty.

"Please keep me informed, Mike." As close to pleading as she ever got, I was sure. "There's just so much at stake."

Something in that hint of vulnerability made me want to help her.

I nodded, finished what was left of my drink.

I had put it off as long as I could. I checked my watch and reluctantly called for the check.

By the time I reached the cemetery, the service had already begun.

I was reminded of how long the Orlandellas had lived on the island when I saw several dozen people had gathered to pay their respects to Ruby's memory.

Edita was beside the casket, a small bouquet of white antherium and orchids laying on top. She stood between two teenage girls I took to be her friends. Tino stood several yards away from the crowd. He also stood between two others, though his attendants were there not to give comfort, but to keep watch on the man suspected of killing the woman in the box. I stood apart from them all.

After some words from a minister, people took turns standing at the head of the gravesite intoning verses meant to comfort the grieving and bless the dead. They just sounded sad to me.

Tino's gaze only occasionally left the ground as he listened to the minister's words, and never once fell on his daughter. There was no comfort to be had, one from the other.

After the service, Tino was hustled into the back seat of an unmarked police sedan, and returned to Hilo County Jail. The dust from his departure still clung to the heavy air as Edita walked up to me.

"I'm glad you were here," she said.

"Your mother was my friend."

Edita looked off toward the girls she had been standing with.

"I think I want to go home with them," she said. "They invited me to spend the night, if it's okay with you."

I knew that she could use the time away from the boatload of adult strangers she had been left to, and I agreed to let her go. I wrote down the girl's phone number in case I needed to reach her.

Standing in unsettled silence, I put my arms around Edita.

"I'm sorry," I said.

She leaned away from me and looked into my face. Her eyes were moist and red.

I held her close while she released the first of many waves of grief.

I drove slowly back into Kona as the sky faded into twilight.

I hadn't seen the sun all day, only the dull gray clouds sealing in a dank humidity that sapped my strength. I followed handwritten directions to Yosemite's new place for a housewarming of sorts. It seemed oddly fitting though. An ending and a beginning.

I found the house at the end of a narrow street that overlooked Honokohau harbor and squeezed into a spot amid a pack of parked cars. I headed toward the sound of loud music holding a bottle of Makers Mark by the neck. It was my gift to him.

The place was crowded and noisy, but I finally spotted Dave in the corner near a makeshift bar. He was wearing another of his T-shirts. This one said: *Don't Be Sexist, Broads Hate That.* I handed him the bottle and poured four fingers of Absolut into a glass of ice for myself.

"Un-fucking-real, huh?" Dave yelled above the noise. He didn't ask about the funeral.

"You throw a hell of a party for a new guy in town," I shouted over the din.

He gestured to a stunning young woman in her late twenties standing beside him.

"They're mostly friends of my roommate here."

He introduced me to her.

"Call me Rosie," she said. I said I would, and she mingled her way back into the growing mob.

Yosemite's sudden rush to leave the *Kehau* was making a different kind of sense.

"Rex here?" I asked.

"He's around somewhere. Maybe out on the lanai."

A pair of young women approached the bar, and Dave moved across to greet them. They both embraced him and he turned to introduce me. Their names were drowned out by the sound of a blender. I shook hands, clapped Yosemite on the back and moved outside.

I was on my third drink, leaning against the lanai rail, having slipped away from a flaky middle-aged woman who had just finished telling me how the NASA moon landings had all been faked as part of a government plot, and how her parrot could swear in Spanish. The night was dark and moonless, but a welcome wind had scattered the heavy clouds. I stood there a long time, staring at the stars, lost in thought.

"Who is she?"

The voice belonged to a thirty-something blond, tan and athletic. I turned toward her.

"Who is who?"

"A man only looks like that when he's thinking about a woman," she said. I felt a twinge of guilt. It wasn't Ruby I had been thinking about.

"Mike Travis," I said, and offered my hand.

"Eve Gildred," she smiled as we shook hands. "You didn't answer my question."

Marti's image flashed through my mind. I remembered the way she smelled, the way she tasted.

"No," I said. "I didn't."

She looked out into the same patch of sky, sighed.

"I hope somebody somewhere is thinking about me with that look on his face," she said and walked away.

I stood there a while longer, rattling the ice in my glass. In a brief silence between songs on the stereo, I heard Dave's laugh cut through the chaos inside. I thought about Marti. I thought again about beginnings. And endings. And I raised my glass to Ruby.

It was after nine by the time I left Dave's party, but the air was warm and dry. I put the top of the Mustang down and made my way back to the Four Seasons. Marti wasn't expecting me, but I didn't feel like being alone.

I self-parked the car and took a shortcut between buildings to Marti's room. Yellow light spilled between louvered doors and across her lanai, so I knew she was awake. I knocked gently.

She answered the door with a look of surprise that softened into something else as I crossed the threshold. She squinted into the dark outside, then closed the door behind me.

"You okay?" she asked.

"Fine."

Marti pulled a face. "You smell like cigarettes and booze."

I explained about Dave's party. As before, I didn't mention the funeral and neither did she.

"Any vodka?" I asked.

"I've got a mini-bar," she said. "I'll make the drinks. You take a shower."

Afterward, I lay and watched the ceiling fan turn listless circles, feeling Marti's breath against my chest. I kissed the part in her chestnut hair, and she sighed contentedly.

I don't know how long we dozed, but later when I woke I saw her standing naked before the louvered doors that looked out over the beach. I heard waves breaking in the distance, and watched blue light dance over her smooth skin.

"You're awake," she whispered.

I nodded.

She came over to me, kissed me softly on the mouth, then walked across the room, closing the bathroom door behind her. Pale light and the sound of a running bath as I lay back into the pillow.

I started when the phone rang. I looked at the bedside clock as it rang again. Eleven-fifteen. It rang twice more before I picked it up.

"Hello?"

Click. Dial tone.

A few moments later it rang again. The bathwater turned off as it rang a second time. I heard Marti pick up the bathroom extension.

As I fell back to sleep, I heard the sound of the sea blend seamlessly with the muted tones of an indistinct conversation.

17

I had a little over two hours' drive to my interview with Dennis Farr, so I used the time to figure how to get what I wanted from him. The meeting could easily be a waste of time, but I had to find the tapes. If they existed.

The two-lane highway traced the rugged coast of the island, and I got periodic glimpses past steep volcanic cliffs reaching down to the ocean far below. As I proceeded south, the lushness of coffee and macadamia nut plantations abruptly gave way to vast stretches of barren lava fields. Some of the flows, I knew, were very new, dating back to the mid-1970s when a sea of molten lava had destroyed the town of Kalapana before it ran down into the Pacific in huge gray clouds of steam. The remains of a few volcanically devastated houses were still visible, metal roofs protruding from a hard black layer of new rock.

Following the directions Farr had given me over the phone, I located the studio with no trouble. It was tucked into the corner of an L-shaped retail center, and struck me as a damned nondescript location for the engineer of such high-profile recordings like Stone Blossoms to end up.

The darkly tinted glass doors were bordered with laser etchings of *maile* leaves. The name of the studio, Haile Maile, was similarly etched in bold capital letters, one word at the center of each of the twin entry doors. As I set foot inside, a wall of refrigerated air reminded me how humid the day had already become.

There was a small, unoccupied reception desk directly before me. A plastic nameplate read Angie Faini Gee. A pair of well worn black leather-and-chrome sofas, with an equally used-looking end table and lamp between them, filled the corner of the room. Four or five old music industry magazines sat in a jumble atop the table amid the ringed stains of condensation and old coffee.

A closed door separated the anteroom from the rest of the studio. A hand-lettered sign had been taped to it. It said to press the buzzer on the wall and someone would be right out.

The buzzer looked like an old fashioned doorbell and I noticed the twisted red-and-white electrical wire that led up around the door jamb, and through a tiny hole in the faux-wood paneling that covered the walls.

I pressed the button, and a few seconds later, the receptionist came through the door.

"Can I help you?"

She was wide-eyed, anxious to please.

"I've got an appointment with Dennis Farr," I said.

Her eyes lost a little glow then, and she made a sorrowful face.

"I'm sorry," she said. "He told me to let you know he's running a little late."

"How late?"

She looked uncomfortable, reluctant to give me the bad news.

"About an hour and a half."

I checked my watch, shook my head, and told her I'd be back.

I figured I might as well use the time to grab some lunch, so I cruised the side streets until I found someplace that might make a good burger. I stopped in front of a gray wooden building whose last paint job had probably been done during the Truman administration. A cracked and peeling sign on the window said Bar and Grill. If it was still in business looking this shabby, it had to be good.

On such freak notions decisions are made, decisions that can sometimes give you trouble.

The inside was as worn as the outside, close and humble. Neon buzzed an ad for beer. There was a chalkboard menu, a couple of professional drinkers at the bar, and a pair of skinny young locals sitting with a large-breasted girl in a tank shirt. The whole scene was supervised by a heavy, grizzled bartender wearing a yellowed apron. I didn't like the look of the empties that sat on the table in front of the locals.

I ordered a burger and a Bud from the bartender, picked a copy of the day's paper off the bar, and took a table near the window facing the door. Cop habits die hard. The bony beer drinkers stopped talking and watched me.

I turned to a story about a banana virus, and made a show of reading while I palmed a heavy glass pepper shaker from my table. I unscrewed the lid with my fingertips and let it fall quietly into my lap as the locals swaggered over.

"You don't belong in here."

They all had the same look, these guys. But the big-breasted girl was tugging at the taller one's arm.

"I'm reading here," I said. The glass shaker felt solid in my fist.

"You wanna start some kinda problem?" He asked.

"I can tell you how it'll end," I said.

He was quick, I'll give him that, the way he back-handed her across the mouth. She landed hard against a table, bloody, eyes stung with tears.

I jacked the pepper into the tall one's face, then caught the side of his head with the empty shaker. He clawed his eyes as he twisted away from me. I was on my feet and ready to use the heel of my hand up under his nose, but his turn put his back to me. I gave him a kite to the kidneys that would have him pissing blood for a week, then reached between his legs and grabbed the waistband of his pants. I somersaulted him onto his back, where he curled up and cupped his crushed balls. I looked at the girl as he rolled on the floor.

"You okay?"

She just stood there, shaking.

I looked across at the other skinny local.

"No," I said. He stayed put.

As I was leaving, I asked the bartender if the burgers were any good.

"Number one," he said evenly.

"Maybe next time, then."

I was walking back through the doors at Haile Maile studios. The receptionist was nowhere in sight, and the handwritten note had been taken off the door. It was unlocked, so I let myself into a short corridor that had one door at the opposite end, and another off to my left. As I was deciding which one to try, the one on my left opened, accompanied by the sound of rubber scraping roughly against the carpet.

"Hey, man, Jesus!"

The guy I'd startled was somewhere in his late-forties, loose-limbed and tousled.

"I didn't mean to scare you," I said. "I'm Mike Travis, I'm here to—"

"Yeah, cool," he interrupted. "I'm Dennis."

He seemed to bristle with nervous energy. Or maybe something manmade and chemical.

I extended my hand and he gave it a cool, limp squeeze. He turned and led me back into the room he'd just come from.

Given Farr's appearance, it was surprisingly orderly. A mixing console occupied the length of one side, and was lined with row after row of colored knobs and lighted dials. It looked like something off the Enterprise. Beside it was a computer monitor and several different types of tape recorders, some with open-reels, some that looked more like cassette recorders. A patch bay, protruding with thick colored wires, looked like old-fashioned telephone switch gear and was built into the wall between the console and another rack of electronic equipment. Each of these was decked with lights of red, orange, yellow and green. An ash tray beside the console held a smoldering cigarette. Blue smoke rose toward a ceiling fan like a twisted vine.

"Have a seat, man," Farr said, and pointed to a black leather swivel chair next to the one he plopped down into. "You want something? Coffee, a Coke?"

"No, thanks," I answered. "So what is it you do here, Dennis?"

I liked to start an interview casually, get to know how my interviewee responds to questions, how he looks when he's telling the truth about things that are safe. It also gets the person accustomed to talking to me, gets him used to answering my questions so that silence or stonewalling feels foreign to the conversation.

"It's a studio, man," he said. "We record stuff."

His tone said, *what an asshole.*

"I can see that. What I meant was, what kind of stuff do you record?"

"This and that. Mostly local music—you know, Hawaiian music, local garage bands, stuff like that. We cut alot of demos for young groups wanting to shop for a contract. Sometimes we help 'em make their own CDs and tapes to sell at gigs."

"So you manufacture tapes and CDs, too?"

"I guess you could say that. We have some high-speed duplication equipment, but it's not really our main thing."

"Business pretty good?"

He lit a fresh cigarette off the dying butt of the last one, squinted as he sucked down a lungful.

"Yeah, it's okay," he said. "You know, kinda slow right now, but we stay busy enough I guess. We got a pretty good reputation around the island, yeah?"

Farr spoke with an easy local cadence, occasionally ending statements with the unnecessary *"yeah?"* that wasn't really a question.

"You the owner?"

He laughed.

"Naah. I'm just the engineer. I don't own the place."

"Been here long?"

"You mean this place? Naw, just a few weeks. I was over on Maui before, yeah? I was over there, like, a year or something."

"You work with Tom Foster over there?"

He tensed, eyes pressed into wary slits. He took another hit off the cigarette.

"Hey, man. What *is* this?"

"Just a question," I said.

"Who *are* you, dude? You a cop or something?"

Funny how the people who ask you that never want you to be one.

"Because I ask you about Tom Foster, you think I'm a cop? Why's that?" I wanted to see which way he would go. We watched each other in the blue haze of the room.

"'Cause the dude's *dead,* man," he said finally. "Somebody killed him."

I nodded.

"You know anything about that? Anybody talk to you about his being murdered?"

"No, man," Farr shook his head. "And I don't have nothing to say about it, either. I don't know nothing about that."

He stood up and started pacing in the confined space of the control room. I remained seated with my back to the only exit door. He had nowhere to go and I wasn't about to let him out just then.

"I mean *fuck!*" Farr said. He stubbed out his smoke, then began shaking another one out of the pack. "That Stone Blossoms gig, man. Everything went to shit after that."

"What do you mean?" I asked.

"Gimme a fuckin' break, dude," he said with a nervous laugh. "Like you don't know about the famous 'Lost Tapes.' That's what this is all about, isn't it?"

"Look, Dennis—"

"*Isn't it!*"

His voice was reedy and vibrated with his anxiety. His eyes showed genuine fear.

I stayed quiet. I wanted to dissipate some of the tension, try to get the conversation back on track. The guy was scared, really scared, but I didn't know why.

"The tapes," he said after a few seconds. "Every few years some asshole tracks me down and wants to know this or that about the goddamned *tapes*. Fuckin' things ruined my *life,* man. Ruined my career. Who wants to hire an engineer who lets tapes get stolen, or lost, or what-the-fuck-ever else they think happened to 'em? I ended up over here 'cause there was nobody gonna hire me in L.A. or New York, or damn near anyplace else. Tom Foster called me a while back. He said they were cool around here—the islands, I mean. That I'd be able to forget about it, man, put it all behind me..."

He paused to catch is breath, and I studied his face. The tip of the cigarette glowed red.

"...But now people are fuckin' *dead* because of 'em," he finished. His voice was gone, his energy spent.

"So what about it, Dennis? What do you know about them?"

He shook his head firmly.

"I got nothin' more to say, man."

"If you know something —something about Tom Foster and Danny Webb's murders—"

"I don't know nothin' about it, okay?" I got nothin' more to say on it, man. They're dead, and that's all. Maybe it'll all finally be over now."

Farr shook his head and stared at the floor.

"You gotta leave now," he said. "I got nothin' more to say."

He pointed to the door. He didn't look at me. Or couldn't. It was hard to tell.

Applying any further pressure was going to get me nowhere at that moment, but I gave him one last push. A nudge to keep him on edge, a reason to come back to me when he couldn't think of anywhere else to go.

"I can help you, Dennis," I said. "Call me when you feel like telling me the rest. You know I won't be the last one here asking."

He looked up at me, startled again.

I took a business card from the holder beside the console and wrote my cell number on it. I reached out to give it to him, but he just stood there. I tossed it on his chair.

I knew there was a lot more there, but it was going to have to wait for now. Farr would need to stew in the anxiety I had caused him before he'd give me the rest. It was bullshit, and a little cruel, but you do what you have to do.

Before I left Hilo, I stopped by the county facility where they were holding Tino. It was small, old and worn, surrounded by layers of rolled razor wire. A green corrugated-metal roof left dirty tears of rust down the sides of the main building.

I left the Beretta locked in the glovebox and made for the main entrance. I could smell it before I even got inside. The odors of sweat, food, disinfectant and hopelessness. I couldn't see Tino lasting long inside.

I filled out the paperwork the guards gave me and they told me to have a seat. I paced the narrow waiting area for almost half an hour, getting to know every crack in the linoleum floor, every scuffed and peeling tile. When the gun bull came back out, he told me Tino had refused my visit, no reason, no excuse, no nothing. I nodded to the guard and walked back to the car.

The glare off the window reflected hot against my face as I unlocked the door and got in. I cranked the air conditioning and sat there in the parking lot, thinking about it all, reminding myself why I was doing all this, even if Tino didn't seem to give a shit about saving himself.

I had heard it said once that a cop's job is to speak for the dead. And I guess that's right. Except this time the living didn't seem much more capable of taking care of things than the dead ones did.

18

I kept my cell phone on the seat beside me in case Dennis Farr changed his mind about talking to me. I figured it could take him a couple sleepless nights, but, hell, you never knew.

By the time I returned to the *Kehau* a light rain was falling, backlit by rays of a late afternoon sun. I went up to the wheelhouse to make some phone calls, and watched as sunbeams poured through cracks in a broken ceiling of clouds.

I flipped through the pages of my legal pad until I found the number for Lyle Sparks, the former keyboardist for the Stone Blossoms. I punched in the digits and waited through several rings. I was about to give up when a female voice finally answered.

"Sparks residence," she said.

"Is Lyle there please?" I asked. I always used first names because it sounded like I knew the person I was calling. It usually got me right through. "And who may I say is calling?"

It didn't sound like she was buying it.

"Mike Travis," I answered. I tried using a tone that suggested any more questions would be unwelcome.

"I'm afraid he's out at the moment, mister, ah, Travis—" she said. She made it sound like she was already forgetting my name.

"Listen," I interrupted. I knew I was getting the bum's rush from the Sparks' household staff. I had to talk fast. "I'm a detective working on a case that involves a former business partner of Mr. Sparks'. I need to speak with him immediately."

A white lie.

"One moment, please, sir."

I smiled to myself. *Detective* almost always works.

Seconds later, a nasal and breathless voice came on the line.

"This is Lyle Sparks."

"I'm sorry to bother you, Mr. Sparks," I said. "My name is Mike Travis—"

"Uh huh. Uh huh," Sparks interrupted. Rapid-fire, like he was in a big hurry.

"—I'm working a case that involves Danny Webb and Tom Foster—"

"Uh huh," he interrupted again. "Yes. Uh huh."

This was one hyperactive sonofabitch.

"Are you aware that they were both recently murdered?"

"Yes. Uh huh," he said. "I am. I mean, I read it in the paper."

I deliberately took a breath, dragged out a little silence. The guy's pace was making me nervous.

"Can you tell me where you were last Tuesday when they were killed?"

"Yes, Uh huh," he answered quickly. "I was, uh, here in L.A. Working. In the studio. Been here for the last month."

"Can anyone verify that?" I asked.

"Uh huh. Yes. My assistant. Cookie. Cookie Knapp. She was here. She's always here."

He spoke in bursts, like the wheezy ruffle of an Uzi. My blood pressure was going up just talking to him on the phone. I couldn't imagine working with him every day.

"Tell me, Mr. Sparks—"

"Uh, Lyle," he said. "Call me Lyle."

"Okay," I said, spacing my words even farther apart. "*Lyle,* is there anything you can tell me about the tapes from the last Stone Blossoms album?"

"Uh huh. Yes."

I waited, but that was all I was going to get.

"Lyle," I prompted. "About the tapes?"

"You mean the ones that were stolen?"

Interesting response.

"Why did you say they were stolen?" I asked.

There had certainly been no shortage of conjecture over the years about what had happened to them. But from what I'd read, most people thought they'd been erased. I was surprised to hear such a bald statement from someone so close to the project.

"Sure. Yeah," he allowed. "I guess they could have been. That could happen."

"But you used the word *stolen,*" I said. "Why?"

"That's, uh, just what we all thought at the time," he rattled off. "That they were stolen. We all figured that, you know, they were being held for ransom or something. But they never *did* show up, did they? So, I don't know, maybe they *were* erased."

"Have you had any contact with the band since then?"

"Uh huh. Yeah—"

A blare of loud music washed over the conversation from his end of the connection.

"—Hey, turn that down!" He yelled, and the sound stopped as suddenly as it had started. He continued without any prompting from me.

"Uh, I heard from Chris Morton and Danny Webb a while ago about doing some kind of reunion tour. But that's been, like, I don't know, five or six years ago."

"What happened?" I asked. "Did you do it?"

"No way. I got my soundtrack gig happening here," he said quickly. "I do movies. Plus, I don't want the nostalgia trip to be played on the Stone Blossoms thing."

"What do you—?"

"It's *over,* you know. Hell, man, everybody's *dead* now anyway. It just wouldn't be the same without Harley Angell, you know?"

"And you haven't heard from either Webb or Morton since?"

"No. They were kinda pissed at me, I think. But, hey, you gotta move on, man."

I could almost hear the shrug.

"How about Dennis Farr?"

"The engineer? I haven't heard *that* name in a while."

Sparks' voice sounded wistful.

"You haven't spoken to him?" I asked.

Sparks laughed.

"*Spoken* to him? I haven't even heard *about* him since the last Blossoms gig."

Sparks covered his mouthpiece and handled something on his end. He apologized and told me I had his attention again.

"I spoke with him earlier today, Lyle," I said. "He seemed pretty upset at the mention of the tapes. And Foster."

"Tom Foster?" parks asked.

"Yeah," I said. "Any reason those things should bother him?"

"Uh huh. Yeah. That doesn't surprise me. That gig ruined him, man. Couldn't get a job in L.A. after a monumental fuck-up like losing the *Lifeline* tapes. Or letting them get erased. Or whatever. Industry people just looked at him and Foster like complete assholes after that."

"Foster, too?" I asked.

"Yeah, but not so much. Foster had a hot reputation as a producer already. Had a couple of Grammys on the shelf at home. It was easier for him to lay off most of the blame for the tape fiasco on the engineer—on Farr. Poor kid…"

Lyle Sparks ran out of rapid-fire words.

"Do you have any idea who would want to hurt Danny Webb or Tom Foster?"

He squeaked out another laugh.

"Are you kidding? People *hated* Danny Webb. He could be such an arrogant a*sshole*, you know?"

Yeah, I knew.

"But Foster's something else," Sparks concluded. "He was cool. Most people liked him. Real mellow guy."

"Foster?"

"Uh huh. Yeah. Foster. As a matter of fact, it's kinda surprising that they were even together, you know? It's not as if Foster liked Webb much, either."

"Why's that?" I asked.

"The last recording sessions were pretty tense, man. Real hairy. Everybody was on everybody else's nerves. Especially Webb and Chris Morton. And Harley Angell. Those two were pissed that Angell had so many songs on the album. Pissed about all the publishing money he'd be getting. They were constantly fighting about album content. Foster was cool, though. He kept things moving. Right up to the very end."

"What about Webb and Foster? I don't think I follow."

"Foster was the producer, right?" Sparks said. "Well, a producer's like a free agent. He didn't work only on Stone Blossoms stuff. He sold his services to whoever could pay his going rate."

"So it's in Foster's best interests to get the best work recorded that he can," I ventured. "Is that it?"

"Uh huh. Yeah," he said. "It reflects well on him to be producer on a prestige product, you know? So he was as interested in the quality of the album as any of us. The fees for his next project would go *way* up if albums he produced sold well."

"I'm with you," I said.

"All right. Then you can see that if Harley Angell's songs were the best songs, Foster wasn't about to advocate lesser material from Webb and Morton for the album. Or me. Or anybody else, for that matter."

"Foster would arbitrate fights among the songwriters, then?"

"Uh huh. Exactly. Except Webb and Morton often thought a lot more highly of their songs than Foster or Angell did."

I'd faced an inflated ego or two.

"So there were some hard feelings?" I asked.

"Fuck yeah, there were hard feelings," Sparks squeaked his laugh again. "A song on a multi- platinum album is worth alot of money to the writer, man. Foster had a big say in who was going to get the big writers' royalties because he had such a strong voice in the band's choice of songs."

"And he liked more of Angell's songs?"

"Uh huh. A lot more. And that pissed Webb off in a big way. Lots of fights and yelling and shit. Very ugly towards the end. Like I said, that's why it's hard for me to see them hanging out together."

That struck me as odd, too. But time can heal a lot of wounds.

"It's sad, though," Sparks said.

"What's sad?"

"About the album, I mean. *Lifeline* was really damn good. It would have been *huge.*"

I scratched some notes on the legal pad, thanked Sparks for his help, and gave him my cell number in case he thought of anything he wanted to add. The rain was falling harder, and the sun was coming down on the horizon. I watched as it began to disappear behind a line of low clouds and punched in another number.

A female voice with a thick accent picked up on the third ring.

"Meester Morton residence."

"Is he there, please?"

"I soury. No here now meester Morton," the voice struggled.

"Do you know when I can call back to talk to him?"

"Yayss. Yayss. You call back talk to heem."

She was about to hang up, relieved to be ending the conversation.

"Wait!" I said.

"Yayss?" She said expectantly.

"Where *is* Mr. Morton now?"

There was a long silence as she pondered.

"Meester Morton no here now," she said. "Other house."

I wracked my brain trying to remember where else Hans had told me that Tim Morton had homes. I flipped quickly through the dog-eared pages of my legal pad.

"Is he in Los Angeles?" I asked.

"No een Los An-hay-lace. Other house."

I finally found the page I was looking for.

"Caracas?"

"*Si,*" she said, relieved again. "Caracas. He there now. You call heem."

"Do you have the number—"

"You call heem in Caracas now. Bye-bye," she finished cheerfully. And hung up.

"Shit," I muttered into the dead phone.

I punched in the New York number again, let it ring twenty times before I gave up and killed the connection. The woman sure as hell wasn't going to make the mistake of answering the phone again.

I climbed the short stairway to the afterdeck, opened a locker and extracted a bucket and a bunch of rags. I took off my shirt and decided to let the rain help me polish the salt off the boat's brightwork. I needed a mindless chore to clear my head. There was something troubling my subconscious, and I wanted to give it some room to work.

A little over an hour later, I had rinsed and mopped the decks, and put a nice glow on the chrome railing and cleats. After putting away the cleaning gear, I took a cold Asahi from the refrigerator, cracked it, and let it slide down my throat.

The rain had finally stopped, so I took a seat on the afterdeck and watched Kona begin to light up for the evening. I hadn't heard from Rex, but I figured he and Dave were over there somewhere. But before I had finished the beer, my subconscious did that thing it does sometimes. That niggling feeling I'd been nurturing shot a message to my tired brain. It was vague and fleeting, but I caught the gist. It was something Lyle Sparks had said about things not being the same because Harley Angell was dead. I couldn't put my finger on it exactly, but there was something there. And the knowledge that there was all that money involved. Back to that. Love or money.

I grabbed another Asahi on my way to fire up the laptop and find out about Harley Angell. He was the one Stone Blossom I hadn't spent any real time on. He'd been dead a long time.

It took me less than an hour on the Internet to learn that Angell's death back in '77 had been ruled a suicide by the coroner. He'd taken a header out the window of the hotel he was living in, and there was a little dope in his system. But there had been no note. It wasn't only me who felt that was odd, either. According to what I was able to find, an umbrella of suspicion of foul play had lingered long after the coroner had closed his files on Harley Angell. I kept turning it over in my head. It was damned odd that the man was an artist, a musician that made his living with his words, yet there was no note to explain his final living act.

I looked at my watch. Hans was probably gone. I shut down the computer and made a note to myself to call him in the morning and ask him about Angell.

I was undressed and ready to take a shower when my cell phone rang. "Travis? This is Captain Cerillo."

"What can I do for you, Captain?"

There were no pleasantries.

"How soon can you come to the substation?"

"How about an hour?" I said. I really needed that shower.

"The sooner the better," he responded.

I wondered what the hell the rush was.

"The prints come in?"

"Yes. They did."

He offered nothing more, and sounded unusually terse under the circumstances.

"Something wrong?"

"Did you see a man named Dennis Farr today?"

I had no idea where this was going, but I was suddenly on guard.

"Yes, I did."

"I need to talk to you," he said. "See you in an hour."

19

Captain Cerillo closed his office door and motioned me to a seat in front of his well-ordered desk. Moon half-sat on the ledge of a window that looked out into the encroaching darkness. Their expressions betrayed the tension that filled the place.

Cerillo leaned across his desk, his head resting on his fists, fingers intertwined.

"You carrying?"

I glanced at Moon. His face was impassive.

"Yes," I said.

"Put it on the desk."

"What the—"

"Gimme a fucking break, here, Travis," Cerillo said. "Just do it."

I took the Beretta, holster and all, and put it on the desk in front of me. It sat there, menacing and dangerous.

Cerillo cleared his throat.

"How do you know this Dennis Farr character?"

"How do you know that I do?" I asked. I had already admitted on the phone to having seen Farr, but I wanted to know how Cerillo knew.

"Because your name was on his appointment calendar at a time very near to when the medical examiner estimated the time of death. And a card with your name and number written on it. That's how."

"Time of death?"

Moon nodded.

"Farr's dead? Why don't we start with you telling me what the hell happened?" I said.

"Humor me, Mr. Travis," Cerillo said.

"You're the captain," I said.

Moon eyed me.

I'd told Moon that I was going to interview Farr. I'd even asked the detective to come with me. But I couldn't tell if that was part of the beef they had with me or not. I figured I wouldn't offer that up as a part of my story. If Moon admitted he already knew I was going to see Farr, then it wouldn't be too hard to insert that detail after the fact. If he didn't, then I could assume that Moon was covering his ass about letting me go without him.

"Go on," Cerillo prompted.

"I've been following up on an angle on the Webb/Orlandella murders. I thought Farr might be able to help. So I went to see him, ask him a few questions."

"Care to share your new theory with us?" Cerillo asked. He nodded vaguely toward Moon as he spoke.

I looked past Cerillo's shoulder at Moon. The detective's face remained impassive, so I recited chapter and verse about the possibility that the five people who had been massacred in my family's home had been killed over the *Lifeline* tapes. I went into some detail about the money that was potentially involved. I also told them about the role they might play in an even bigger potential business deal—the IPO for Planet Entertainment. As a motive for murder, there was more than enough money involved to explain the bloodbath.

I left out the fact that the business deal was being spearheaded by a company run by my brother. I also omitted that I'd had this same conversation with Moon already, and that he thought I was full of shit.

For his part, Moon remained still, arms crossed in front of his chest. He looked like he was hearing it all for the first time.

"Any reason why you didn't let us in on this little story?" Cerillo asked, giving me sarcastic.

I made momentary eye contact with Moon. *Your balls are in a vise, Detective.*

"I thought it was a long shot," I said. "I mean, no one really knows for sure if the tapes even exist. I figured it would be better to check out the possibilities before I got you guys all worked up over something that might not pan out. You've only got so much manpower."

Moon's shoulders sagged slightly with the release of tension.

"As it turns out, Travis, the man was killed because of your judgment. Or lack of it," Cerillo said.

I felt my ears getting hot. A man was dead, and that was a tragic thing, but there was a limit to how much crap I was willing to take for it personally. Frankly, I was pissed that Farr had died without ever telling me what was going on with the tapes.

"That, Captain, is absolute weapons-grade bullshit," I said. "You can't possibly hold me accountable for this." Hell, I wanted to know the reasons he'd been killed as much as anybody did.

Cerillo stared hard at me, and I held his gaze. Another standoff. Gilley at the projects with a rapist; Cerillo across a clean and orderly desk with me.

"Okay, let's all cool down," Moon offered.

Smart move. If it was going to go much farther down that road, I wasn't going to stand quietly by and be the whipping-boy for Moon's earlier lack of investigative imagination.

I put my hands in the air in a pantomime of surrender.

Several seconds of silence.

"Okay, let me see if I get this," Cerillo began. His voice was level. "You thought that maybe those people were murdered because of a business deal—"

"Because of the Stone Blossoms tapes," I interrupted.

"Right," he said. "Because of a business deal involving some rock band's tapes. So you decided to follow up on that by talking to Dennis Farr. Help me here, Travis…"

"Gimme my gun back first," I said.

Cerillo started to say something, but I cut him off.

"If we're going to sit here like cops, give me my gun," I said.

Cerillo cut a sideways glance at Moon, then slid my holstered Beretta back toward me. I stood and put it back where it came from. Its weight was a familiar comfort.

"Farr," I said, "was the engineer on the recording sessions for the tapes we're talking about. They happened a good while ago, back in seventy-seven."

Cerillo nodded.

"I wanted to ask Farr what he knew about the tapes. Where he thought they might be, who he supposed might have them. Hell, I wanted to know if they even existed. It wouldn't be much of a motive for murder if the goddamn things are just a figment, don't you think?"

"That's all you talked to Farr about?"

"Farr was one of only three people left alive who would know anything about them. Everybody else is dead."

"Well, now there's only two. Because so's Dennis Farr," the Captain sighed. "Now."

"So what did he tell you, Travis?" Moon asked. There wasn't a trace of the condescension that usually colored his conversations with me.

"Not too damn much," I said. "I lit a small fire under him and hoped he'd call me back. He wasn't real happy to be talking about the tapes."

"Well, somebody learned something," Cerillo said. "Somebody tortured the poor son of a bitch before they did him."

He handed me a manila file folder that contained a stack of eight-by-ten photos.

"They duct taped his wrists and ankles and went to work on him with razors and cigarettes."

I looked at the pictures, shook my head. "He didn't strike me as a guy who'd hold out long under that kind of pressure."

"Looks like they enjoyed doing it," Moon said.

"What about noise?" I asked. "Didn't anybody hear anything going on?"

"It was a recording studio," Moon said. "You could shoot off a cannon in there and nobody'd hear it."

"The secretary?"

"She's okay. Already went home by the time they came after Farr."

I looked past the captain out into the black night. In the distance, yellow headlights traced the highway north to Waikoloa.

"All I can tell you is that he got real nervous when I brought up the tapes. Said they ruined his life, his career. When I mentioned Foster, he real got squirrelly. But he didn't tell me a damn thing."

I handed the photos back to Moon. He stacked and straightened them, put them back in their folder.

"So, whaddaya think, Captain?" Moon said. "You think this is related with the Webb thing?"

"Let's play it out," Cerillo answered. "But, I've got to say that in the absence of Travis here being connected to both homicides, I'd probably never put them together. It still might turn out to be nothing. Pure coincidence."

I gave him a skeptical look.

"How long you been a cop, Captain?" I asked.

"North of twenty five years," he said.

"And you still believe in coincidence?"

I was in the parking lot, unlocking the door to my rental car when I heard footsteps approaching from behind me.

"Hey Big City," Moon called out. "Wait up."

I opened the car door and turned to face him, leaned over the rolled-up window.

"I…uh…wanted to tell you I think it was pretty stand-up of you in there," he said.

I started to get into the car.

He made a show of consulting his watch.

"How about I buy you a beer?"

A peace offering.

"Why not?" I said finally. "Where?"

"Honokohau," he said. "Coldest beer in Kona."

"I'll follow you."

He walked over to a late model Bronco parked several spaces down from mine. He started it up and pulled quickly from the lot and out toward the highway.

Five minutes later we were at the bar of the Harbor House, an open-air beer bar and sandwich joint that overlooked the charter fishing fleet that jammed the boat basin. A warm breeze blew freely across the water, dappling its surface and rattling the palm fronds outside. A handful of raw, sun-darkened men were engaged in a story that involved alot of arm waving and rough laughter. Skippers from the working fleet.

"Howzit, detective?" The lady bartender asked.

She was trim, dark-eyed, on the blissful side of thirty. She had a smooth olive complexion and the solid, athletic build of a surfer or paddler. Thick black hair fell nearly to her waist, and a plumeria blossom was tucked behind her right ear. The girl was a velvet painting.

Moon answered in easy pidgin rhythm.

"No complaints, Lani," he said. "How you?"

"No worries," she smiled. "So who's your frien'?"

She firmed the flower behind her ear.

"'Dis one mainland *hapa haole* name Mike Travis," he said.

I flashed her a smile and extended my hand. Hers felt firm and warm in mine. My mind flashed to Dennis Farr, the limp handshake. Crime scene images, razors and cigarettes bore down on the memory.

"Where you from, Mike Travis?" She asked me.

The ugly vision vanished with the sound of her voice.

"Here, now. I just sailed over from California."

"Well, then, maybe I see you around, yeah?"

"It's a good bet," I said.

She turned back to Moon.

"So what are you boys having, eh?"

"Longboard Lager," Moon answered for both of us.

"Right on," she said, then stage-whispered to Moon, "He's cute."

Moon blinked as she walked away.

We sat in silence watching Lani fill two frosted schooners. She topped each one off and delivered them with a smile.

Moon and I both drank.

I wiped the foam from my lip with the back of my hand.

"Damn good," I said.

"One of the best around, you ask me," Moon said. "They brew it right here in town."

There was an awkward silence, the kind you experience with people you don't know very well, but made all the worse with prior animosity. Moon finally broke it.

"I appreciate what you did with the captain, Travis."

"Forget it."

Moon looked away, out toward the boat basin. White dock lights reflected off the rippling water.

"I probably deserved you frying me," he said. "I can't say I wouldn't have if the roles were reversed."

I took another drink, then turned around on my bar stool, leaned my back against the bar.

"Yeah, well…"

The night became still and hung with the smells of fried food and salt water. The charter boats pulled at creaking dock lines.

"Whatever happened with the reconstructed prints I had sent over from L.A.?" I asked after another awkward silence.

Moon looked up, grateful for the question.

"Nothing's come back yet. Usually takes a couple of days."

I nodded.

"Maybe tomorrow, then?"

"Yeah, probably," he said.

We ordered another pair of schooners and talked cop talk. We traded war stories, commiserated about tight budgets and poor press relations. After about an hour, Moon paid the tab and excused himself to go home to his wife and two young sons. A quick flash of wallet photos and a handshake.

I returned to my seat and ordered another Longboard while I watched Lani work. When it was gone, I left some bills on the counter sufficient to cover my beer, and a respectable tip. I planned on coming back.

I was almost to the door when Lani called out after me.

"Hey, Mike Travis!"

I turned as she reached across the Formica countertop and handed me a folded scrap of paper.

"I work most nights at Lola's, over in town," she said.

I thought I knew what the paper was.

When I got back to the *Kehau,* Rex was grilling a steak on the hibachi that hung from the stern railing out over the water. Thick smoke roiled in the wind and reminded me how hungry I was.

"Hey, Mikey, I just got this going. Want one?" Rex said, gesturing with a barbecue fork.

"Hell yes," I answered, and went down to the galley for another steak and two cold beers.

"Thanks, pal," Rex said. His eyes were red and tired. He didn't look quite right.

The clouds that had carried the rain had dissipated to reveal a purple blanket of sky. The night was quiet, and the wind blew only occasional sounds from the waterfront bars our way.

"I been feeling kinda hinky, man," Rex said suddenly.

He prodded the steaks with the fork, avoiding my eyes.

"What do you mean?" I asked.

"I don't know. It's like this feeling I used to get in the bush. It's fucked. The skin on my scalp starts feeling tight. Too small for my head."

I nodded, and understood why he looked so far away. Maybe half a world away, somewhere in southeast Asia.

"Fuck it," he said dismissively, shaking his head. "Forget I said anything."

"Go on," I said. "What's up?"

He was more agitated than I'd ever seen him.

"It's just a feeling I used to get before the shit came down," he answered. He looked out into the dark, where the horizon should be, eyes squeezed to narrow slits. He looked like a man chasing devils around in his head.

I kept quiet.

His head and shoulders shook with an involuntary chill, then he reached down and tossed off the remainder of his beer.

"Fuck it, man," the big man said again. "Never mind."

He still had the distant look. The thousand-yard stare. I didn't know where he was just then, but I sure as hell knew where he wasn't.

After we finished our steaks, I called Marti at the Four Seasons. The phone rang several times before it bounced back to the hotel operator.

"I'm sorry, the guest is not answering. Would you care to leave a message?"

"No thanks," I said. "I'll try back tomorrow some time."

"Good night, then," the operator said. *"Mahalo."*

I fell into an uneasy sleep brought on by too much beer and a lingering unease. I knew it was the backwash from the monsters that lived in Rex's head. I knew all about them. They were the kind of monsters that came back from time to time as a reminder that there are some things that change you forever. And there's not a damn thing you can do about it.

20

The scream comes from outside. A sense of icy panic.

I move for the door.

The night is ink black and the air thick, heavy and wet, swollen with humidity. In the near distance waves break against a gravel shore.

"Oh, my God—"

Sounds of struggle, and something more. Fear.

I run toward the voice, the shoreline. Legs pumping, heart pounding. Sounds of surf competed with my own labored breathing. Blood rushes loud in my ears.

More noise. Limbs flailing, beating against the ocean's surface.

"Somebody—"

Flesh against black water.

My legs are aching, driving hard against coarse sand.

"—please—"

Noise from a different direction. I am disoriented. Dense jungle clawing clammy skin.

I gasp, breaking free of tangled vines. Here is the source of my growing dread.

It is here. In the shadowy shore break. A man, his back turned toward me. A sheen of sweat shines on his thick neck, arms working hard beneath the roiling black surface.

I try to call out, my throat is dry, constricted. An impotent croak.

The man turns toward me, a face cloaked in shadow. He stares at me a moment, taunting, challenging.

I claw for my Beretta. I reach it, but the holster is empty. I am frozen in my tracks.

Ignoring me now, white foam around muscled thighs. Striding from the surf across black sand, he disappears into a grove of ghostly palms.

I can move. I high-step the incoming tide.

A form floats just offshore.

A woman. Dead. My mother.

Her eyes are open, her face distorted. A grotesque mask of terror. Long dark hair floats like strands of Spanish moss. I carry her to the beach, lay her there. A bubble emanates from her purple lips.

She whispers to me.

"Hele aku," she says. *"Waiho ia."*

An aqueous voice. My skin goes cold.

Go, she says. *Leave it.*

I woke with a start, my breathing ragged.

I was thirteen when I discovered my mother's drowned body floating in the bay. My family had been taking a vacation at our home near Honaunau, the Place of Refuge, the house last occupied by Danny Webb.

It had been early on a still morning whose sky was steel gray with overcast. My father was doing business on the phone, my brother still sleeping. I had gone out to join my mother who had gone out for a solitary swim. She called it her morning communion.

My recollections of that day have come back in broken, kaleidoscopic pictures. I'm still denied a seamless whole. My most vivid memory, though, is standing beside my fifteen year old brother, stoically watching the ambulance attendants pull a white sheet over my mother's ashen face. We watched them load her into the back of the vehicle, red lights blinking against the clouded sky.

Later, at the funeral, I couldn't bring myself to look at her so the last glimpse of my mother would forever be a lifeless contour beneath a limp white sheet. And these prowling nightmares.

I picked up my watch from the bedside table and tried to focus on its glowing face. It was four-thirty a.m.

The sheets on my bed were twisted and damp with sweat. I disentangled them and laid back, stared at the ceiling, concentrated on regulating my breathing. I closed my eyes and tried to focus on nothingness, letting the gentle sounds of the sea lapping against the *Kehau's* hull act as a balm for my jangled nerve ends.

The sounds aboard my boat were familiar and comforting. I knew every one, every whisper she made. That was why I sensed the change.

It was while I was trying to get back to sleep. A creak from somewhere above, in the galley or salon. Not an errant cross breeze or a wake from a passing vessel slipping free into the night. Something else.

I waited, staring hard into the dark.

Creak.

Much closer this time, near the companionway stairs.

I reached for the Beretta, twisted my legs out from under the sheets, my bare feet pressed into the carpet.

It was bad, too, because Rex was aboard. The bulkheads weren't meant to take nine millimeter rounds. Standard practice says let the intruder come to you, get behind some iron, a bedframe, protect your head, heart, femoral arteries... But Rex was across the hall. I had to engage.

A stronger sound, a footstep, not Rex's. His I had known and absorbed into my boat's rhythms during the crossing. I thumbed off the safety and grasped my door handle.

Movies have it wrong. There is no time for barking commands. You'd be dead before the second word crossed your lips. I yanked on the door and let myself fall, the Beretta blasting, a cannonade of rapid fire. Even then, I wasn't quick enough. The shotgun blast found me, whipping me around. I struggled back up on my good arm, swapping hands with the Beretta, which did a bloody slide in my grip. I was dead...

Hearing returned, I stared out at the body, the angled shotgun. He had cottonwool plugs in his ears. Shit. The laugh came loose around the pain coming in over the adrenaline. I watched, but the body stayed still. It would get a sheet, just like my mother. I was still staring when Rex's door cracked open. I watched it from a hundred miles away, fascinated. I steadied the Beretta. It kept sliding in my blood, and firing left handed, I'd take the ejected brass in the face. Not good, I mumbled to myself, not good. A hand came around Rex's door. The old man on his arm looked worse for wear. More blood. Everywhere blood.

I don't remember the rest, except Rex leaping across the companionway and onto me.

"Fuck," is all he said.

I wanted to speak. But I watched as his finger came up to his lips.

"Recon," he whispered. "Be right back."

"I hit you," I said. "Through the bulkhead. Goddamn it, I'm sorry..."

The former SEAL's finger came up again. He took the Beretta from me. Then he was gone.

Kehau was strange to them. The crime scene unit, the emergency medical techs, even Moon walked around the cabin and gangway tentatively. They were used to mansions with expensive artwork splattered with blood, the lush silk sheets offering still, empty shapes; and they were used to coffee shacks and crumpled bodies spilled against secondhand furniture. I thought about Tino, but I had problems of my own now.

The medics had shot me full of painkillers. Reason had returned, but clarity was out of reach. I had my left arm strapped against my chest. Across from me, Rex was getting his wound dressed with a heavy bellyband. My nine millimeter had gouged a furrow under his arm. The medics said it was a fleshwound, but it didn't help much. He sensed my eyes on him, looked over at me and gave me a nod. I had always known he was a SEAL, but I'd never seen him in action. The instant the shooting began, he was rolling off his bunk, taking my round, hitting the floor. I'll never forget the sight of that arm coming around the door, Rex taking my gun off me and vanishing.

He had done it all. Phoned the cops, Moon, the medics.

I looked around. *Kehau* was injured too. The shotgun blast had punched a hole in the cabin door, and left the companionway a mess of blood. I watched the crime scene people edge around the staterooms, checking out the deckhead camber, the stowage, the compactness of everything. They moved around each other, photo flashes going off, camera mechanisms whirring.

Moon approached me.

"Dead guy's a Hispanic male, about five-eight, one-forty. Young. Maybe eighteen, nineteen, something like that. We've rolled his prints."

"A teenage kid? He had cotton in his ears."

"Television. You can pick up a lot. Ever see McQueen in *Bullitt?*"

"No," I said.

"Good movie. So, how you doin'?"

"Painkillers helped."

"You're going to the hospital. Of course, you probably already figured that."

I nodded, looked toward Rex.

"Your friend is too," Moon said.

Someone from the harbormaster's piloted *Kehau* to the pier and we offloaded. In all, I wasn't too bad. An earnest looking EMT said I had pellets in my arm and gut that needed to come out. The arm, he said, would be all right.

179

The EMT was very young.

"Your big friend over there? He said the door took most of the pattern. You were lucky."

I nodded again.

"They'll need X-rays."

"Sure."

Rex came over.

"I just thought of something," he said to me.

"What."

A smile stole across his face.

"All that time on the job and you never got shot. You retire and sail to Hawaii…"

Moon stepped over, flipped a notebook closed.

"So, no idea who the kid is?"

"No," I said.

He looked at Rex. "When you looked around, nothing?"

"Nobody. No boat, nothing."

Half an hour later we were at the hospital waiting out the X-rays when the doctor came into the room.

"Bad news, Mr. Travis. Looks like we're going to have to give you a general anesthetic to get some of those pellets out."

He slipped the X-ray films into metal brackets on the wall, and switched on a light behind them. They showed several black spots spread through my upper left chest.

"You'll have to be admitted."

"For how long?"

"Maybe overnight. We'll see how it goes. If all goes well, though, I might be able to let you go home when you're all stitched up."

"How about my friend, here?" I asked.

The doctor smiled, looked at Rex.

"You'll outlive us all," he said to him. "You're remarkably fit. Special Forces?"

"SEAL," he answered.

The doctor studied him a moment longer, then moved on.

"Let's get the admissions paperwork done. You'll have to sign a couple of things, Mr. Travis. After that, we'll prep you."

Moon said, "We can finish up when you're out of surgery, Mike."

The doctor gave him a sharp look. "If he's up to it."

"Sure. Right. If he's up to it."

He used that tone cops use when they mean they'll do whatever they damn well want.

The jungle is fetid and close.

I look across the clearing toward the houses. A girl in her late teens sitting cross-legged, playing some kind of game with a boy about her same age. Too far away to hear the words. They both look familiar.

A tap on my shoulder and I turn.

Rex, his face painted the green and black camo that matches the sodden fatigues he wears. He cradles an AR-15 in the crook of his arm, the muzzle pointing at the jungle canopy. He points off to our left, puts a finger to his lips.

I look away from the kids in the clearing, follow his eyes. I see it now too, deep in the jungle shadows.

Rex leans in close, and I catch the rank smell of the bush in his sweat soaked fatigues. A bead of thick sweat runs down my own back as he whispers in my ear.

"Charlie," he says.

A knot in my gut, but I say nothing.

"Charlie's inside the wire."

I regained consciousness in a small room, my head throbbing, vision blurred, sweat soaking my back. Soft blue light bathed unadorned walls.

I heard a voice from far away.

"I think he's coming around," it said.

I tried to speak, but a dryness in my mouth prevented anything but a clicking sound. I closed my heavy eyelids and fell back into a half-sleep that was filled with unintelligible sounds and snippets of conversation.

When I opened my eyes again, I was in a different room.

"Is he gonna make it, doc?"

A concerned voice was asking about me through the fog I was coming out of. I couldn't make out the response.

As consciousness overtook me, I saw Yosemite's face. When my eyes opened, he cracked into a wide grin.

"I was just fuckin' with ya," he said. "I saw you waking up, and I just wanted to mess with your head a little."

"How you feeling, Big City?" Moon's voice said.

"Okay," I croaked. "Thirsty."

Moon poured some water from a plastic pitcher on the bedside table into a matching orange cup.

"Drink it slowly," the doctor said.

The water moistened my throat and soothed my queasy stomach.

"What time is it?" I asked.

"'Bout ten o'clock," Dave said.

"In the morning?"

"Yeah, it's still morning, Dave said. "Kinda confusing when they put out your lights like that, ain't it?"

I tried to prop myself up, but was caught short by a stab of pain in my side and a sudden wave of nausea.

"Just take it easy there, Mr. Travis," the doctor said as he entered the small room. "It's going to take some time for you to recover. Just try to relax."

I shifted position on the bed, more slowly this time.

"I'm not going to have to stay here all day am I?"

"No," the doc said. "Everything went just fine. I want you to rest in bed for at least a couple more hours, then we'll see how you're doing. If you're up to it, I'll discharge you and let you go home. Sound all right?"

I nodded and my brain felt loose in my head.

"Where's Rex?"

"He's being treated right now. It'll be a while longer."

"You've got my clothes?" I asked. Strange what you worry about when you're half out of your mind.

"I'll have the nurse bring them in and hang them in that closet over there. Anything else?"

"I don't think so," I said. "I just want to get the hell out of here."

The doctor looked at me like he heard that a lot.

"We'll all do what we can," he said. "For now, though, just rest. I'll check in on you in an hour and a half or so."

He nodded to Dave and Moon as he left. "You figure out who shot me yet?" I asked Moon.

"His fingerprints are in the system as we speak."

I pointed to the water jug, and Moon obliged me.

"I thought you'd like to know," he said. "We're treating this as an officer involved shooting."

"Thanks."

Moon shrugged, a little embarrassed maybe.

"How'd you find me here?" I asked Dave.

"Rex called me. It's all over the TV and radio, too."

"Already? Shit…"

"I don't get the feeling that Hawaii's too accustomed to the volume of shootings it's been doing lately. The media is paying a lot of attention."

A nurse entered the room holding a small bundle of clothing. She acknowledged my two guests then turned to me.

"How are we feeling?"

The royal 'we' common to hospitals and grade schools.

"We're just dandy," I said.

The nurse ignored my sarcasm, or missed it. She smiled and hung my clothes in the cramped closet near the door.

"Oh," she said. "There's someone else to see you if you feel up to it." "I feel fine," I said. "Send 'em in."

I hoped it was Marti Batteau. I needed to see her, needed to see her eyes, feel her skin, her lips on me.

The nurse left the room and moments later Edita came in. She was with two others about her age. I recognized them both.

Edita held a small bouquet of wild orchids in her hand. She hugged Dave, glanced at Moon, then stood beside my bed.

"I brought these for you."

"That's real nice of you, Edita," I said. "They're pretty. You mind putting them in that orange pitcher? It's already got water in it."

As Edita slid the stems into the water. I looked over at her friends, but they both glanced away uncomfortably.

"This is my girlfriend, Mele," Edita began. "She's the one I've been staying with. And I'm sure you remember my boyfriend Peter."

Her eyes were anxious, gauging me.

Sure, I remembered the little bastard.

"You got everything all worked out between you, then?"

The question was aimed at Peter Kalima.

Kalima's face flushed.

"Yeah. Everything's okay," Edita answered. "I heard about you on TV. They made it sound like you might die or something, but you don't look so bad. I was real worried."

"Thanks," I said. "I'm doing a hell of a lot better than the other guy."

Edita tensed, then looked at her flowers. She had a long way to go.

"There's something else, though, too…" she said, looking sideways at Moon.

Peter Kalima shifted from one foot to the other.

The detective stole a glance at me.

"Uh huh…?" I prompted.

A few more seconds of silence passed.

"Well, go on, tell him…" Edita said. She nudged Kalima with her elbow.

"Okay," Peter said impatiently. "I t'ink I might know the dude got shot on your boat."

Moon's expression mirrored mine.

"How do you know the guy?" Moon asked immediately.

Kalima was surprised by the urgency in Moon's voice, and more than a little intimidated.

"Saw his picture on the TV," Kalima said. "I don't exactly know him, but I think I know, like kinda, who he is."

"Could you identify him if you saw him?" Moon asked.

"I might… I mean, I guess so…"

"Then we're gonna go on a little walk," Moon said.

Kalima looked like he wanted to bolt. Moon saw it and finished his thought so the kid would relax a little.

"I want to take you to the morgue here at the hospital. I want you to take a look at the body. If you know who he is, it'll be a big help."

Kalima hesitated.

"I guess that'd be okay."

Moon looked at Edita and Mele.

"You ladies can wait here," he said. "We won't be long."

Moon and Peter Kalima left the room. Three pairs of eyes stared back at me, no one knowing what to say.

21

Dave was keeping the three of us entertained when Moon and Peter Kalima came back to the room. The boy was ashen faced and a little shaky. They had been gone about an hour, and since it didn't take all that long to walk to the morgue and back, I assumed Peter had spent some time in the bathroom driving the porcelain bus.

"So?" I asked.

"Says he doesn't know the guy's name, but he knows where he hangs out," Moon said. "Or used to."

I looked at Kalima.

"He go to your school?"

"No," he began. "Dude lives with a buncha guys over in Pohana, I think." Pohana was a small village on the opposite side of the island from Kona, not far from Hilo.

"They sell rock and batu, man," Kalima added. "Pretty scary dudes."

I shot a questioning look at Moon.

"Batu is ice," he said. "Crystal meth."

Crack and methamphetamine. That is some scary bad shit. The stuff is so toxic it leaves scars on the skin when users sweat it out. It is not uncommon for people who do crystal meth to stay awake for three or four days at a stretch, getting more psychotic and frayed with every passing hour. Run into a meth junkie on a three day jag, you'll wish you were in a different area code.

"So how do you know these guys?" I asked.

"I seen 'em around," Kalima answered vaguely.

I was being as patient as I could, but I didn't feel up to playing high school counselor with him. I had a shoulder full of buckshot wounds and I wanted the answers to come a little closer together.

"Gimme a break," I said.

Kalima shrugged.

"Small place, brah," he said. "You see people."

I glanced at Moon, but he shrugged too.

"How'd you know it might be the guy in the first place?" I asked again.

Kalima looked exasperated.

"I heard some guys talkeen', man. They was saying like those were the dudes who wasted that guy over in Hilo. The musician."

Moon shifted on his feet.

"You mean the recording engineer?" I asked. "Dennis Farr?"

"Yeah, that's the guy," Kalima nodded. "The *haole*."

He was trying to be helpful, but I couldn't credit Kalima with an over-abundance of brains. As far as I was concerned, it was probable that whoever killed Farr also killed Edita's mother and the others. Edita hadn't made that leap in logic yet, either.

"Then we've got to go to Pohana," I said to Moon. "Get a positive ID on the one in the morgue, then wait and see what materializes." I was being intentionally vague because I didn't want to tip my hand to Edita that these were probably the same ones who had killed her mom. I didn't need that kind of mess on top of everything else.

"'*We*' who?" Moon asked.

"'*We*' you and me," I answered.

Moon started to say something, but I cut him off.

"And Peter," I added. "He's going to have to show us where to find these guys."

Moon shook his head.

"You're all bandaged up, Big City. Doctor's not going to let you go anywhere but back to your boat."

I smiled a little at that. It felt good to have something resembling a firm lead to follow.

"Doctor's not going to know. He's going to be discharging me within the hour. It won't kill me to ride along with you to Pohana."

"I don't think—" Moon began.

"Listen, Moon," I interrupted. "This is the first real break we've had. So I got my left arm in a sling? I shoot right handed."

Moon's face relaxed a little, and I knew he understood. If he were in my place, he'd be as adamant as me. We both knew it.

"All right, Big City. As soon as you're out of here, we'll take our young friend on a ride to Pohana."

The detective turned to Kalima.

"How's that sound to you?"

The kid blanched.

"Uh... I don't think..."

"The question was rhetorical, Peter," I said.

Kalima looked at me, a question in his eyes.

"He means it wasn't a question that needed an answer," Moon supplied. "You're coming along. You're the only one that knows who we're looking for, remember?"

Kalima shot a look at Edita, shook his head.

"Shit, man," he sighed. "That's what I get for tryeen' to help, yeah?"

Moon reached over and clapped him, a little harder than necessary, on the shoulder.

"You *haven't* helped yet," Moon said with a smile.

It was closer to two hours later before I was released.

While I waited, I phoned Marti Batteau out at the Four Seasons again. I was trying to figure out why it was beginning to annoy me that I hadn't heard from her. It wasn't really like me. After ringing several times, the hotel operator came on the line and asked if I wished to leave a voicemail message.

That time I did. I told her that I was fine, and I'd be back aboard the *Kehau* by late afternoon. I didn't tell her not to worry. Maybe I was just feeling sorry for myself.

When I was finally finished with the hospital's discharge paperwork, the doctor came to wish me well one last time. He told me that my left arm and shoulder would need to stay in a sling for a week to ten days, and reminded me that I'd been extremely lucky. I nodded, but I had a pretty good understanding of that before I had even arrived at the hospital. I'd seen shotgun wounds at close range before.

He asked me how I felt, and I told him. There was some tightness in the areas that had required stitches, but surprisingly little pain. He smiled a small doctor smile and walked off down the hall.

Dave drove the girls to the pier in Peter Kalima's car. When the rest of us returned from Pohana, Kalima would pick them up again.

Moon, Kalima and I drove south in the detective's Bronco. I rested my head against the window as the miles clicked by. The painkillers were slowly wearing off, and I felt the first touch of a dull throb in my shoulder. Kalima sat in the back in a stony teenage silence that neither Moon or I paid too much attention to.

Unable to sleep, I used the cell phone to call Hans. I needed to know about Harley Angell. There was part of the Stone Blossoms story I didn't understand. I told Hans I'd been shot, and he called me an asshole. I knew he was concerned, but that's how it goes. Partners. But he finally agreed to try and find the old case file on Angell, and called me an asshole again before he hung up.

The early afternoon was turning a heavy gray as we finally headed into Pohana. In the distance, jagged streaks of lightning stretched from horizon to the top of the sky.

The town itself was a loose collection of small, roughly paved streets that branched off Pohana road. Worn buildings held shops that barely stayed in business, while people sat in small groups, smoking on lanais and stairwells. The whole town had unemployment and crime written all over it.

"Turn right up there," Kalima said, as he pointed to a small paved road that led off the main highway toward the sea. They were the first words he'd uttered since we left the hospital. He was having grave doubts about the possible repercussions of his good citizenship. Fear shone through a sheen of sweat on his face.

Moon turned onto the road as he had been instructed.

Kalima leaned forward over the seat.

"Just go down to the bottom of this hill and the road, like, dead-ends. You have to go either right or left at the bottom."

"And?" Moon said.

"And go left." Kalima's voice was testy.

Moon nodded.

"Sure."

As we wound down the narrow road, the boy shifted nervously in the back seat.

"People can't see in these windows can they?" Kalima asked.

I turned around as best I could, and looked him in the eye.

"Try to relax, Peter," said. "You're going to be okay. Nobody's going to see you."

He crossed his arms and sat heavily against the backrest, tight with tension. The sheen on his forehead was becoming a flop-sweat.

I faced forward again as we reached the dead-end and turned left.

"Now go kinda slow," Kalima said. "I gotta figure out which house it is."

Moon slowed the Bronco to a crawl. I thought Kalima was going to climb out of his skin.

"Not *that* fuckin' slow, man," he hissed. "Everybody's going to notice. Aw, *shit*..."

"Peter, chill," I said. "I told you, nobody's going to see you with the cops, okay?"

He shot me a look meant to be tough.

"Just try to relax."

Moon cut a sidelong glance at me, a smirk on his face. I tried to contain one of my own.

The boy mumbled something unintelligible and stared out the tinted windows, keeping his head behind the elevated headrest of my seat.

The area was dotted with modest, single-story houses. Some looked as though they had once been cared for, but the majority had the bare and neglected look of a neighborhood going to seed. There was no sidewalk, and the street was cracked and potted, barely wide enough for two lanes.

"That one!" Kalima whispered. "The blue and white house right there. There that dude's sitting."

There was a skinny kid in his late teens or early twenties sitting on the front steps of a small, ragged house that sat between two vacant lots. His hands were folded together, as if in prayer, except that a burning cigarette protruded from the fists. A forty-ounce bottle of beer sat on the stoop beside him.

He was staring vacantly into the heavy sky and didn't notice our approach. He jumped when he heard the twin slams of the Bronco's doors closing behind Moon and me. I saw the muscles in his legs tense. But then he thought better of it. *Good boy.*

"Howzit, brah," the young man said, giving us nonchalant. He gave me a quick once-over, eyeing my bandaged left arm, then the Beretta in the holster at my side. I'd made no attempt to conceal it.

"Howzit," the detective answered.

I nodded, but said nothing.

"You got a minute?" Moon asked.

The young man's yellow eyes darted from Moon to me, then back again.

"Yeah, sure."

"I got a problem I think you can help me with," the detective said easily.

"We all got problems," he wise-assed.

"True enough," Moon answered evenly. "But some people's are bigger than others, know what I mean?"

The guy shrugged, took a slug off his forty.

"You got a name?" I asked.

"Everybody got a name," he said.

"This guy's a stand-up comic," Moon said.

A short, husky man wearing a pair of cutoff jeans and no shirt came out through a torn screen door behind where the younger one sat. He had a pair of tattoos wrapping around his biceps. Black ink. Jailhouse art. A head of thick, black hair was cropped close to his bullet-shaped head. His neck and arms were pink with meth rash.

"The fuck's goin' on out here?" Bullet-head asked, his eyes darting.

I tensed. The big guy was amped, jagged. I could sense Moon next to me. He was thinking the same thing. We both knew we had to be careful or it could get out of hand.

Moon withdrew his shield.

"HPD," he said. "And we were just asking this young man for some help."

The big one looked suspiciously from the two of us to the younger man still seated on the stairs. "Five-oh."

"Right."

"What kind of 'sistance you need, brah?"

Moon extracted a pair of Polaroid snapshots of the kid who shot me. They had been taken on my boat. I recognized the carpet beneath the dead kid's head.

"You know this person?" he asked. Moon held the photos at arm's length toward the shirtless man. He made no move to look at the pictures.

"No," he grunted.

Moon took the first step up the stairs.

"Here, take a closer look ..."

I watched the younger one eye the sling on my left arm. A flicker of light crossed his face, and he grabbed the neck of the quart bottle beside him.

"Moon!" I hollered as I reached for my Beretta.

The detective ducked and took a step forward. He caught the bottle in the fleshy area at the small of his back, instead of his head where the kid was aiming. The kid didn't have a good enough angle to get any lethal force behind his swing, but it was enough to push Moon toward the big bullet-headed man. He waited for him there with a cocked fist.

"Don't fucking do it!" I yelled. The nine-millimeter was in my hand.

Both men froze.

As Moon reached for the big man I trained my gun on the younger one. He was breathing hard. So was I, but I tried not to show it. My arm throbbed inside the sling.

Moon swung the big man around by the arm and slammed him, face first, against the flimsy wall of the house. He pulled his arm up high between the shoulder blades.

"Move and I'll break it, motherfucker," Moon said. He was panting with the release of adrenaline.

Still holding the man in place, he reached around and pulled a pair of handcuffs from his back pocket. The detective slapped them roughly on the other man's wrists and swung him around to face him.

My pistol was still pointed at the younger one's chest.

"Assaulting a police officer," I said. "Good start, asshole."

The guy worked his jaws, but nothing came out.

"All we wanted to know is who the guy in the pictures is," I said. "Now you've gone and put yourselves in a world of hurt."

The big man shot the young one a brief, hard look.

"Face down on the ground, hands behind your head," I said. "Don't even think about moving."

Moon glanced at me over his shoulder. He was still holding bullet-head against the dirty wall.

"I got this shitbag under control," Moon said to me. "There's an extra pair of cuffs in the glove box of my truck."

The detective stood back and drew his gun, pulled the big one down beside his young friend. He covered them both while I holstered the Beretta and went to get the handcuffs.

When I opened the door, I could hear Kalima breathing hard in the back seat. He was down on the floorboards where he couldn't be seen. I whispered to him that everything was under control.

I walked back to Moon, knelt and slapped the cuffs on the young skinny one. I patted him down with my one good hand and found nothing, but I left him lying there, facedown.

"Just stay on the ground," I said.

Moon was putting the Polaroids in front of the big man again.

"All right, fat boy, who's this in the picture?"

"I don't know," the man spat.

"Bullshit," he said. "Let me put it to you a different way. The kid in this picture is dead. He tried to murder a cop. The cop he tried to snuff was on a boat moored out in Kailua bay."

The big guy stared razors.

"The thing about it is that *somebody* had to take this kid out to that boat. We know that because there was no skiff at the crime scene for the kid to escape on. So whoever took him there is an accessory to attempted murder."

The young man on the ground was craning his head around to get a look at Moon and the big guy.

"Turn around and keep to yourself, asshole," I said. "You'll get your turn in a minute."

Moon leaned in on the big guy.

"What was that you said?" Moon said. He had his hand cupped to his own ear. "You want me to come *inside your house* with you?"

I smiled. It was getting thick.

"Hey, Travis," Moon said. "This guy just invited me inside his house."

Bullet-head tensed with fear.

Ordinarily, it required a warrant to enter a person's home. Unless that person invited you in. Anything you found as a result of that invitation, narcotics, paraphernalia, whatever, would be cause for arrest and admissible as evidence. If Peter Kalima was right, and these guys were dealing batu, there was some serious jail time lying around in the house.

Moon grabbed the chain between the man's handcuffs and made toward the door.

The big man stopped in his tracks and resisted Moon.

"Wait a second, goddamnit!"

The younger man attempted to twist to see what was going on. I cuffed him on the back of the head.

"Ow!"

"I told you to wait your turn," I said.

I turned and watched Moon work the big guy.

"You have something to say to me?" Moon asked.

He lowered his voice.

"I know the kid in the pictures, okay?"

"What's his name?"

"Paco."

"Paco *What?*"

"I don't know, man."

Moon tugged at the cuffs.

"Bullshit. Time to go inside," Moon said.

The big guy winced.

"Ramierez."

"Better," Moon said. "And how do you know Paco Ramierez?"

"Him an' his brother stay here sometimes."

"That Paco's brother on the ground here?"

The big man hesitated. The younger guy started squirming, mumbling something in Spanish.

"Yeah," Bullet-head said finally.

"Shut up!" Paco's brother screamed.

"*You* shut up, asshole. It's over. Your *brother's* fuckin' *dead*, you spic shithead."

The skinny one twitched and squirmed with impotent rage.

"I didn't do nothing," the big one said to no one.

"Keep going," Moon said. "You may be getting yourself out of some very deep shit."

His eyes worked back and forth now, nervous.

"It was the bitch, man."

"Shut the fuck up!" the younger one screamed.

I turned back to him, trained my gun on a spot between his shoulder blades. "What's your name, Paco's brother?"

"Fuck you," he spat.

I pressed the steel barrel against his spine and he recoiled in pain.

"I asked you your name," I repeated.

"Guillermo." It came out as a grunt.

"What bitch would your friend there be talking about, Guillermo?" I asked gently.

Moon looked from the big man to me.

"I don' know what he's talking 'bout, man."

"Bad answer," I said.

"If I talk to you, can you cut me some slack?" Bullet-head asked quickly. "I didn't have nothin' to do with nothin', man."

"Whoever talks first," Moon said with a smile.

I could see the wheels turning inside the big man's head. Finally he spoke.

"This bitch, she paid money."

"Try to speak in full sentences. I can't understand a thing you're saying," Moon said.

"The woman," he repeated insistently. "She paid for Paco and Guillermo to follow a cop."

I looked at Moon uncomprehendingly.

"What woman?" I asked impatiently.

"I don't know."

"What cop were they supposed to be following, then?"

"I don't *know,* man."

"Listen, you son of a bitch," Moon threatened. "You'd better start doing a lot better than this. Real fast."

"I don't fucking *know.* It's the truth. I never saw her, only talked on the phone."

"How did she get in touch with you?" I asked.

"She called my beeper. Exactly fifteen minutes later, I was supposed to call back on the number she'd leave."

"What did she sound like?" It was Moon this time.

"I don't know. Like a woman."

I shook my head.

"Do better."

"Like a *white* woman."

"Old? Young?" I said. "C'mon, asshole."

"In between. Not like a young girl, but not like an old woman, neither. But she talked real good."

"You still got the numbers she left for you to call?" I asked.

"Fuck no. I flushed 'em right after I talked to 'er," the big man said.

"How many times?" I asked.

"What?"

"How many times did you *talk to her?*" I said. I was losing my patience again, and he knew it.

"Three different times."

"When?"

"Like two times last week, and one more time night before last."

"How did she pay you?" Moon asked.

"Cash. In the mail."

"Regular mail?" Moon asked.

"Yeah. Regular mail."

Smart. No tracking numbers. No way to identify the sender. The only flaw was that you had to trust that your cash wouldn't get stolen along the way. Murder by mail.

Moon withdrew the notebook from his shirt pocket and flipped it open.

"Gimme your pager number," he said.

The big man recited it and the detective wrote it down.

"Wait here," he said, then strode back to his Bronco. I imagined Peter Kalima was sweating bullets right about then. I knew he could hear everything being said.

Moon stood beside the open drivers' side door as he spoke into the microphone of his police transmitter. I couldn't make out the words, but I figured he was calling for backup to take these two in for booking, but he was taking a long time doing it.

When he was finished he came back to where I stood covering the skinny one.

"Okay, Guillermo, get up off the ground and go sit on the stairs," he said. "You, too, ah…"

Nobody said anything.

"He wants your name, dickweed," I said.

"Gee-Dawg," the big man supplied.

"Gee-Dawg?" I repeated.

"Yeah," he said indignantly. "Like the letter 'G.' It's my street name."

Moon stole a glance at me, amusement at the corner of his eyes. "Well then, Mister *Dawg,* you sit down on the stairs with your buddy. We're gonna wait here for a few minutes until another patrol unit comes to get you."

The younger man's eyes burned into him.

On the way back to Kona, Moon stopped off at the first pay phone he could find. It was at an old wooden grocery from the 1930s. My cell was in a dead zone. After he finished his call, he went inside the store. Moments later, he climbed back into the truck with a bag of soft drinks, handed one each to Kalima and me. He started the truck and pulled back onto Highway 11.

"Good job, son," he said to Kalima.

"Yeah," the boy responded unenthusiastically.

Moon gave him a look of assurance.

"Don't worry, not anybody gonna know you had anything to do with this, okay?"

Kalima's expression was both skepticism and relief. He nodded and leaned back in his seat, closing his eyes.

"What was the pay phone about?" I asked.

"I passed the big dude's pager number along to a friend at the phone company. She's going to run a trace-and-match for me."

My curiosity showed.

"What they do is, they take the number they're looking for— in this case, the pager number—and run it against all of the phone bills for the preceding billing period looking for a match. That way, we can find out what phone numbers the calls came from."

"From anywhere?" I asked.

He shook his head.

"Only if the calls came from the local phone system."

"It's a good place to start."

"She said we were lucky because the billing cutoff is day after tomorrow. After the bills get printed, all that data goes away."

I looked out the window at the stands of wild ginger that grew among the tree ferns along the road. I could smell them in the air.

"So, *if* the calls were made from within the boundaries of the island," I said. "And *if* they weren't all made from pay phones, then we might get a lead on *where* the call came from. But still not *who* made the call."

"Listen to the pessimist," Moon said. "Besides, all the island's pay phones have one of two prefixes. Easy to eliminate. I mean, we'd never be able to identify a caller who used a pay phone anyway, right?"

"How long?" I asked.

"She said she'd call back in two or three hours."

"You'll call me when she does?"

"'C'mon, Travis. After all this you gotta ask me that?"

We drove the rest of the way in a silence that was punctuated only by the static and chatter from Moon's scanner. Each of us was contemplating his own set of worries. The drive seemed shorter going back, and before I had a chance to nod off, Moon was pulling to a stop sign at the south end of Kona.

"Let me off here," I said. Jake's Diving Locker was right there. I wanted to catch Yosemite, kill some time while I waited for Moon's phone company contact to come through.

"What about the kid?"

I adjusted my holster, and pulled my aloha shirt loose so it would cover it as I walked.

I glanced at Kalima.

"He can come with me."

Jake's was crowded with sunburned tourists filling out paperwork at the desk. I finally found Dave in the gear locker outside, fitting divers with wetsuits, weight-belts and tanks. A fat couple with a heavy Midwest twang was regaling him with stories of their expertise. Yosemite was saying "hmm" and "ahhh" to fill the empty space.

"Yosemite," I interrupted. "How long 'till you're off? I'm looking for a beer and some lively conversation."

Dave glanced at my sling, then over at Peter Kalima.

"Can't, bro," he smiled. "Doin' the night dive tonight. Mantas. Talk to the kid."

It was my turn to look at Kalima. "The kid doesn't have much to say to me right now."

Kalima just shook his head and walked off into the parking lot.

"How about Rex?" I asked. "He's back on *Kehau*?"

Dave nodded.

"Took him back there a couple hours ago. He's doin' all right."

Dave returned to his work and I motioned for Peter to follow me. My shoulder was pounding and my mind was buzzing with the burnoff of adrenaline and the nagging weight that tells you your business is unfinished. I should have felt good about taking Guillermo and G-Dawg down, but somebody was pulling the levers, and we still didn't know who.

"Slow down, man," Kalima said.

I stopped and waited for him to catch up. Late afternoon sun tore through broken clouds and popped sweat on us both. The Beretta felt heavy and hot against me. I looked out at *Kehau* and saw her pulling hard at her moorings. A swell was picking up and beginning to break white water over the seawall.

Kalima paced me as we cut through the open market, but didn't speak. The smell of ripe mango and papaya filled the air, mingled with sounds of half-hearted bartering. Tee shirts and beach towels hung in the doorways of the shops we passed, and a kid played ukulele on the sand across from Hulihee Palace. Through it all, the waves pounded a growing rhythm that made my mind race.

I glanced at my watch. I checked the battery on my cell phone. Looked at the time again. I wanted to hear from Moon. We were close. I could feel it.

I picked up my stride, my eyes fixed on the pier, and kept on walking.

Kalima untied the *Chingadera* from the quay after I started the motor, and we swung out onto the rippling blue bay toward my boat. I could see Edita and Mele sitting on the bow.

Rex came out from below when he heard the skiff approach. He waited at the top of the ladder.

"So who's your friend?" He said to me.

"This is Peter Kalima," I said. "Edita's boyfriend."

"Welcome aboard, son," Rex said flatly. "Edita's on the bow."

"Yeah," the boy said.

"Not real social, huh?" Rex said, staring after Kalima.

"No. But he helped us out some today."

Rex grunted and watched Kalima and the girls on the bow.

"How's the arm?" I asked.

He looked me in the eye, made sure I heard him.

"Forget it, Travis."

I nodded and started to go below when my cell phone rang. I flipped it open before it could ring a second time.

"Travis, it's Moon."

"What've you got?"

"The prints we took of the kid who shot you?"

"Yeah…?" I asked.

"They match the set your forensic tech pieced together in L.A."

I felt the hair stand up on the back of my neck.

"You're shitting me," I said.

"Not," he said. "And there's more. They match one of the sets they rolled at the Farr scene. Dollars to doughnuts Guillermo's end up matching, too."

The little pukes had been busy.

"Anything from the phone company?" I asked.

"I said I'd call you when I hear back."

"You know where to find me."

I snapped the phone shut and looked back toward the island. Waves beat against the rocky shore and I was overcome by desolation. My shoulder began to ache in earnest, and I went below to grab an Asahi. I came back to the afterdeck and watched Kalima talk to the girls. It made me feel old.

I wiped the foam off my lips and thought again of Ruby. And Marti. And where the hell was she? It stung when I realized that Tino was an afterthought. God damn, I was wired. I had another hit of beer, and tried to shake it off.

22

I was slicing the *Chingadera* through a series of swells that were coming up from the south. The deck vibrated with the speed and power of the twin Evinrudes, and seaspray soaked my face. The stereo was blasting, Pink Floyd doing *Run Like Hell.* The release that only loud music and pounding through the waves could give me. An illusion.

I had just returned from dropping Kalima, Edita and Mele at the pier. They were going to drive back to Mele's house. Edita was staying there again that night. My shoulder throbbed, and my arm ached. Someone had tried to kill me aboard my own boat. My head spun with facts I could make no sense of. I felt the need to fool myself into a sense of control if only for a few minutes, and if only on something as pointless as throttling my skiff to full-tilt and pushing its pointed bow through a succession of blue rollers. It was stupid and childish, and before long, I turned her around and throttled back to idle. I sat there awhile pondering the shoreline, wondering how things had gone so bad so fast.

I had some threads to follow, but my best one, Farr, was gone. I thought about Guillermo and G-Dawg. Thought about how, after a day or so of lockup, we should go back and scramble their eggs a little more. Get them to turn. Young Guillermo hadn't done any time before, as far as I could tell. He'd find out fast how it went for a new fish. Fresh meat.

I wanted to know about Harley Angell, too. Something there hung onto me like a parasite.

I was about to call Hans when the cell phone rang in my hand.

"Travis, Moon again."

I asked him what was happening.

"I think you oughtta come on down to the sub. They just faxed me the list from the phone company."

"And?"

"And the call G-Dawg said he received night before last? It came through the Four Seasons' switchboard."

I was still for a moment, looked out toward the *Kehau* rolling slowly on the incoming tide.

"Nothing else that night?" I asked. "No other calls?"

"Nothing. Only four other incomings that weren't from pay phones, but they all fall outside the time frames we're looking at. Probably drug deals. We'll run 'em down later, but the hotel call is hot."

...she talked real good...

My stomach turned to ice. I had relied on my intuition all my life. At least in my life as a cop. Now I found myself fighting it, and I didn't know why. Or maybe I did, and I didn't want to face it.

"Travis? You there?"

"Yeah," I said. "I'm on my way."

I killed the line and sat for another minute before I punched in the number for the Four Seasons. I knew it well. I had dialed it often enough in the past few days.

"Four Seasons Hualalai." A soft feminine voice.

"I'd like to speak with a guest, please," I said. "The name is Marti Batteau." I spelled her last name.

There was a moment of silence, and the clacking of a computer keyboard. Lobby noises drifted across the line.

"I'm sorry, but that guest has checked out. Is there anything else I can do for you?"

I squeezed the phone in my hand.

"When?"

"Excuse me?"

I cleared my throat and tried again.

"*When* did she check out?"

"I'm sorry," she said finally. "But it looks like you just missed her, sir. It's showing that she checked out about an hour ago."

I thanked her and snapped the phone shut.

I rammed the throttle forward and the *Chingadera's* bow rose in a tight turn that brought water over the transom, and sped back toward the pier. David Gilmour's guitar hammered the deck beneath his feet.

Moon was in the open area, behind the wired glass wall that separated the station's waiting room from the offices in back. He was hunched over, absorbed in reading from a thick manila file. He caught me in his peripheral vision, looked up and motioned me in. The uniformed officer at the desk buzzed the security door, and I passed through.

I didn't wait to speak.

"I know someone who was staying at the Four Seasons," I said. "Her name is Marti Batteau. I called out there on the way over. She's just checked out."

Moon looked at me uncertainly.

"And what is that supposed to mean?"

"I was thinking about it on the way over. The woman I'm talking about was involved in the business deal with the Stone Blossoms tapes."

"The deal you told Cerillo and me about."

"Yeah," I said. "She was staying close to me. Close to the case."

"Christ."

"I thought she'd been sent here to take care of the public relations mess," I said. "But there may have been more to it."

"How so?"

"I had told her I was going to concentrate on trying to locate the tapes."

"So you could vindicate Orlandella," Moon said.

I looked across the empty room and felt like a complete fool.

"She could have had you followed," he said.

I nodded. I didn't want to believe it.

"The timing's too coincidental," I said. "She went dark on me right after I was shot."

Moon shut the manila folder.

"When did she check out?"

"About an hour ago."

"She have a car?"

"Not that I know of. I've driven every time we've been together."

Moon reached across the gray steel desk and pulled a phone toward him. The silence was tense as seconds ticked by. Moon held his ear to the receiver, and I recited the number to the Four Seasons.

"Bell desk, please," he said finally. We waited a few seconds more, then he said, "Is Kimo there?"

"Hey, braddah," the detective lapsed into a pidgin patois. "'Dis Kapono Moon, cuz. I need yo' help."

Moon went silent as he listened for a moment then interrupted.

"Hey, cuz, I'm gonna put a frien'a mine onna phone. He gonna ask you about one guest, yeah?"

I took the receiver from him.

"My name's Mike Travis," I said. "I need to know if you can tell me where one of your departing guests went?"

"Do my best," the voice said. It was an open, helpful voice, his talk-to-the-tourist voice. "Who you lookeen' for?"

"A woman, very attractive, late thirties. Dark hair and eyes."

"Got a name?"

"Batteau. Marti Batteau."

"Sure, I seen Miz Batteau. She checked out just a little while ago."

Moon stared at me as I listened.

"Yeah, right," I said. "Any idea where she might have gone."

"I can fin' out," he said. "Jus' one minute, yeah?"

The phone banged against a desk, then the sounds of muffled conversation. The man came back on the line.

"One of our guys saw her," he said. "He says she was in some big-kine hurry, so we took her in the hotel shuttle. The driver, he says he dropped her at the airport."

I didn't know what this was coming down to, but I felt the wheels coming off.

"Which terminal?"

Kona International Airport isn't large by any stretch, but there wasn't time for a blind search. I heard his hand cover the phone again, and the sound of more muted discussion.

"Private terminal," the bell man said.

"Private terminal?"

I parroted what he said and looked at Moon to see if he knew what that meant. He nodded.

"Thanks," I said and handed the receiver back to Moon.

"Thanks, brah. Gotta go, eh?" He paused as the other man spoke words I couldn't hear. "Yeah. Later," he finished and hung up.

"Let's go," he said. "If she's got a private flight, she could already be gone."

"Don't you have some patrolmen out there?" I asked.

Moon made a face.

"You seen the size of this place. You kidding?" He said.

Moon went quickly to a small office in the back, rummaged in a desk drawer for his keys. I saw him reach down to check his weapon. I checked mine.

We pushed through the glass doors and out to his Bronco. Dust curled into the air behind us as he pulled out onto the two-lane highway and headed north

"Flasher?" I said. I pointed to the roof.

"No, better go in low-key."

A minute later we passed a sign that said the airport was only three miles away. Three long miles. I tried to put it together, but the pieces fought me. Or maybe I didn't want them to fit. Either way, it felt surreal.

Moon looked over at me.

"You all right?"

"When we get to the terminal," I said. "I'd like to go in casual. Alone."

"What's the point?"

"This whole thing could be nothing. There's gotta be two hundred rooms at the Four Seasons—"

"Two-forty," Moon interrupted.

"Whatever. Point is, there's no way to know what room the call to Gee-Dawg's beeper came from." It was true. I wanted it to be true.

Moon glanced at me again. The look on his face said Bullshit.

"You're the one that talked about coincidence, Travis."

Justification is a waste of time. Always has been.

"There's a chance I'm wrong," I said. "I don't want to go in with guns blazing, know what I mean?"

Moon thought about that for a minute.

"Let's just see how it lays when we get there."

I didn't have to wait long. We were speeding down the two-lane drive that led to the airport. The beacon on top of the control tower pierced the darkening sky.

Moon brought the truck to a halt into a narrow parking space next to the private charter air terminal. It was small, not much more than a shack, with a pair of windows that faced out onto the parking lot.

The building was set apart from the inter-island terminal by a good two hundred yards, maybe more. Still, I saw the lines of tourists and inter-island commuters manhandling baggage and checking in for their flights. The private terminal, by comparison, was deserted.

I approached one of the windows from an oblique angle, one I hoped would afford me a glimpse inside without being fully visible to anyone indoors.

When I poked my head above the sill, I saw Marti Batteau sitting on a black, faux-leather couch, a purse and small briefcase on the seat beside her. She was staring out through the glass curtain wall that faced the active runways. She looked absorbed in the fueling and loading of a sleek Gulfstream V private jet. Her hands nervously tapped out a rhythm on her knees.

She wore a stark white blouse beneath a dark blue business suit whose pleated skirt stopped just short of her knees. I looked at the well-muscled calves I had held in my hands more than once. She didn't seem like the same woman now.

I looked around the rest of the terminal and noticed only an unoccupied kiosk. The back wall had a stylized logo: *Island Air.* A private charter desk.

I was surprised at the absence of an airport security magnetometer. But that was a good thing for me. Nothing to give me away. I touched the Beretta again.

There was no one else inside the building.

I turned to Moon.

"I'll go in first," I said. "Come in behind me, don't let her see you."

I'd done it the other way, too. Storm the suspect, arrest them without preamble. There were a lot of questions that needed answering, and maintaining her right to remain silent would get us exactly nowhere.

But I wanted her alone. I wanted to hear from her that she knew nothing about any of it. That she was who I thought she was. That she knew nothing about the houseful of dead in Honaunau, Dennis Farr, and me.

No, my way was better.

But I knew she was smart. Smart enough to know she'd clam if we placed her under arrest and read her Miranda. I knew her silence would be followed by the appearance of a high-priced lawyer who would close off any other opportunity we might have.

I knew Moon understood my reasoning, even without an explanation. I knew he'd be somewhere behind me and out of sight, close enough to cover me if things got squirrelly. He'd also be a witness to the conversation Marti and I would have. "There's no metal detector?" I whispered. I hadn't seen one, but I wanted to make sure. Nothing would fuck this up faster than Moon and me entering the terminal and setting off a blaze of whistles and buzzers.

"Not in this area," he said. "It's only used for private aircraft."

"Okay, then," I said.

Moon nodded.

"Go."

The angle of the short corridor would afford only seconds after I entered. Moon would need all of it to go in without being seen by Marti. He needed to time it perfectly.

I opened the glass door and moved toward her. She caught me in her peripheral vision, but I couldn't tell if she had seen Moon. She turned toward me.

There was brief surprise in her brown eyes. Then she was just looking at me. I gave her that. No silly talk. No, 'What a surprise.' Now I knew.

"Got winged, I see."

"And your boy is dead."

She looked out beyond the window to the Gulfstream. The black hose was being hauled down, rolled up. She stayed that way until the fuel truck slowly pulled away.

"Whatever you think happened, Mike, it's over."

I shook my head.

"No. It's not."

Marti smiled.

"You're alive. Be happy with that."

The jet sat silent, stairs down. Its shiny skin reflected the burning purple sky.

"The tapes," I said. "You found them. You had Farr tortured and he told you where they were."

"You led me right to him, Mike."

"Where are they?"

She smiled again.

"Long gone."

"You're not following them. It's finished."

She looked out the window again, maybe measuring her chances.

"I'm not going to prison."

"Set the handbag to one side, Marti. Do it slow."

"Mike, I'm this close to more money that even you can possibly imagine…"

She was fast going for the bag, but she had to know it wouldn't be enough.

I stepped to one side and reached for the Beretta while her hand tangled in the bag, trying to track my sideways move.

No time for words, for warnings.

My shot hit her in the chest.

People screamed outside as Moon ran up from behind me.

I just looked at her as the red bloom spread obscenely on her white blouse. Then she was gone.

Moon went to her. She with her red rose, her hand in the bag.

Moon reached in, pulled out a Glock compact 9 millimeter. He looked it over, then slanted it toward me in his hand.

"Custom tuned," he said. "New York trigger."

I tried to look out the window, but only saw Marti reflected in it.

"She would have had you, Mike."

I shook my head.

"Not today. Maybe some other time, but not today."

In the distance, I heard the sirens approach.

23

I spent the next two days in the Kona substation giving my statement and trying to put the final pieces of the story together. Moon had reports to finish, and there was the internal investigation of an officer-involved shooting to be put to bed. My self-defense arraignment for shooting the kid on my boat would come later.

Toward the end of the second day, Moon was told that the investigators had cleared my shooting of Marti Batteau. Justifiable Homicide. A pair of words that still seem strange together.

As for me, I was numb. The depth of the betrayal I felt nearly sickened me.

Steps had also been taken to have Tino Orlandella released from jail. G-Dawg and Guillermo, the two batu dealers from Pohana, had not only rolled over on one another with respect to the drug charges against them, they had also implicated each other, and Guillermo's dead younger brother Paco, in multiple homicide and conspiracy counts. They never stood a chance. The fingerprint work that Vonda Franklin had done turned out to be the lynchpin in tying the three of them to the killings.

Because Paco—the kid I'd killed aboard my boat—had only been fifteen years old, there were no prints on file in any of the systems they had run them through. Which is why they had never come up with a hit when they ran them the first time. The boy had never applied for a job, let alone one that required finger prints. Hell, he hadn't even applied for a drivers' license yet. He never would.

Moon looked at me across his paper-strewn desk.

"What'd you hear from your brother?"

Ever since my initial call to Valden, the one where I told him I had shot Marti, I had been speaking with him several times a day.

The whole thing set off a storm in VGC's New York offices. My brother and I spoke often during that time, while VGC's public relations people attempted to stave off the press who were beating down their doors. The story was a big one. It had it all: Sex, drugs, rock and roll, murder and big, big money.

As for VGC, it looked as though their two billion dollar IPO was going down in flames. Valden was doing what he could to spin the story and salvage the reputation of the firm. A hard job even for him, a world-class bullshitter.

When I had told my brother of Marti's death, the first thing the firm did was pull her personnel file. They needed to locate next-of-kin for us so they could be notified. The only person that had been listed in her file was Danny Webb's old song writing partner, Christopher Morton. A few hours and several publicly-recorded documents later, Valden's legal staff uncovered that Morton and Batteau had been married several months earlier, a fact that had been withheld from everyone. An intricate secrecy.

I explained the "Love or Money" theory to Valden, and asked him to give some thought to how Christopher Morton and Marti Batteau could profit from the deaths of Danny Webb and the others. It still wasn't clear to me, but given how close they were to the Planet Entertainment deal, I knew the whole damn thing would begin and end there. My brother called me back a few hours later and filled me in on what they had come up with.

It was Moon's turn to hear the story.

"First off," I said. "The deal with VGC was for both Danny Webb and Chris Morton to get two-and-a-half percent of the stock in Planet Entertainment."

"To share?"

"Each," I said. "About fifty million apiece."

Moon whistled low.

"But I guess it wasn't enough for Chris Morton," I said. "Valden's lawyers found an old agreement between Morton and Webb that dated back to 1969. They had mutual ownership of song writers' publishing rights to everything they wrote. Even songs that one or the other wrote individually were to be jointly owned."

"Like Lennon and McCartney," Moon said.

"Exactly. I'll spare you all the legal crap, but the short version is that all their song writing royalties belonged to a company that each of them owned one-half of."

Moon caught right on.

"So what happens when one of the owners dies?"

"The surviving partner get's the dead one's shares."

Moon leaned back in his chair, looked up at the ceiling.

"Don't tell me, their 1969 company was going to be the owner of their interests in Planet Entertainment."

I nodded.

"What about a will? Couldn't they give their shares away in the event of death."

I had asked Valden the same thing.

"The agreement between the two of them precluded it. All of the remaining stock was to revert to the surviving shareholder."

"Jesus Christ," Moon said. "You'd better trust your partner in a deal like that. It's like walking around with a target painted on your back."

I wadded up a piece of paper and tossed it in a trash can about six feet away. It hit the rim and bounced against the wall.

"I imagine that back then, they both thought the other was indispensable—"

"And I'm sure they didn't think there'd ever be so much money involved," he interrupted. "You gotta be pretty fucked up if fifty million dollars, and half the publishing of a multi-platinum bunch of music aren't enough."

I knew better. I had seen unbridled greed in all its ugliness. It knew no bounds or limits. The fact human beings would murder one another for money was one of the few absolutes on the planet. People killed each other for a hell of a lot less every day.

"I think there's more, though," I said.

"Like what?"

"I think the missing tapes were going to be a huge boon for Christopher Morton personally."

"How so?"

"Since the tapes had never been published at the time of their disappearance back in the late '70s, no one really would have known with any certainty who the writers of the individual songs were. Morton could have claimed that he and Webb had written virtually all of them. At least the one that Lyle Sparks didn't write. After all, who was going to be able to prove otherwise. That would've been a huge windfall. A big boost for their artistic reputations too."

Moon thought about that for a minute.

"The only ones who would have known, besides Morton and Webb, would have been the producer, Foster," Moon said.

"And Dennis Farr."

"Right."

"But I don't think that's why Farr was killed, just a profitable by-product."

"Then why?"

"Because I think he was the only one who knew where the tapes were. My guess is that Farr was supposed to have delivered them the night Webb and Ruby Orlandella were murdered. But something went wrong and Farr never showed. The shooters came to rip off the tapes, but the tapes weren't there."

"And they had no idea where they were," Moon said.

"That's what I think. So, when I told Marti Batteau that I was going to try and find them, she had me followed."

"And they tortured Farr until he copped."

"I think that's how it went."

"But why would he hang onto them all these years?"

"I don't think he had them until recently. But it looks like we'll never know."

I left out the part that Hans had told me about Harley Angell. It wasn't pertinent to our case, but it was a hell of a sidebar. Evidently, in the case file that Hans had found, there was some widely-held contention to the theory that Angell had killed himself. Not only was there some compelling testimony by those close to him, but there was some forensic evidence that suggested that he might have been pushed out of his hotel window. If Angell had actually been murdered, then it was the catalyst to everything that followed. And that this whole fucking mess, or something much like it, might have been planned all along.

It was still unclear to me why Ruby Orlandella had been with Webb and the others that night at all. My best guess, though, was that she and Tino had fought again, like they had so often lately, and she'd simply gone next door for a little distraction from the tension at home. And while it didn't really matter, I doubted that there had been any relationship between Ruby and Danny Webb. That was also what I wanted to believe.

The missing Stone Blossoms tapes were an embarrassing thorn in Valden's side, and he asked that I do what I could to track them down. It seemed to me that the goddamn things somehow weren't meant to be heard. I told him I'd think about it.

When police searched through Marti Batteau's hotel charge records, they listed and identified every single phone call that had been made from, or charged to, her room. One of these was to Kona Copy and Mail Center.

I asked my brother to fax me a good head shot of Marti. VGC's Public Relations department kept photos on file for senior executives, for those occasions when they might appear in newspaper articles.

I looked at that face again, those eyes. A face I had trusted; eyes that had deceived, then defrauded me.

I took the photo to Kona Copy and Mail and inquired if any of the employees recognized the person in the picture. One did. He also remembered that she'd paid a considerable amount to have a heavy package sent overnight to somewhere outside the U.S. He went to look for the records. I knew right away what I'd find when he located them.

I was right. The package had been sent to Caracas, Venezuela. New permanent address of Christopher Morton.

Venezuela has no Extradition Treaty with the United States, so as far as Morton was concerned, he was untouchable by U.S. law. But he'd have to remain outside of American jurisdiction for the rest of his life. Unless someone wanted him bad enough to get real creative. He'd need to stay away from any other country that had a treaty with America as well. Forever.

Interpol, the FBI and every friendly government's national police agencies would watch for Morton until the day he died. He'd traded his country and his wife for what? I wondered if he felt it was worth it.

Lyle Sparks, the only other surviving member of Stone Blossoms, was a class act. Though reporters literally camped out in front of his Malibu house, he made only one appearance and read a prepared statement. In it, he voiced his shock at the violence that had been visited on Danny Webb and the others, and a deep sadness at whatever had overtaken Christopher Morton to perpetrate it. Sparks said that he wished that the band's legacy could have been something more. It was meant to have been something more. Harley Angell had always wanted it to be.

I looked at my Tag Heuer watch then over at Moon.

"It's five-thirty," I said.

He looked up from the paperwork he was finishing.

"Yeah?"

"Let's go get a Longboard at the Harbor House."

"Thanks, Big City," he said, fatigue lacing his voice. "But I gotta stay here 'til this is done. You go on ahead. You look like you could use it."

I stood and started for the door. I was halfway there when Moon called after me.

"Hey, Travis."

I turned.

"I just wanted you to know," he said. "It's a motherfucker, but you did right."

My head throbbed with exhaustion, and all I wanted to do was start over.

"Not yet," I said finally, and turned for the door. Not yet.

EPILOGUE

We sat on the worn wooden lanai of Tino Orlandella's house. The three of us were settling into easy conversation while racks of pork ribs smoked on Tino's grill. Stray sparks drifted into the evening sky as drippings from the meat fell into the fire. Edita was tossing a salad, throwing bread and scraps to Poi Dog who ran in excited circles around her bare feet.

The *Kehau* rocked gently in the bay at Honaunau, and I admired it with paternal satisfaction. My plan was to sail around the islands, stopping wherever I wanted, with no particular itinerary. I still intended to explore the rest of Polynesia, but I was sure it would be some time before I felt up to another long crossing to Tahiti, the Marquesas, or the Cooks. I was in no hurry.

That night, though, there was something I needed to finish.

"Daddy, did you tell Mike about your new job?" Edita asked.

"Naw."

I looked over at Tino.

"New job?" I said.

He scuffed his sandals against the dirt.

"Big contractor hire me for one project up *mauka*."

Since his release from jail, he'd started going to meetings. We toasted with soft drinks.

Edita was doing better than I imagined possible, and it looked to me like Tino was no longer taking anything for granted. Especially the time he had together with his daughter. They both seemed to sense that it wouldn't be long before she would be out on her own, maybe even off the island entirely. Graduation was not far off.

Over dinner, I gave Edita a gift-wrapped box. She took it with a smile, and tore into it. It was the photo album she had let me borrow, but I had added one of my own at the very front.

She looked at me and smiled, then leaned the book so her dad could see. Her eyes filled with tears as she hugged me. It was a picture of Ruby, Tino and me that last summer so long ago. When we were all sixteen.

After dinner, Edita did the dishes, and I asked Tino to follow me to the beach. I wanted our conversation to be private.

The night was still and smelled of ocean and approaching rain. The last night noises of mynah birds came from the trees.

"Tino, there's something I want you to do for me," I began.

"Anything, brah. Name it."

"Valden and I have been talking, and we've decided to get rid of the house."

"What do you mean?"

"After everything that's happened, we aren't likely to use it anymore. We want to sell it."

Tino looked away. Our families had been neighbors since before either of us were born.

"But the thing I want for you to do is take charge of selling it for us. I want to pay you a commission if you'll handle it."

He didn't say anything for a long moment.

"I don' know nothing 'bout selling houses, brah."

"Then hire a real estate agent," I said. "We'll pay their commission, too.

I don't want anything more to do with it. Neither does Valden. We just want it gone."

Go. Leave it. That's what my mother had said in my dream.

"I don't know what to say…"

Tino heaved a ragged sigh and looked away. I knew that some of it was gratitude for the money. It made me feel awkward.

"There's something else, too," I added.

He turned to face me.

"When the house sells, Valden is going to want his half. You can have the money wire-transferred to him in New York—"

He started to say something, but I held up my hand.

"—I'll make sure you have all the instructions. But I want you to take my half and put it away for Edita, okay? Put it in the bank. Send her to college, see that she gets what she needs."

I had enough money for the life I had planned.

Tino stared at the sand between his feet.

"She's a good girl," he said. "She deserve something good li'dat."

"But there's one condition," I said.

He nodded.

"You can't tell her where the money came from. You've looked after this place for a long time. The money's yours."

He didn't answer.

"Promise me."

"I promise," he said.

He gripped me in a bear hug that reminded me I'd only been a week without the sling. I winced when the pain hit my shoulder and he let go. He shook my good hand in both of his. Like the brother I wished I had.

We made our way back across the coarse white beach to his house where we talked late into the night. From time to time, I would catch a glimpse, a toss of the head or a smile, of Ruby. And I know that Tino saw it too.

A couple days later, I called over to the dive shop and found Yosemite. It was late afternoon and I knew his work day was almost done.

An hour later, Rex, Dave and I were drinking cold schooners at Lola's. It was good to talk of ordinary things.

It struck me again that I had come to Hawaii to reclaim my life, distance myself from violence. I wondered now if I carried it with me like a virus. Like a disease.

I looked across the table at my friends, though, and felt things come back into balance. Dave was beginning a new life, and seemed more content than I had ever seen him.

Rex was going back to California; back to Avalon to get his business back in shape. He said he had had enough vacationing, and absently fingered the bandage that still covered the bullet wound I gave him. Dave told Rex that he'd give him ten percent for selling Dave's boat and equipment, since he wouldn't be needing them in Kona. Dave also gave him permission to take over his charter book if he wanted. He'd built a good reputation and client roster back in Catalina, and Rex jumped at it.

The jukebox was playing *Samba Pa Ti* as the sun slipped below the razor sharp horizon. As always, it reminded me of Ruby. A group of tourists lined the railing and waited for the green flash.

I looked past the crowd sitting along the bar and caught Lani's eye. As she had told me before, she bartended at Lola's most nights. I waved casually and she tossed me a smile.

I put my fist to my ear like a telephone receiver.

She nodded and smiled again.

Rex caught the whole thing, called me an asshole, and bought another round of beers.

I looked out across the sand and saw us dancing.

In my head Santana played, and the younger, gentler versions of ourselves held each other and laughed even though we were leaving something behind. She touched my face with her fingers, and I smelled the flowers in her hair. She stood on her toes and kissed me softly on the cheek. But as I pulled her closer, she vanished into nothing.

And in that moment I knew what Ruby had left me.

Check out these other fine titles by
Durban House at your local book store.

Exceptional Books
by
Exceptional Writers

BASHA
by John Hamilton Lewis

Set in the world of elite professional tennis and rooted in ancient Middle East hatreds of identity and blood loyalties, Basha is charged with the fiercely competitive nature of professional sports and the dangers of terrorism.

Ben Weizman, who has grown up believing his blood parents were killed by Palestinian terrorists. He's handsome, talented and destined to become one of the greats of the game. Nothing seems to be standing in his way: marrying Jenny Corbet, the love of his life, or becoming the number one player in the world. Nothing except the terrible secret his adopted father, Amon Weizman, has kept from him since he was five years old.

Basha, an international terrorist, suddenly appears and powerful members of the Jewish community begin to die. Is the charismatic Ben Weizman on the terrotist's hit list?

The already simmering Middle East begins to boil and CIA Station Chief Grant Corbet is charged with tracking down the highly successful Basha. In a deadly race against time, Grant hunts the illusive killer only to see his worst nightmare realized.

HOUR OF THE WOLVES
by Stephane Daimlen-Völs

AFTER MORE THAN THREE CENTURIES, THE *POISONS AFFAIR* REMAINS ONE OF HISTORY'S GREAT, UNSOLVED MYSTERIES.

A nameless woman's sexually mutilated corpse is unearthed in a Carmelite abbey. A penniless aristocrat has his lover's wife poisoned. A cardinal poisons a communion wafer. A banker poisons a travestied castrato. A priest breaks the seal of Confession to reveal a plot to poison the King of France. A fortune-teller brags about her aristocratic clients.

MUNDANE INCIDENTS GALVANIZE HISTORIC EVENTS.

The worst impulses of human nature—sordid sexual perversion, murderous intrigues, witchcraft, Satanic cults—thrive within the shadows of the Sun King's absolutism and will culminate in the darkest secret of his reign: the infamous *Poisons Affair*, a remarkably complex web of horror, masked by Baroque splendor, luxury and refinement.

In the eye of the storm is the king's German sister-in-law, Lislelotte, a creative, compelling and much too prolific writer. In turns humorous, serious, self-effacing and scatological—yet always keenly observant—she has an opinion on any-and-everything: social and religious conventions, life at Court, political intrigues, but most especially, on the insane cast of characters who populate the story.

DISCOVER THIS WHOLLY ORIGINAL, YET PLAUSIBLE, SOLUTION TO THE MYSTERIOUS *POISONS AFFAIR*.

PRIVATE JUSTICE
by Richard Sand

After taking brutal revenge for the murder of his twin brother, Lucas Rook leaves the NYPD to work for others who crave justice outside the law when the system fails them. "Mobbed-up" Harry Raimondo's young daughter is murdered, and to find the killer, he needs just the sort of compelling, deep-seated anger which drives Rook.

Rook's dark journey takes him into Inspector Joe Zinn's precinct and on a collison course with Homicide Detective Jimmy Salerno. The Raimondo case was his, and though it has long gone cold, it still haunts him.

Then another little girl turns up dead. And then another. The nightmare is on them fast. The piano player has monstrous hands; the Medical Examiner is a goulish dwarf; an investigator kills himself.

The FBI claims jurisdiction and the police and Rook race to find the killer whose appetite is growing. Betrayal and intrigue is added to the deadly mix as the story careens toward its startling end.

DEADLY ILLUMINATION
by Serena Stier

It's summer 1890 in New York City. Florence Tod an ebullient young woman in her mid-twenties—more suffragette than Victorian—must fight the formidable financier, John Pierpont Morgan, to solve a possible murder.

J.P. Morgan's librarian has ingested poison embedded in an illumination of a unique Hildegard van Bingen manuscript. Florence and her cousin, Isabella Stewart Gardner, discover the librarian's body. When Isabella secretly removes a gold tablet from the scene of the crime, she sets off a chain of events that will involve Florence and her in a dangerous conspiracy.

Florence must overcome her fears of the physical world, the tensions of her relationship with Isabella and deal with the attentions of an attractive Pinkerton detective in the course of solving the mystery of the librarian's death.

The many worlds of the turn-of-the-century New York—the ghettos to the gambling dens, the bordellos to the bastions of capitalism—are marvelously recreated in this historical novel of the Gilded Age.

DEATH OF A HEALER
by Paul Henry Young

Diehard romanticist and surgeon extraordinaire, Jake Gibson, struggles to preserve his professional oath against the avarice and abuse of power so prevalent in present-day America.

Jake's personal quest is at direct odds with a group of sinister medical and legal practitioners determined to destroy his beloved profession. Events quickly spin out of control when Jake uncovers a nationwide plot by hospital executives to eliminate patient groups in order to improve the bottom line. With the lives of his family on the line, Jake invokes a self-imposed exile as a missionary doctor and rediscovers his lifelong obsession to be a trusted physician.

This compelling tale stunningly exposes the darker side of the medical world in a way nonfiction could never accomplish and clearly places the author into the spotlight as one of America's premier writers of medical thrillers.

THE SERIAL KILLER'S DIET BOOK
by Kenvin Mark Postupack

Fred Orbis is fat—very fat—which is an ideal qualification for his job as editor of *Feast Magaine,* a periodical for gourmands. But Fred daydreams of being an internationally renowned author, existential philosopher, râconteur and lover of beautiful women. In his longing to be thin he will discover the ultimate diet.

Devon DeGroot is one of New York's finest with a bright gold shield. His lastest case is a homicidal maniac who's prowling the streets of Manhattan with meatballs, bologna and egg salad—and taunting him about the body count in *Finnegans Wakean.*

Darby Montana is heiress to the massive Polk's Peanut Roll fortune. As one of the world's richest women she can have anything her heart desires—except for a new set of genes to alter a face and a body so homely not even plastic surgery could help. Then she meets Mr. Monde.

Elizabeth Aphelion is a poet, but her "day job" is cleaning apartments. Her favorite client, Mr. Monde, lives in a modest brownstone on East 54th Street. Elizabeth would sell her soul to quit cleaning toilets and get published.

Mr. Monde is the Devil in the market for a soul or two.

It's a Faustian satire on God and the Devil, Heaven and Hell, beauty, literature and the best-seller list.

WHAT GOES AROUND
by Don Goldman

Ray Banno was vice president of a large California bank when his boss, Andre Rhodes, framed him for bank fraud.

Ten years later, with a different identity and face, Banno has made a new life for himself as a medical research scientist. He's on the verge of finding a cure for a deadly disease when he's chosen as a juror in the bank fraud trial of Andre Rhodes, and Banno knows the case is so complex he can easily influence the other jurors. Should he take revenge?

Meanwhile, Rhodes is about to gain financial control of Banno's laboratory for the purpose of destroying Banno's work. Treatment, rather than a cure, is much more lucrative—for Rhodes.

Banno's ex-wife, Misty, who is now married to Rhodes, discovers Banno's secret. She has her own agenda and needs Banno's help. The only way she can get it is by blackmail.

It's a maze of deceit, treachery and non-stop action, revolving around money, sex and power.

MR. IRRELEVANT
by Jerry Marshall

Sports writer Paul Tenkiller and pro-football player Chesty Hake have been roommates for eight career seasons. Paul's Choctaw background of poverty and his gambling on sports, and Hake's dark memories of his mother being killed are the forces which will make their friendship go horribly wrong.

Chesty Hake, the last man chosen in the draft, has been dubbed Mr. Irrelevant. By every yardstick, he should not be playing pro football. But, because of his heart and high threshold for pain, he perseveres.

Paul Tenkiller has been on a gravy train because of Hake's generosity. Gleaning information vital to gambling on football, his relationship with Hake is at once loyal and deceitful.

Then during his eighth and final season, Hake slides into paranoia and Tenkiller is caught up in the dilemma. But Paul is behind the curve, and events spiral out of his control, until the bloody end comes in murder and betrayal.

OPAL EYE DEVIL
by John Hamilton Lewis

From the teeming wharves of Shanghai to the stately offices of New York and London, schemes are hammered out to bankrupt opponents, wreck inventory, and dynamite oil wells. It is the age of the Robber Baron—a time when powerful men lie, steal, cheat, and even kill in their quest for power.

Sweeping us back to the turn of the twentieth century, John Lewis weaves an extraordinary tale about the brave men and women who risk everything as the discovery of oil rocks the world.

Follow Eric Gradek's rise from Northern Star's dark cargo hold to the pinnacle of high stakes gambling for unrivaled riches.

Aided by his beautiful wife, Katheryn, and the devoted Tong-Po, Eric fights for his dream and for revenge against the man who left him for dead aboard Northern Star.

ROADHOUSE BLUES
by Baron Birtcher

From the sun-drenched sand of Santa Catalina Island to the smoky night clubs and back alleys of West Hollywood, Roadhouse Blues is a taut noir thriller that evokes images both surreal and disturbing.

Newly retired Homicide detective Mike Travis is torn from the comfort of his chartered yacht business into the dark, bizarre underbelly of LA's music scene by a grisly string of murders.

A handsome, drug-addled psychopath has reemerged from an ancient Dionysian cult, leaving a bloody trail of seemingly unrelated victims in his wake. Despite departmental rivalries that threaten to tear the investigation apart, Travis and his former partner reunite in an all-out effort to prevent more innocent blood from spilling into the unforgiving streets of the City of Angels.

TUNNEL RUNNER
by Richard Sand

A fast-paced and deadly espionage thriller, peopled with quirky and most times vicious characters, this is a dark world where murder is committed and no one is brought to account; where loyalties exist side-by-side with lies and extreme violence.

Ashman—"the hunter, the hero, the killer"—is a denizen of that world who awakens to find himself paralyzed in a mental hospital. He escapes and seeks vengeance, confronting his old friends, the Pentagon, the Mafia, and a mysterious general who is covering up the attack on TWA Flight 800.

People begin to die. There are shoot-outs and assassinations. A woman is blown up in her bathtub.

Ashman is cunning and ruthless as he moves through the labyrinth of deceit, violence, and suspicion. He is a tunnel runner, a ferret in the hole, who needs the danger to survive, and hates those who have made him so.

It is this peculiar combination of ruthlessness and vulnerability that redeems Ashman as he goes for those who want him dead. Join him.